EMPTY HOUSES

EMPTY HOUSES

Betsy Thornton

Severn House Large Print
London & New York

This first large print edition published 2015
in Great Britain and the USA by
SEVERN HOUSE PUBLISHERS LTD of
19 Cedar Road, Sutton, Surrey, England, SM2 5DA.
First world regular print edition published 2015 by
Severn House Publishers Ltd., London and New York.

British Library Cataloguing in Publication Data

Thornton, Betsy author.
    Empty houses. – (Kate Waters series)
    1. Murder–Investigation–Fiction. 2. Arizona–Fiction.
    3. Detective and mystery stories. 4. Large type books.
    I. Title II. Series
    813.6-dc23

    ISBN-13: 9780727872999

Severn House Publishers support the Forest Stewardship Council™
[FSC™], the leading international forest certification organisation. All
our titles that are printed on FSC certified paper carry the FSC logo.

Typeset by Palimpsest Book Production Ltd.,
Falkirk, Stirlingshire, Scotland.
Printed and bound in Great Britain by
T J International, Padstow, Cornwall.

For Alix Jane

ACKNOWLEDGEMENTS

Thanks again to my weapons expert Tom Glass for his always helpful advice. Any weaponry errors I may have made have been entirely my fault.

Work, for the night is coming.

—Sacred hymn

One

The place was a beach town near LA; the event was lunch at La Casita, a Mexican restaurant Harry and Kate went to from time to time. Tiled floor, wooden tables and red vinyl booths. Serapes and sombreros on the walls. Kate particularly liked the *caldo de queso*. She was from back east and had only been in California for three months. She'd had a good job as the director of a community arts center in Vermont, but it had faded to almost nothing along with the economy until it was, in fact, nothing at all. And during this time her long-term relationship with the sculptor Rick Church had – well, she could hardly stand to think about it much.

She'd met Harry Light, a California poet, five months ago back in Vermont at a poetry workshop she'd organized, part of a series. Kate wrote poems from time to time, and he singled out a recent one of hers about the impending break-up of her long-term relationship to read at the workshop: *Mother-Riddled Men are Engines of Pure Regret.*

As he read her poem out loud to the workshop group, his voice had picked up not only every nuance intended by Kate but also found even more she hadn't realized were there. He was so dynamic, seductive, so ready to show emotion.

They had a fling. After all, at this point, even though Rick was the owner of the house where they lived, he was spending four nights of the week somewhere else. Her name was Hannah.

Harry had gone back to California but called Kate several times. He commiserated with her about Rick and Hannah. 'But,' he said, 'you're better off without him. He doesn't deserve you. Get away from the whole situation. Your job's gone, so why stay? Come to California. We don't have all that—' his voice turned scornful – 'weather.'

So she did. She got in her old Honda and drove cross-country to be with Harry Light: poet. He'd assured her there were good jobs in California, he knew all the right people, but so far nothing had transpired.

'Patient,' he'd always say, 'you have to be patient.'

Harry Light, poet, was dressed in black: black jeans, black shirt – a hint of the fifties and Kerouac in the cut of the shirt. Now he looked at his watch impatiently, then looked around the crowded restaurant with disgust. 'So?' he said to Kate. 'So?'

'So, what?' she said.

'This was a lousy idea to come here. I should never have listened to you.'

Kate couldn't recall it being her idea, but she arranged her face to look pleasant and non-committal. She refolded her napkin then unfolded it again. 'Why not?' she asked.

'Why not?' Harry said in fake astonishment. 'Why not? I see people here – customers. I see lots and lots of customers, but there's one thing I don't see.'

Kate's shoulder and back muscles tensed up. 'What's that?'

'A waitress.' He smashed his fist on the table, making Kate jump. Several people at other tables looked over. 'A goddamn waitress.' He looked around the room. His voice rose. 'Are we fucking lepers here?'

Harry smashed his fist down on the table again. A man appeared suddenly behind his shoulder, a fit, muscular-looking man. Harry was not, after all, in the best of shape. 'Sir?' the man said.

Kate knew what was coming. Reaching into her purse, she pulled out her sunglasses. Ray-Bans, big and dark.

'Sir, I'm going to have to ask you to leave,' the man said.

'Fine.' Harry threw down his napkin and stood up. 'That's fine. We were about to, anyway.'

Expression obscured by her sunglasses, Kate followed Harry through the swinging door.

Outside in the warm California sun, he said disgustedly, 'Now we'll have to go to some crummy fast food place; it's too late for anything else. Thanks a lot, *Kate*.'

Turning, he headed for his car, but Kate stayed where she was.

Harry stopped halfway and looked back. He saw: a fortiesh woman in big sunglasses. She was tall and auburn-haired with a little more make-up than his students wore. She saw that despite the fact that he told her he loved her almost every day, the expression on his face as he looked at her now appeared to be pure loathing.

This was what she had discovered about him.

3

There were two Harrys – Harry Light and Harry Dark. Tomorrow, or even later this evening, Harry Light would show up again as if nothing had happened.

But right now it was Dark Harry.

'Come on, come on, I don't have all day,' he said. 'I've got a workshop at one thirty.'

'I don't want to go to a fast food place,' Kate said.

'Then where the fuck do you want to go, little miss spoiled brat!' he shouted.

'Nowhere. I'm not really hungry.' She kept her voice light, airy. She was trembling now but didn't let it show in her voice, out of some intuition that if he felt her fear, like some snarling dog, he would attack. 'I'll just walk back to the house. I feel like walking, anyway.'

Kate walked the three blocks back from the Mexican restaurant to the pleasant wood-frame house painted white with green trim that belonged to Harry Light. The spark that had brought her here from so far away was gone, but down the block the Pacific Ocean still glittered.

Inside she went to the bedroom closet and took down her suitcase. Most of her stuff was back in Vermont, in the attic of a friend; all she had in the world right now were the clothes hanging in a line in the closet and in one drawer of the chest of drawers, a few books, and a jar of raspberry jam, dated some years ago, made by her mother and stepfather Bill from the raspberries that grew in the patch behind their house.

She wanted to vanish into thin air – the thought

of a farewell scene gave her the creeps. So many things set Harry off: inattentive clerks in stores, people who drove too slow or too fast, bad service in restaurants, inattentive colleagues at work.

Who knew what her leaving like this would do?

Because she'd found the gun.

It wasn't even hidden, not really, just in the bottom drawer of his bedside table. She'd opened the drawer, looking for something else, and there it was. Was it loaded? How could you tell? She had little familiarity with guns – it might just as well have been a bomb. She was afraid to even touch it for fear it might go off.

But it was best to leave a note. Otherwise he might think she'd been kidnapped, had left involuntarily (such ego he had!) and involve the police. Well, maybe not, but you never knew.

Too much, she wrote. *Had to leave.*

Suddenly, she had a little picture of Harry after one of his workshops – she'd driven over to surprise him – talking in what seemed to her an overly intimate way to one of his students, a beautiful young woman named Anna Marie Romero. It brought back that memory of Rick, her ex, saying earnestly, 'We didn't plan on this happening. Hannah really admires you, Kate. She feels terrible about all of this.'

She didn't ask Harry about Anna Marie because what would be the point? She'd already made her decision to leave him and leave him very soon.

She paused at the door on her way out, for a second imagining herself in the kitchen, smashing all the cups, the plates, the bowls; throwing the contents of the fridge on the floor in a soggy mess; then on to Harry's office, his row of arty chapbooks full of crummy poems, everything in his desk, all ripped to bits.

But no. She got in the car, texted her artist friend Dakota in Dudley, Arizona who had promised to put her up. Harry didn't know Dakota, or where she lived.

On my way.

Hurry, hurry, hurry. The first hour or so, tense, she kept glancing at the rear-view mirror in case he'd come back early, seen her leave, was following her. But by the time she reached Yuma, Arizona, she was more relaxed. The sun was going down in a spectacular display of orange, indigo and purple as she pulled up to the window at a McDonald's and ordered a Big Mac, fries and a Diet Coke.

She parked her car by the kiddie play area, got out and sat on a bench near a dinosaur statue not far from her car. As she ate the greasy salty food, she watched the cars, the big trucks rocketing by, all going seventy-five, eighty miles an hour on the I-10 Freeway.

Her phone chimed. Dakota.

'Where are you now?'

'Yuma.'

'Three hours away. Call me when you get to town and I'll guide you to my house. Listen, I wanted to tell you. I think I got you a job – you said you'd take anything, remember?'

'Ah,' said Kate.

'It's at the local food co-op. It's – it's not like just a grocery store. It's political and stuff.'

'Why not? Sure.'

'See you soon, then.'

Afterwards, Kate sat for while longer. The piquant smell of burning gasoline filled the air, the night was balmy, the sky indigo and full of stars. Oddly in the dark, lit up the way it was, the McDonald's resembled a fantasy house from a book of fairy tales. How had this happened? Everything that had seemed permanent in her life, vanishing just like that: her job, her relationship. But wait, didn't disasters come in threes? Harry, did Harry count as number three? Maybe it was true, things were taking a turn for the better. After all she would be in a new place, a town where no one would be gossiping about Rick leaving her for another woman, that hint of glee because, before the economy went bust, she had been quite successful at her job – a person of note in the little Vermont town of Rustic.

Now she was nowhere, a woman close to forty, thoughts jumbling in her head, phrases from her possibly useless education, from her life with her mother, who read a lot and had lived in Paris as a child, and these things seemed to have no connection – *ou sont les neiges d'antant* and, *I am dying, Egypt, dying*.

Her cellphone pinged, a text coming in. More from Dakota? No, Harry. She opened it. It read:

Mistake.

7

Two

Malcolm MacGregor, a detective with the Mesa Arizona police department, had lived with his wife Cindy in an older subdivision in Mesa, a suburb of Phoenix, for the last fifteen years, until a few months ago when Cindy had checked into a motel nearby, wrote a note saying, *I'm so sorry, Mac*, swallowed a whole bunch of pills, and died.

It was a shock but not a surprise. She'd been fighting depression for years. Had he not met Cindy in college, fallen for her badly, and then later married her while he was in law school, he might have finished and become an attorney like his brother Ian, instead of a detective with Mesa PD, but saving Cindy took all his psychic energy.

Now some people might say it had been for nothing, quitting law school to save Cindy. Look where he was now. But he liked police work; it had taken him away from Cindy's problems in a way that law school could not. And he'd been handling her death as well as could be expected, hadn't he?

Okay. He was *okay*.

He worked hard at work, and at home he kept busy. When, during a rare early rain, he discovered the leak in the roof of the guest bedroom (where Cindy kept the expensive exercise equipment that she never used), that very next weekend he hauled the half-full five-gallon bucket of roofing tar out of the shed in back, set the bucket by the ladder already in place against the side of the one-story stucco house and wiped his forehead – it was hot.

It was always hot in Mesa. He should have tackled this job earlier in the day, instead of finishing re-grouting the tiles in the bathroom, which had needed to be done for the last ten years. He knew that now, but it was something he should have known the minute he got up – do outside chores early in the morning. It wasn't that he didn't know things any more, he would just forget them temporarily.

The roof sloped, ridged on the front and sides so that all the water drained to the back. When he climbed up he saw that the honeysuckle vine in the back yard had grown up on to the roof. He would have to prune it quite a bit before he could patch the leak. He climbed back down. He was already tired, in a way of being tired that had nothing to do with the fatigue of overexertion.

People kept saying to him: take some time off, *relax*. That was exactly the last thing he wanted to do – what he wanted to do was to go to work and stay there, preferably sleep at his desk at night in his office, bathe down the hall in the restroom. Never go back to this carnival fun-house where ghosts popped out of the walls when you least expected them.

Malcolm went back into the shed, brushing aside some insect – probably, with his luck, a brown recluse spider – and found the pruning saw. He paused. Maybe clippers would do the job better. He found the clippers, carried both tools outside, climbed back up the ladder. His plan was to fix everything that needed fixing, then put the house on the market. With the economy the way it was, it was the worst possible time to sell, but at least he had a plan.

Fix up house, move to some apartment closer to work.

Certainly not take time off. For what? But if he did take time off, his brother Ian kept saying he could go stay in his wife Sally's investment house, down in Dudley, Arizona, a tourist town not far from the Mexican border. Maybe do a little work on that house for the rent, or maybe even not. Whatever. *Just get rid of old Malcolm so we don't have to see him all the time and worry about him.*

He was tired of being treated like an invalid, someone who couldn't function. Ian had pointed to that fender bender he'd had just last week in the Safeway parking lot, as if it meant something, but everyone had fender benders – that woman's car had been parked perfectly in his blind spot, just a freak thing. Of course, Ian didn't know about the stop sign Malcolm had run in his unmarked police car; he just hadn't noticed it, was all. He must not have handled the patrolman who stopped him very well, because he had actually been issued a citation. Anyway.

Malcolm reached the top of the ladder, set the pruning saw and the clippers on the roof. Even though it was shaded here in the back by an overgrown mesquite tree, the roof was hot, hotter than he'd expected. Probably, he should give it a squirt with the hose. For a second, just one fleeting second, he almost called down to Cindy, 'Hey, hon, could you turn the hose on this—'

Never mind.

Actually, he could get pretty close to the worst of the vines without going on to the roof. Clippers looked like the best bet. He grabbed them, then leaned over, got hold of the closest vine and pulled it toward him. The clippers were pretty good, still sharp, and they cut right through the stem. He threw the cut vine down on to the yard and saw he could just reach the one next to it.

He leaned as far as he could, maybe just a little too far because the ladder began to tilt. He grabbed the edge of the roof with one hand to right it, dropped the clippers he was holding in his other hand, tried to catch them and lost his footing. Then the ladder was falling, and he was falling with it.

Uh,oh, Cindy, here I come, was the last thing he thought before he hit the ground.

After the accident, Malcolm's chief, Ray Friendly, once again suggested he take time off.

'*Why?*' Malcolm asked.

He and Ray had known each other since Malcolm was a rookie, and Malcolm trusted Ray generally speaking, but now nothing anybody said to him made any sense.

'I mean, I can still function. I just have some shoulder pain,' Malcolm protested.

11

Ray said nothing. There was what you might call a pregnant silence.

'Time off for what?' Malcolm said finally. 'So I can stare at the walls?'

'Or go fishing. Whatever.'

Malcolm had never fished in his life. 'Jesus Christ, Ray. Can't you do better than that?'

'Okay, okay,' Ray said. 'What I'm saying is, you got to take time off before you hurt yourself or, god forbid, somebody else. That's an order. And here's another piece of advice. There's too many memories for you here right now. Get out of town for a while.'

'No – I mean, why?'

'For one thing, you have to drive by that motel every day on your way to work. How does that feel?'

'I don't drive by that motel. I get up a little earlier and take an alternate route.'

Ray put a Friendly hand on Malcolm's shoulder.

Malcolm flinched.

'Oops,' Ray said. 'Sorry.' He paused. 'Just do it, okay? Leave town.'

So he did.

Three

Two months later

Maybe I'm wrong, Carrie thought. She felt sick to her stomach. *God, of course I am.* She'd tried

12

to call Rose, her sister, back in Pennsylvania, but Rose wasn't answering her cell.

It was Brewery Gulch Days in the small Arizona town of Dudley; bands were playing, and there were art galleries and street artists, the Miz Dud beauty contest, and street dances at night. The hotels were all booked up, and the town full of tourists, Carrie Cooper and her husband Wes among them. Wes had taken early retirement from his job selling insurance; Carrie had a crafts store she ran with her sister. They were middle-aged people; not young, but certainly not old.

'In our prime!' Wes would say, and Carrie would laugh.

She laughed at all his jokes whether they were funny or not. Though not newly-weds, they still sometimes acted as if they were. He was tall, with medium-brown hair, muscular but with a bit of a gut now. He'd worn a full beard for years, but had shaved it recently. She thought he looked even better without it.

Carrie had her light-brown hair streaked every three months with gold highlights. She'd just had it done before they came here. Carrie was something else, despite what she would jokingly call her advanced old age. She was fine boned, her delicate features perfectly symmetrical. She still brought looks from men wherever she went.

Carrie was beautiful.

That afternoon Wes had decided to go on the mine tour, but Carrie had been queasy about going way underground where it was dark and cold, so she stayed behind. Carrie was prone to jumping at loud noises and slept badly without a man in the bed beside her, which in her younger days had caused her to make some mistakes. And right now she was scared.

She'd been scared since last night, their first night in town. They were staying at the Copper Queen Hotel. Wes had gone up to take a shower before dinner, and Carrie had taken a walk. That was when it happened. What she saw.

She'd hurried back to the hotel. In the lobby she'd had a conversation with one of the waitresses, then Wes had showed up.

She hadn't told him what had happened, what she'd seen on her walk last night. *Should I have?* she wondered now. She tried her sister's cell again, but still no answer. *You think you can get away with things*, she thought, *but maybe you can't.*

There was music in the air, mostly drums, some guitar riffs. Despite Wes's usually comforting presence Carrie hadn't slept well last night, worrying. Melatonin – her sister swore by melatonin. The woman behind the desk at the Copper Queen had given Carrie directions to the Natural Foods Co-op. They would probably have some there. So Carrie put on her baseball cap and sunglasses and took a walk.

She left Main St and turned down a side street, taking pictures with her cellphone: she took one of the sign at the Silver King Hotel, and one of a man in a long black frock coat and a cowboy hat. After she took his picture, the man in the black frock coat followed her for a while.

'I'd love to show you around, ma'am,' he said. 'I know some interesting places the average tourist never sees.'

'No, *please*,' Carrie said. 'Thank you.'

She walked and walked. Walking was good for anxiety – that was all it was, anyway, anxiety. Last night had been her imagination. The more she thought about it, the more she realized she had to have been mistaken, and she had always had some anxiety issues – she hated that word, issues – but she was much better than she used to be.

So get over it, she told herself.

She turned a corner, walked a stretch, and then another corner and there it was: the Dudley Natural Foods Co-op.

There was a sign in the window saying 'We Are Not Racist Here' over a circle with the letters 'SB1070' for the anti-immigration law recently passed in Arizona and a slash across it. Next to that a sign said 'Humanitarian Aid Is Never a Crime'. *Humanitarian aid*, thought Carrie. I could use some of that.

By the door a young woman with bright-red hair in a long batik skirt was dancing, swaying and bobbing to the faraway drums: thumpety thump, thumpety thump.

The young woman dancing was Posey, an employee of the Food Co-op in charge of produce, on her break. She was skinny, angular, with a dragon tattoo like the girl in the book on her left arm.

'Look at her dance!' said Windsong behind one

of the cash registers. He was in his sixties, with a gray beard and a red bandanna round his head. 'See!' he said to Kate. 'We don't need YouTube in Dudley. We got our own YouTube here. It's called life!'

'*Life*,' Kate said.

'Hey there, you. Lighten up,' said Windsong. 'One life is all you get.'

Kate smiled. Windsong was always making her smile. She almost resented it. 'What?' she said. 'You don't believe in reincarnation?'

Now she watched as a pretty woman wearing a baseball cap, sunglasses, pink T-shirt, khaki capris, big fat silver athletic shoes – standard tourist uniform – walked past Posey dancing and into the co-op.

The automatic doors hissed: doors installed by an ambitious manager (now gone), along with a point of site cash register-computer system such as they used at places like Walmart, using a twenty-three percent interest loan that would cripple the Co-op's bottom line for years.

'What does that mean?' the woman asked Kate, taking off her sunglasses. She had beautiful eyes, startlingly blue, but she looked tired. 'Humanitarian aid is never a crime?'

'People were getting arrested for helping illegals that were crossing the border in the desert,' Kate explained. 'Giving them water, that kind of thing.'

'But that's good, isn't? Giving people water in the desert?'

Kate shrugged. 'I would think so, wouldn't you?'

16

'Yes.'

'Let me know if you need any help finding anything,' Kate said.

On the back wall was a mural depicting a couple in a red pickup, merry faces looking out the windows as they drove through desert to a green oasis, where a farmer in a straw hat stood surrounded by bushels of (certainly organic) fruits and vegetables.

'Oooh. Nice.' The woman took a picture of it, then frowned. 'I didn't get it all,' she said.

'Here,' said Windsong. 'Let me try.' It was slow today, everyone down on Main Street dancing.

She handed him the phone. 'Do you guys have melatonin?' she asked Kate, voice going up on the word melatonin.

'Of course. Here, I'll show you.' Kate led her to the right aisle. 'Let me see,' Kate said, scanning the supplements. 'Here it is!'

The woman reached over to the shelf for the bottle. Her hand was shaking just a little bit. Something about her was wrong, off. Stress? The dreadful stress of being a tourist? Or a panic attack, Kate thought. *Maybe she's having a panic attack.* Kate's mother had had panic attacks when Kate was a little girl, before her mother met Bill, now Kate's stepfather.

The woman dropped the bottle of melatonin.

Kate stooped to pick it up. 'Are you all right?' she asked her.

'Yes. No. I mean, I don't know.' She paused. Kate looked concerned.

'My name's Carrie,' the woman said suddenly.

'I'm Kate. Are you sure you're okay?'

17

'Oh, I'm being stupid. I'm sorry.'

'For what? I mean—' Kate began but she didn't finish because Windsong came hustling over, cellphone in his hand.

'Got a good one,' he said to Carrie. 'The whole mural.'

'Thank you.' She held out her hand for it.

'No, wait.' He stepped back. 'Another picture is called for here. Two beautiful ladies.'

They stood together, grinning cheesy smiles as he took the picture.

'Kate!' someone called from the back.

'Ryan wants you, Kate,' Windsong said. Ryan was the manager, at least this week, Windsong liked to joke. The co-op went through managers every three or four months.

But Kate turned to Carrie, concerned. 'Are you sure—?'

'Yes, yes, of course.'

Carrie's cellphone rang.

'Hey, Kate,' called Ryan again.

'That was strange,' Kate said to Windsong later.

'What?'

'That woman? That you took the picture for?'

'Uh huh.'

'The woman in the baseball cap?' Posey asked from the produce section. 'Pretty?'

'Yes.'

'She *was* a little stressed,' Posey said. 'I noticed too.'

'I asked her if she was all right,' Kate said. 'I don't know—'

'Maybe she'll come back,' said Windsong.

18

'Purchase some of our fine all-natural stress reducers.'

'Maybe,' said Kate, standing in the aisle where the herbs were kept in giant glass jars: mugwort, sheep sorrel and skullcap. *Mugwort, sheep sorrel and skullcap*, Kate sang in her head. *Oatstraw and gotu kola.*

Witchy stuff.

From way in the back of the store, Kate heard her cellphone ping. A text coming in. Not Harry, she hoped. She deleted his texts before she even read them, ever since that first one: *Mistake.*

Who cares, thought Kate. *Bully for him. He has no idea where I am.*

'Actually, not so much stressed,' Kate said. 'More like scared.'

'Let's take a walk,' Wes said. 'Before it gets dark.'

He took Carrie's hand, and they left the Copper Queen Hotel. She was feeling better now – it was just stress, she told herself now, making her imagine things. Stress, anxiety, whatever it was, it wasn't real. She planned to tell Wes – not right now, but later – and they would laugh about it.

They climbed the crumbling WPA stamped cement steps behind the hotel. Shadows had begun to lengthen, making mysteries out of alleyways and corners. The air had taken on a renewed vitality, full of interesting smells: fennel and creosote and marijuana. Later, in the dark, the town would begin to glitter.

They passed a big three-story building with a

19

bell tower, then climbed another long flight of steps. It was a mile high, and the altitude made them stop from time to time to catch their breath. They peered down the little alleys that led off on either side, curious about the tiny houses that lined the steps.

From a house nearby, music; it sounded Mexican.

'Salsa,' said Carrie. She loved music.

Last night, she remembered, music from the bars had throbbed in the dark till midnight.

'Wes,' said Carrie. She stopped, suddenly deciding. '*Listen.*'

He stopped too, two steps up from her, one hand on the railing. 'What?'

'There's something I want to tell you.'

'Wait till we get to the top!' he said. 'Almost there. Come on!' In a burst of energy he began to run up the steps.

'Wait up,' she called. 'Come on. Wait.'

He stopped again and turned. She could see his face, his new face without the beard. He seemed to be smiling. He waved at her and turned back. Then she heard a popping noise, barely audible over the salsa music.

He stumbled. He must have missed a step when he stumbled, because he fell.

'Wes,' she called urgently, thinking: what? Oh no, heart attack? The altitude, the climb? 'Wes, are you all right?'

She hurried up the steps, fast, fast.

She'd almost reached him when there was another popping noise. She fell too. One hand stretched out in front of her so that she was just touching his ankle as her blue eyes dimmed, her newly streaked blonde hair still bright.

Four

It was almost dusk when the sirens began. Windsong and Kate heard them as they were closing up. They walked outside together. Windsong was getting on his bicycle and Kate into her car when an ambulance whizzed by on the highway above, red lights flashing, siren full blast.

'Wow!' Windsong teetered on his bike.

Kate started her car and headed for the High Desert Market where she'd pre-ordered a dinner to go. On Main St the noise of sirens grew louder, insistent. Three police cars, lights flashing, went right by the Grill at the Convention Center.

The street was packed, the sound of the sirens like an urgent backdrop. Cars were almost at a standstill, inching along. Damn. Kate usually walked to work, but she'd been running late that morning. She edged along then lucked out and found a parking place just down from the High Desert Market. She pulled in and got out.

People, oddly dressed, crowded the sidewalk. A couple of contestants for the Miz Dud contest, of indeterminate sex, sashayed by. One of them wore a tight black sequinned skirt and feather boa, the other a long purple jacket and leggings.

The air thrummed with tension. What was going on? Kate wondered. People passed by, to and fro, seeming to walk a little faster than usual.

A man in a cowboy hat jostled her arm and hurried on without apology. The sidewalk narrowed a bit just before the market, and someone bumped right into her from behind.

'Excuse me?' someone said.

Kate turned and saw a tall blonde woman in a long black dress. The woman's blonde hair was shiny, well cared for, but didn't match her ageing face, made her look hard. She looked familiar, but Kate had met so many new people lately that she'd lost track of who was who. For a moment they stared at each other, then the woman looked away.

Kate was certain now she must have met her. 'I'm sorry,' she began. 'I've forgotten your name. I—'

'My purse,' the woman interrupted: whisky voice. 'I dropped it.' She pointed down. There it was on the ground, a black suede pouch, next to Kate's foot.

'Oh.' Kate stepped away. 'Do you happen to know what those sirens—?' she started to ask, but the woman was already gone.

Two teenage girls giggled at some lame teenage joke, nudged by, and then Kate was at the market.

Inside it was jam packed, people talking all at once, half tourists, half locals. Peyton, the owner, recognized her and handed over her dinner. Kate took it to the cash register to pay.

'What's going on,' she asked the cashier, a young woman with Rasta braids, as she paid.

'Somebody got shot.'

Shot. Kate felt a little sick. 'How? Was it an accident? Are they okay?'

The girl shrugged. Customers were waiting. 'That's all I know.'

Outside, Kate's cellphone chimed. Dakota.

'Hello?'

'Where are you?' Dakota asked.

'I'm standing by my car at the High Desert Market.'

'Well, get in your car, lock the doors,' said Dakota. 'Then go home and lock yourself in. Someone shot and killed two tourists. That's what those sirens are about.'

'No. *Two* tourists? My god. Who?'

'I don't know who shot them. I don't know if anyone knows or if someone's been arrested or anything. It happened on the steps that go up to High Road past the Central School. Not like a drunken bar thing. It's kind of panicky around here right now. You need to play it safe.'

Kate pulled in her carport and got out. She'd only lived in this house, a renovated miner's shack bought on spec by an out-of-towner, for a month. Before that she'd stayed with Dakota. A small house on a narrow winding street, almost quaint but not quite. So the rent was pretty low.

When she'd first moved in, the shabby little house on her left had housed a portly bass player, who practiced long into the night. One night the police came and talked to the bass player, Kate watching through her bedroom window, and then he was gone and now a 'For Rent' sign hung crookedly on the wire fence that surrounded the front yard.

In the house on the other side, a line of bright zinnias grew along the little picket fence. It was twilight now, and the lights were on inside. An elderly woman, Estelle, lived there alone with her two cats. 'Hello, cats,' Kate would hear her say in the early morning. 'You're the most beautiful cats in the *whole entire world.*'

If anything happened she could scream, and Estelle might even hear her. Still, it was scary. She unlocked the door and went inside, slamming the door behind her. If she didn't slam it pretty hard the lock wouldn't catch. She rented the house furnished and hadn't done much to make it her own, except throw a Mexican shawl over the couch. Spiders had spun their webs in the corners, and occasionally a tiny packaged insect would fall on to a countertop or a table or the floor.

Kate checked the side door to make sure it was locked, and then went round to all her windows to make sure they were all closed and locked. She put the dinner, tandoori chicken, in the microwave for two minutes. Her laptop was on the kitchen counter, and she opened it to check her email while the dinner was heating. Not much except yet another email from Harry – he sent them once or twice a week.

She usually deleted them right away, but this one she started to read.

I don't care how awful this letter is, he wrote, *it's just too damn bad. What you are is a self*

24

centered, inconsiderate, unthinking, spoiled princess and you—

She stopped reading and hit delete.

The microwave pinged, and her cellphone chimed.

Bill, her stepfather, calling from Long Island. Her mother had died three years ago, but she was still close to her stepfather.

'Bill,' she said. 'What's up?'

'You okay?'

'Yes. Why?'

'Saw something on my Google home page – you know I have the Arizona section, 'cause of you living there. Said two people got shot right there in Dudley. That's about all it said though.'

'I can't tell you anything else.' She went to her home page on the laptop. 'I'm home, don't worry, I'm safe. Everything's fine,' she lied.

'Good, good.'

She typed in 'Dudley, AZ shooting', got nothing that was newer than what Dakota had told her. 'So, Bill,' she said, 'how are *you*?'

'I'm all right.' He paused. 'But the other day, I was thinking, I don't know why. You remember, Kate, how me and your mom used to play Scrabble all the time?'

'Of course.'

'I was just thinking, what a bad sport your mother was.'

'She was,' Kate said. 'A terrible sport.'

'It made her so happy to win,' said Bill. 'I should have let her win more. I see that now.'

'Bill, it's all right. You were the best thing that ever happened to her.'

25

There was a pause.

'How are you, Katie?' Bill asked. 'I know things have been rough these last few months.'

'I'm okay. Better. I like this job I have. It's maybe not my future, but it lets me rest for a while.'

'Well, hang in there. You deserve the best. Don't forget that, okay?' His voice broke a little. 'Gotta go, Kate. You be careful now.'

'You too,' Kate said, but he was already gone.

She ate the tandoori chicken in front of the television, feeling nervous, unfocused, too alert, as if she were waiting for some reason to act.

The house felt stuffy with everything locked up. She needed some air, so she opened the door that led out to the porch. It was on the side of the house by Estelle, so relatively safe, the street light close by. Crickets chirped in the cool dark. Somewhere down the street a neighbor she had never met had the television going, an audience, eerie in the dark, erupting in laughter at some comedian making a joke.

She saw the headlights of trucks above on the bypass faraway: first the front headlights bright white, then the red as the trucks receded. She saw her mother from twenty years ago, standing in her garden, wearing a big floppy hat. She had a spade in her hand, and she was laughing.

Then someone knocked on her door.

Five

Lupita Flores, a waitress at El Serape restaurant, heard the commotion too, the sirens of the police cars going up the hill. Suddenly, it seemed like everyone in the restaurant was on a cellphone, followed by a mad dash to the door.

'What's happening?' she asked the Lonely Man. That was what Lupita called him to herself, though she knew his real name. Malcolm, Malcolm MacGregor. He was a cop from Mesa, on some kind of sick leave. Somewhere in his forties, not too bad-looking for an old guy, nice, always polite, good tipper.

Malcolm was checking out his cellphone. 'Some tourists got shot.'

'What. *What*?' said Lupita. 'Got shot where? Here? Here in Dudley?'

'Looks like it.'

'Oh my God,' said Lupita. 'Where? Who did it?'

He stood up. 'Think I'll go see.'

He'd been coming in a lot in the last few weeks, always by himself. He and Frank the owner got along really well; one night when it was slow they'd serenaded Lupita with a terrible rendition of 'Twenty Four Hours from Tulsa'.

'Wait,' Lupita said. 'Take my cell number, okay? Five five five, two three zero zero. *Text me* when you find out.'

27

'Then here's mine,' Malcolm said and gave it to her. 'Text me if *you* find out.'

It was kind of a joke, really. They were always kidding around.

He put a ten-dollar bill and a five on the table and left.

Drunks, thought Lupita, a bunch of drunks, probably, that killed those tourists. Drunks shooting off their guns down on the Gulch, showing off. Assholes.

The restaurant was pretty much emptied out – nothing left inside now but Lupita, Frank in the back, and silence.

Lupita imagined all the tourists jumping into their cars, their trucks, their SUVs, driving away from Dudley, heading for home. She surveyed the tables with their red-checked tablecloths, silverware and napkins neatly laid, a tiny glass vase with one fake red rose on each table. The smell of oregano and poblano chili lingered in the air – Frank's *posole*, and no one to eat it.

No customers, no tips.

Her nana's birthday was coming up. She'd planned to buy her two CDs – one by the mariachi singer Jose Maria Solis and one by Vicente Hernandez – but now maybe she'd just get one. She and her brother Chico lived with their nana Ariana, who had raised them after their Anglo mother ran off with a beer distributor. Their father had pretty much lived in the bars until he died. They still lived with their nana – partly to look after her in her old age, and partly because it saved them a lot of money.

'Jesus. Benny just called, told me what happened.' Frank, the owner and chief cook, short, rotund and bearded, came out from the kitchen, out the front door, leaving it open as he lit a cigarette. 'Two people got shot! Both of 'em dead.'

'Dead? Oh, *no.*'

Lupita came out and sat down on the empty smoker's bench where normally all the customers they got on busy nights would sit and wait for a table. She was too thin, dark complected, almost but not quite beautiful. '*Who*?' she asked.

'No one we know. They were tourists,' Frank said.

'I mean, who did it?'

'If anyone knows they're not saying.'

'Oh god.' Lupita put her heads in her hands. 'Everyone will be scared off. They won't come to Dudley any more. We'll all be poor.' She paused. 'I mean, poorer.'

Frank laughed. 'No sympathy for the people who got killed?'

'I do, I do have sympathy,' Lupita cried. 'I didn't mean it, the way it sounded.' She crossed herself dramatically.

'He's not gonna forgive you,' Frank said.

'Who?'

'That guy in the sky you're crossing yourself for. In fact, not even is he not going to forgive you, he's not even there.'

'Sinner!' Lupita hit out at his arm, but he danced aside and she missed.

'Go home,' Frank said. 'I'll close up; no use you hanging around. Wait—' He stood up, went

29

into the kitchen and came back with a takeout container. 'Some *posole* for your nana.'

'*Thank you.*' Lupita took the container, smiled and threw him a little kiss.

'You be careful now,' Frank called after her, 'walking home.'

She didn't live too far away if you were young, eighteen and didn't mind a steep hill. She trudged up slowly, tired from her day, carrying the takeout of *posole*. Her brother Chico loved *posole* too; it would be great if he were home, but he usually came in late after she was asleep. He was an artist and had a studio downtown; another artist let him use for free. Maybe she would wait up for him tonight – he would know all about the tourists getting killed. He always knew what was going on downtown.

The house was wood frame and ramshackle and needed a paint job. By the rusty wire gate was a large totem-like figure, painted in an intricate lace of colors, that Chico had made a few years ago. As she came closer, Lupita heard a sound like a baby crying, except there weren't any babies in the neighborhood. She ran up the rest of the steps and into the house.

It was dark except for the light of the television and the light from a votive candle lit under nana's plaster statue of the Virgin of Guadaloupe. The sound was off on the TV, and her nana was standing in the middle of the living room in her nice purple velour running suit, and her hair, always so perfect (she had worked for the city of Dudley for many years before retiring) – her

30

hair was all messed up. Her nana was standing in the middle of the living room, wringing her hands and weeping.

'What's wrong!' Lupita cried. She ran over her and put her arms around her. 'Nana, what is it?'

'They came up here,' she said.

'Who?'

'The police. That Debbie Hannigan and Sergeant Ben Luna.'

'Why? What about?'

'Chico. They told me— They— They *arrested* him.'

'No! For *what*? Chico never does anything wrong. It sounds like harassment. Was it marijuana?'

'No, no. They're saying he killed those tourists.'

Malcolm stood just off the road at a spot with a good view of the crime scene. The ambulances had gone, but law enforcement was still working on stringing yellow crime-scene tape everywhere and gathering evidence. It was dark now, but the crime scene was lit up by the street light.

So much blood.

When he'd first moved here to live in his sister-in-law Sally's investment house in Dudley, he'd read a bunch of old books from his father's library that his brother and sister-in-law had stashed in the house. After a while it wasn't enough, so he gave up on that and started hanging out like some old fool in the El Serape restaurant.

Still, he got a chuckle out of the quote at the front of Willeford's *New Hope for the Dead*, a

31

quote by Pascal: '*Man's unhappiness stems from his inability to sit quietly in his room.*'

So now he was sneaking up on crime scenes for a little vicarious thrill. His shoulder was bothering him, as usual, but he'd learned to ignore it.

A bearded man in jogging clothes came towards him, nodded with his head in the direction of the crime scene. 'Man, oh, man,' he said with a distinct New York accent. 'Can you believe this? Some drunk shot a couple of tourists.'

'That what it was?' Malcolm said. 'Some drunk?'

'Yeah. A drunk with a gun. That's what I love about the great state of Arizona. Everybody and anybody gets to pack heat.'

For a moment they stood together companionably, two strangers united by catastrophe.

The man raised one hand. 'Ciao,' he said and walked away.

Malcolm stood for a long time, watching yet not watching, in a kind of trance. A drunk with a gun.

Something bothered him about the scene, but he wasn't sure what. He turned away and started down the hill, picking his way around the potholes in the decaying asphalt, bits of fluff from the desert broom that flowered along the side of the road following him like the flicker of memories in the brain, just below consciousness.

It was the blood, he thought. There was so much of it. What kind of firearm was it, anyway? An AK-47?

His cellphone pinged a text. Lupita. He

remembered now he'd said he would text her when he found out what was going on. He opened it.

Help, it said. *Call me.*

Six

Kate froze for a moment when she heard the knock. Someone knocked again. She went to the window closest to the door and peeked out. A man and a woman; the woman was wearing a uniform. *The police.* Her stomach gave a little lurch. The police were standing there at her door, and behind them she could see mostly dark apart from a street light a way down, a mist of bugs swirling around it.

Thoughts swirled in her mind like the bugs: a homicidal maniac was on the loose in Dudley and they were going door to door to warn everyone; Harry Light, in a rage, had concocted a false story about some crime she had committed, such as leaving him when all he'd done wrong was to treat her like shit. Or someone somewhere that she loved was dead.

Cheer up, she told herself, it's probably just the homicidal maniac.

She went to the door and opened it.

'Kate? Kate Waters?' said the woman in the uniform. Plumpish with dark wavy hair.

'Yes?'

'I'm Officer Deborah Hannigan, and this is

my sergeant, Ben Luna, Dudley PD.' Sergeant Luna nodded politely, dark hair graying handsomely.

'Yes?' Kate said again.

Sergeant Luna cleared his throat. 'Would you mind answering a few questions?'

'Questions about what?' Kate said. 'I mean, no, please. Come on.'

They came in.

'I know it's kind of late,' said Sergeant Luna, 'but we'd like to talk to you now while things are fresh in your mind.'

Kate led them to the section off the kitchen that might be called a dining room, four chairs around a table. 'What things? Sit down, please,' she said. 'Would you like, um, some coffee?' she offered, before she remembered she'd run out.

'No, thank you, ma'am,' Sergeant Luna said, and Officer Hannigan shook her head. They sat down, so Kate did too.

'What on earth,' Kate asked, 'is this all about?'

Sergeant Luna cleared his throat. 'I understand you're acquainted with Caroline Cooper?'

Kate sat down on the other chair. '*Who*?'

'Caroline Cooper.'

'I don't think so,' Kate said. 'I'm sorry, you must have come to the wrong house. I've never even heard of Caroline Cooper. I mean, why are you asking? Who is she?'

Sergeant Luna leaned across the table at her. 'Caroline Cooper and her husband Wesley were shot to death tonight.'

'The two tourists? Is that who you're talking

34

about?' Kate stared blankly at Ben Luna's nice pleasant face. What he was saying didn't make sense, and she had never in her life heard of Caroline and Wesley Cooper. 'How would I know them?'

Officer Ryan opened the file folder and produced two computer printouts of photographs and slid them over to Kate. One was of the mural at the Natural Foods Co-op, and one was of—

'*Carrie*,' Kate said. 'That's me and Carrie.' She looked up. 'Carrie? Is Carrie—?'

'Caroline Cooper,' Sergeant Luna said.

'Oh, no.' Kate put her hand over her mouth. She looked at the photograph again, seeing how pretty Carrie was, but even in the photo her smile was not quite happy. 'She was scared,' she said. 'When I talked to her at the Co-op, she was scared about something.'

'*Really*,' said Ben Luna. 'And did she tell you what?'

'No. No, she didn't.' She thought of Carrie. She was dead? It really didn't register. 'I'm so *sorry*. I – I don't *know* her. She was at the Co-op, and she wanted some melatonin. She seemed shaky to me, so I was concerned. Then Windsong came and took that picture with her cellphone, and then she left.'

Kate took a breath. 'I don't see – I mean—' She felt herself babbling. 'Someone *shot* her and her husband? She's *dead*?'

Sergeant Luna nodded.

'We hardly talked at all,' Kate said.

'Shaky. You said shaky. Like, how, exactly?'

35

Sergeant Luna's voice was patient. 'What made you think she was scared?'

'She didn't say she was scared, but I could tell she was, the way she acted.' Kate paused. 'That's it. What about who did it? Are they still out there?'

'We have a suspect in custody.'

Kate leaned back in her chair in relief. 'Well, thank God for that. Who?'

They gave her a name, Hispanic. No one she knew. Though she hardly knew anyone in town, anyway. 'Was he drunk or what?' she asked.

She looked at them for some kind of answer, but the faces of Sergeant Luna and Officer Hannigan bore no expression at all, as if they had turned to wax dolls right there at Kate's dining-room table.

'Nothing else you remember?' Sergeant Luna asked.

'Not really.'

Officer Hannigan and Sergeant Luna rose in unison. 'If you think of anything else,' said Sergeant Luna. 'Please let us know. Here's my card.'

Kate took it. 'At least you've arrested someone,' she said. 'Now I don't have to worry about someone coming over and shooting me.' She laughed, a little self-consciously.

'It never hurts to lock your doors,' Officer Hannigan said.

Seven

The initial appearance for Chico Flores took place the next morning, a Sunday, in the justice court over by the county jail. Lupita, Lupita's nana, Ariana, and Malcolm sat on the hard wooden benches inside the courtroom. They were the only people in the courtroom except for a prosecutor from the County Attorney's office, a court reporter and the judge, a Judge Harvey. Chico, looking like a pale ghost, was on a television with a defense attorney who was out of view, except for one arm that appeared from time to time as the judge spoke.

They listened as the judge read the charges. Two counts of first-degree murder, one count of public intoxication. A drunk, a stupid drunk, thought Malcolm, no matter how smart Lupita and Ariana had assured him Chico was as they waited in the courtroom. Bail was set at one million dollars, causing gasps of horror from Lupita and Ariana. Then it was over.

First-degree murder was unlikely to stick, Malcolm was thinking. Cops always overcharged. Negligent homicide was what he was thinking, from his experience as a cop and also his year of law school, before being Cindy's husband had taken away his focus. That's probably what he'd end up pleading to: two counts of negligent homicide. After the brouhaha died down.

Except this was a murder in a tourist town. Lots of pressure. No one outside the system would want a plea bargain.

They went outside and sat on a bench, waiting for Chico's lawyer to show up. Ariana sniffled softly, and Lupita sat pale and rigid.

'I thought his lawyer was going to get him out,' Lupita said finally. 'A million dollars! Who can come up with that?'

'Actually, it would be ten percent of a million,' Malcolm said. He explained.

'A hundred thousand then,' said Lupita in a voice of despair.

It was still early and, even though they were in the desert, muggy. Tiny gnats nipped at their skin. Malcolm was still trying to process how he, a cop, had ended up out here with the relatives of a man accused of committing a double homicide.

'Chico is a very good artist,' Ariana said to Malcolm. 'He always was good at drawing, and then a couple of years ago these artists in town, they saw what he was doing, and they helped him out, gave him a studio for free so he could work.'

'He's even in a show downtown right now,' said Lupita. 'At the Sail Rabbit Gallery.'

'Really?' Malcolm said with interest. 'The Sale Rabbit Gallery? What kind of name is that? They sell rabbits too along with the art?'

'No, it's spelled S-A-I-L. Chico said it's a postmodern name; that means don't ask me what it means,' said Lupita.

'That's all he cares about, being an artist,'

Ariana said. 'This—' She threw out her hands. 'This whole thing is not . . . it's not possible. It is a mistake.'

Lupita patted her on the back.

'Excuse me. I must use the restroom.' Ariana stood up. She walked carefully, with dignity, back inside the building. She was dressed in black pants and a black and white silk blouse, as if about to go to work in an office.

Lupita watched her go. 'My poor poor nana.' She sniffed sadly. 'He hasn't even used that gun for months,' she said, '*years*. It was just an accident.'

'What gun is that?' Malcolm asked.

'It was this twenty-two. He got it when he was sixteen. 'Cause of our father. He would drink a lot and then try to hurt nana. So Chico got this gun at an estate sale. It was this gun-guy's widow, you know, and she hated guns so she was happy to sell it to Chico. He even took a class about how to use it.'

'A twenty-two, you said?'

Lupita nodded. 'Our father died, a couple of years ago, so Chico didn't need the gun any more. He put it some place.' She shrugged. 'I don't know where.'

And took it out one night, went to a bar, got really drunk, waved the gun around and accidentally shot two tourists? 'A twenty-two semi-automatic,' Malcolm mused. 'It would have ten rounds. He must have fired them all. Still—'

Then a car pulled up in front, and a man with a briefcase got out. 'Miss Flores?' he said.

'Yes.'

He strode over, hand out, a roundish man, balding, in khakis and a tan sports jacket that appeared to have been slept in. 'Stuart Ross. I'm Chico's attorney.' He glanced at Malcolm.

'Just a friend,' Malcolm said.

'Bail is *one million dollars*,' Lupita said in outrage.

'Wouldn't expect less with a double homicide,' said Stuart Ross. 'I'll work on getting it lowered, but today was just *pro forma* stuff. Right now I can tell you law enforcement thinks the killings appear to be drug related.'

Drug related, Malcolm thought, beginning to regret being there at all.

'I'll have more to tell you when the reports start coming in,' Stuart Ross said. 'Here's my—' he fumbled in a pocket – 'card.'

'My nana's inside. She'd like to ask you some questions, and we'd like to know when you can get him out of—' Lupita started to say.

But he was gone.

'Drug related is stupid,' Lupita said. 'Chico didn't do drugs. And what does *pro forma* even mean?' she asked Malcolm.

He explained.

Eight

'I don't kill any of them,' the woman was saying at the table next to Dakota and Kate's at Poco's Vegan Cafe.

'Not even scorpions?' said her companion.

'Not even scorpions. Or spiders. Or centipedes. What I do is get a glass jar, put it on top of them, then kind of slide some cardboard underneath and take them outside. They're innocent. Not like humans—' A note of disgust crept in. 'Humans just kill and kill for no reason at all, just the fun of it.'

'What about mosquitoes? You don't kill *them*?'

'Chico's a gentle soul,' Dakota was saying. She took a bite of her gluten-free deep fried Brussel sprouts burrito. 'He wouldn't hurt a fly. The only good coming out of this whole thing is that if people think he's a murderer, they'll probably buy some of his pieces.'

Dakota wore a black tunic and skinny black jeans, her hennaed red hair in a soft frizz around her face. She and Kate were having lunch at Poco's then going over to the Sail Rabbit Gallery to see some of Chico's work.

'But if he was drunk when he did it, it probably wasn't on purpose,' Kate pointed out.

'Nobody thinks he did it, actually.'

'Why would they arrest him then?'

'Come *on*,' Dakota said. '*Chamber of Commerce*? Arrest someone right away so the tourists won't get scared off.'

Kate finished off her quinoa taco and took a sip of healing coconut water. It tasted uninteresting.

'God,' said Dakota. 'I still can't believe you talked to her. That is so *destiny* or something.'

'I didn't really talk to her. I just showed her where the melatonin was,' Kate said. Her hand

41

was shaking, just a bit. 'I keep thinking about her, *dead*, just like that. Everything all over, forever.'

There was a pause.

'If it wasn't Chico,' Kate said, 'whoever did it is still out there. It just kind of freaks me out.'

'Look,' Dakota said, 'if you're so nervous, you can come stay with me again for a while till this blows over. The guy next door – you met him, remember? Biker Bill. He'll look out for us.'

'That's okay.'

Dakota regarded her for a moment. 'You know what you need, is some super sublingual vitamin B. It's fantastic for stress and anxiety. I've got some; I carry it with me all the time.' She reached in her purse, took out a small bottle and shook it vigorously. 'Here. It has a dropper. You squirt it under your tongue, and it goes to work right away.'

Kate squirted. It tasted sweet and bitter at the same time.

'It's that guy,' said Dakota. 'The one you ran away from, Harry. He's made you into a nervous wreck.'

The Sail Rabbit Gallery was down on the Gulch, between Spokes, a bicycle shop and VaVa Boom, a vintage clothing store. A KOLD-TV Channel Thirteen van was parked up a little way from the gallery, and a cameraman was panning a view of the street.

'Hey, Kate!' Windsong swerved towards her, teetered-tottering on his bicycle. He was wearing a tattered vintage bowling shirt with the name

42

PHIL embroidered on one pocket and looked a little dreamy; he probably smoked a number before hitting the streets on this fine day.

'What?'

'The press is looking for you.'

'What press?' She gestured toward the Channel Thirteen van. 'Them?'

'Not them. It was the *Arizona Daily Star* guy. I don't see him right now.'

An artfully hand-lettered sign in the gallery window said: 'Chico Flores: Lost Innocence'.

'Lost innocence. Can you believe it?' Dakota said. 'Let's go in. I want you to meet Melody. She's one of the arts collective members.'

They went inside.

Melody was a pale woman with dense black hair and red-framed glasses. Behind the glasses her eyes were red too, as though she had been crying all night.

'Hi,' she said politely when Dakota introduced Kate. 'Dakota's talked about you a lot. It's nice to meet you.' She extended a limp hand, but clearly her heart wasn't in it.

She faded away into the back somewhere.

A gaggle of people – from tourists in clean bright clothes and running shoes, to punks and Goths, all in black with hennaed hair and piercings – filled the gallery space. The white walls were hung with baby dolls painted bright colors and crucified on crosses decorated with rhinestones and glitter. Kate stood back to get the full effect – it transcended the materials, the crosses sad bright jewels on the gallery wall. That sounded like copy for a press release, something she might have written back in her community arts center days.

'Excuse me?' someone said.

Kate turned, and there was a young man with a dark beard and tiny wire-rimmed glasses. 'Are you Kate Waters?'

She nodded.

'Ben O'Malley. I'm a reporter with *Arizona Daily Star*. I was talking to Windsong, and he said he took a picture of you and Caroline with Caroline's cellphone.'

'So?'

'Did you talk at all?'

'Why, yes, she said to me: someone's going to shoot me and my husband later on and there's nothing I can do about it.'

'Jesus Christ! No kidding!'

'Kidding,' Kate said.

'Hey,' Ben O'Malley said, 'give me a break here. I'm with a *newspaper*, for Christ's sake. We need all the help we can get.'

'I'm sorry,' said Kate, suddenly wary. 'I really don't have any comment for you.' She turned away abruptly, almost running into a man coming in behind her.

'*Sorry.*' He bowed like someone from an eighteenth-century novel. Blue T-shirt under a sports jacket. A tired face with angular features, but a nice smile.

'My fault.' Kate smiled back.

Something zinged in the air. For a second they stared at each other like old friends. Kate felt her face flush.

'Malcolm MacGregor,' he said.

44

'MacGregor,' said Kate. 'Like in Peter Rabbit and the flopsy bunnies.' She couldn't believe she'd said that.

But he laughed. 'And all that soporific lettuce. I think I read that book to my nephew only a year or so ago.'

'I'm Kate. Kate Waters.'

'You like the show?'

'I kind of do.'

'And the artist? Chico? Do you know him?'

Why was he asking all these questions? Kate wondered suddenly. Who was he? Better check with Dakota. And that vitamin B stuff wasn't working at all. 'No,' she said cautiously. 'No, I don't. I—'

'Kate!' Windsong was outside, waving his arms at her.

'Excuse me,' Kate said.

The Safeway was located out of town a way, near one of the newer developments. That afternoon on his way there, in his blue Chevy 1500 truck that was too big for a tiny town like Dudley, Malcolm thought about the woman he'd spoken to in the gallery. Kate Waters. She'd been talking to that reporter; he'd seen her through the gallery window. It had to be something to do with the murder of the tourists, that was why the press was there. He wondered what. She had a kind of – what? – undercurrent of unease that he'd always found attractive. And he liked the Peter Rabbit stuff, dumb as it might be, but that was neither here nor there. It was nowhere.

And where the hell am *I*? he wondered,

45

passing Tin Town, a cluster of houses, tiny like toys, tiny church, big bar. To his left in the distance was a rusted structure from an old mining excavation, abandoned years ago. It looked like some ancient ruined Mayan temple, worshipers long dead in some bloody tribal ritual.

Get a grip.

At the Safeway, he bought a six-pack of Sam Adams beer, a pound of hamburger – eighty percent lean, even though his dead wife Cindy had always bought the ninety percent, 'cause you needed a little fat for the taste – and some Philly Cheese Hamburger Helper. Cindy would be appalled at the way he'd been eating. Yeah, right, Cindy, he thought as he trundled his cart out to the parking lot, your diet was so good, and where did it get you? Jesus Christ.

No more thinking about Cindy.

Better to think about Chico Flores. Much better.

Negligent homicide, he decided, because there didn't appear to be any intent, just a drunk waving a gun around like a total asshole, though of course he hadn't read the police reports yet. According to Lupita, Chico owned what sounded to him like a twenty-two semi-automatic – it would have ten rounds in it, and he'd probably fired them all. Two counts of negligent homicide; hard to plead that down much more with two deaths and an outraged town that relied on tourists for a living.

Chico seemed like maybe an okay guy – whatever you decided about those baby dolls in the gallery as art, just making them had to have been a lot of work. But look what Chico's carelessness had done – not just to the tourists, but to his sister and his grandmother.

Back home Malcolm checked his laptop for updates. The bloggers had jumped in already, he noted, blaming the deaths of Wes and Carrie Cooper on the Democrats, on the Republicans, on the Tea Party, on a lack of gun control, on inadequate security on the border and, by extension, on Janet Napolitano and President Obama, on illegal aliens, on the Mexican drug cartels, on vigilante groups, on terrorists cells lurking everywhere, and finally on Sheriff Joe Arpiao and Governor Jan Brewer.

Malcolm cooked up the hamburger with the Philly Cheese Hamburger Helper, ate it in front of the TV with a bottle of Sam Adams. He hadn't slept well the night before, and he fell asleep on the couch while the Channel Thirteen weatherman was still talking.

He woke up hours later, to the ten o'clock news. They were playing an interview with Belen Acuna, the woman who had initially called the police after the Dudley shooting.

'For a minute I didn't know what was happening,' she said. 'I heard the shots – one, two – and I thought fireworks. Then I looked out my window. I could see the woman, poor thing, she was lying on the steps.'

Still foggy, Malcolm took a swig of Sam Adams, by now warm and lacking any fizz.

'Pretty tough on you,' said the interviewer. 'Thank you, Belen Acuna. The alleged shooter,

Chico Flores, is being held in the Cochise County jail on a million-dollar bond.'

Malcolm stood up, drained the rest of the beer and took his dinner plate and fork out to the kitchen. The window over the sink that looked out on to a cement wall was a dark blank. *Wait,* he thought suddenly, did I hear that right? He set the plate and fork in the sink, went to his computer, to the Channel Thirteen website, and replayed the interview.

Once again Belen Acuna said, 'For a minute I didn't know what was happening. I heard the shots – one, two – and I thought fireworks. Then I looked out my window. I could see the woman, poor thing, she was lying on the steps.'

Two shots, she'd said. Only two shots? Something was off here, seriously off.

Nine

'The thing is, I thought he was going to get out *right away*,' said Lupita, Monday morning.

'Oh, honey,' Attorney Stuart Ross's secretary Ruth Norton said. 'I'm so sorry.' She pulled a Kleenex from the box she kept ever ready on her desk, got up and went to Lupita, who was sitting in the chair by the window, face scrunched up in a grimace, weeping silently.

Lupita took it and blew her nose. She looked at Ruth, who she'd hardly noticed before because she'd started crying as soon she was walked into the office. Middle-aged, thick reddish brown hair with a streak of white down the center. She reminded Lupita of a substitute teacher who used to fill in back when she was in junior high.

'I can see you love your brother a lot,' Ruth said kindly.

Lupita nodded.

Then Stuart Ross came out of his office and gestured at Lupita to come in. She did and sat down. 'You couldn't even get him out?' she said accusingly. She sniffed, and a small tear rolled down her cheek.

He looked at his watch, as if he wanted to get rid of her as fast he could. He cleared his throat. 'Before we lose sight of reality, don't forget that just after the tourists were shot, he was found holding the gun that shot them.'

'Isn't he supposed to be innocent until proven guilty?'

'Of course.'

'So what next?'

'They can only hold him for a week before either a grand jury indicts him or there's a preliminary hearing, but I doubt there'll be a PH.'

'PH?'

Stuart looked overly patient. 'The abbreviation for preliminary hearing. Look, there's probably going to be an indictment, and I plan to file a motion to modify his conditions of release as soon—'

'Modify conditions of release. What does that *mean*?'

'I'll ask the judge to lower his bail or release

him on his own recognizance. The case stinks to high heaven, and the media's swarming – we need to let them see just how lousy the case is.'

'His own recognizance would be best—' Lupita began.

'Not going to happen. Best-case scenario is they lower the bail to fifty thousand, but even that isn't certain.'

'But—'

'Okay. Look, it's a long shot getting him released right away. The most likely scenario – here's the speech. You up for it?'

'Yes.'

'The judge has imposed extraordinary bail. That can't be changed unless we can show extraordinary facts why it should be lowered. That's where an evidentiary hearing comes in.'

'What's that?'

Mr Ross looked at his watch again. 'It's a hearing for the purpose of determining what evidence should be suppressed or whether claims made by the prosecution in seeking such high bail are supported by evidence at all.' He paused.

'And?' said Lupita.

'It's not a one-step dance. First, the court will have a hearing to decide whether or not to grant the motion at all. Then, after determining that, how much time it will take, whether or not depositions must occur, how much time for written response prior to the hearing—'

'Wait!' said Lupita. 'Can't you just tell me how long it will take?'

'No.'

'*No*?'

'Welcome to the legal system. This case is too hot right now – he's accused of killing two tourists in a tourist town. That's why a strategic release hearing right away is best, so pertinent facts can come to light for the benefit of the media and at least let in some doubt. But frankly, unless by some entirely unlikely miracle the grand jury doesn't indict, he's going to be in jail a while.'

Lupita sighed. Outside the window she had a good view of the shop across the street, vintage clothes on display: a pair of cowboy boots leaning against each other, an old prairie dress covered with ricrac. Junk. Junk, she thought, the clothes and the tourists who bought them; then she thought of her Nana, her heart broken, and Chico, her beautiful good brother who had never ever been in trouble in his whole life.

Except that one time, no, twice, actually, when he was sixteen and got caught with some marijuana. But he was a juvenile, and the record was sealed so it didn't really count. And neither did that school detention stuff either.

Stuart Ross whooshed out a sigh. 'Look,' he said, 'you may not know as much about your brother as you think you do. You're going to have to trust his attorney. That's me.'

'But what—' Lupita began, but Mr Ross held up a hand.

'Not now,' he said. 'I've got a court appearance in ten minutes. And one more thing. You're entitled to come to all the hearings, but you need to control yourself. It's not going to help Chico if you make a scene.'

51

'Kate!' said Windsong and Posey, excited, in unison, as Kate came in the hissing sliding doors. 'Look at this!'

'What?'

'You're famous,' Posey said.

'Hey!' said a customer. 'Are you planning to ring me up or just socialize?'

'Sorry.' Windsong rapidly weighed a bunch of grapes, rang up some Brown Cow yogurt. When the customer left, he reached under the counter and brought up a copy of the *Arizona Daily Star*. 'Read this!' he said, pointing to an article.

She scanned the article; it was about the murders and contained mostly information she already knew. She paused at the line: *Many Dudley residents doubt Flores' guilt. 'It's the Chamber of Commerce,' Doreen Davies, an aromatherapist, commented, 'deciding who's guilty and who isn't.'*

'Last paragraph,' Windsong said.

Kate Waters, a Dudley Natural Foods Co-op employee, she read, *had her picture taken with Caroline Cooper's cellphone earlier in the day but would not comment on the encounter.*

'What!' Kate said. 'I didn't tell him anything, and he still has to go and mention my name?'

'He's an asshole. He talked to me too,' said Windsong in a hurt tone. 'I said almost exactly the same thing Doreen did, and he never mentioned my name once in the whole article.'

'Well, I wish he mentioned you instead of me,' Kate said.

'Why do you care?'

'It might show up online.'

'So?' said Windsong. 'Aren't you kind of over-reacting a bit?'

'It's a long story.'

'That crazy ex?'

'Who, Harry?'

Windsong smiled. 'Ha! I knew there was one.'

'How do you know that?'

''Cause there's something about you that's ever so slightly paranoid.'

'God! You know what? People in this town are crazy. I thought Vermont was bad, but this is worse.'

'Hey.' Windsong looked stricken. 'I'm sorry, I really am. Maybe it's true what my ex used to say, that I have Asperger's syndrome. I really am sorry. Look, I honestly think this has to do with drug cartels and stuff like that. Carrie seemed like a very nice person, but that doesn't mean she wasn't dealing drugs. I don't think you're in any danger.' He paused. 'At least, not from whoever killed the tourists. Don't worry, we'll protect you here at the Co-op. It's part of our basically non-existent benefit package.'

'Comforting,' said Kate.

'Where is he, anyway?'

'California.'

'What I think is, you're a nervous person. You need to learn how to chill. You might try yoga; there's a really good yoga teacher, Marsha— Wait.' He stepped out from behind the register. 'I've got something for you. They just came in, a whole line of mists.'

'Look,' said Kate. 'I've already tried the sublingual vitamin B complex. That didn't do anything.'

'Oh ye of little faith,' said Windsong. 'You have to keep trying. Now, these mists, they have to do with chakras and stuff like that. Here—' He handed her a blue bottle. 'It's on me.'

Kate held it in her hand, read the label out loud. 'Ghostbuster Mist: generously mist in closets, around windows, behind furniture, under and above beds to prevent bad dreams and banish any unwanted monsters of all shapes and sizes.' She stopped and looked at Windsong. 'Come *on*.'

'I know, I know,' Windsong said, 'but it might work, what if it does? Besides, what else is working? Economies are crashing all over the world except in China, the Middle East is one big uprising, Iran is making atomic weapons, and three houses on my street have gone into foreclosure. So tell me that: what else in this whole world is really working?'

Maybe it would be better to stay at Dakota's for a while, Kate thought when she got home, after that newspaper article. She could leave her car here and walk to Dakota's. She collected some things to take with her and then checked her email: one from speak-of-the-devil Harry with the subject line *Sorry*.

She opened it – *I think in the end you'll be sorry for what you've done with your life, you're not young any* – closed it and hit delete.

And who was this? The subject line said: *Hi Kate?*

Hi! Is this the right Kate Waters? This is Ellen Wilson, we knew each other in New York City? Or did we? I've been trying to find you (your

54

facebook page is old old old) and suddenly there was your name in a Tucson newspaper.

Ellen Wilson. New York City. Back before Vermont, long ago.

Yes, Kate typed back, *it's me. Hi Ellen! Hope you're well. What's going on with you?* and hit send.

Suddenly, she felt more grounded, as if she were not just a person in the present but also someone with a past.

Ellen answered immediately. *I live in the suburbs outside the city now. Just inherited a house from my aunt in New Jersey. I'll probably sell it when the market settles. In the meantime I've been searching out old friends – we can all get together and kind of camp out for a couple of days at auntie's house. How about that? ☺ Ooblecks forever!!*

Kate smiled. Ooblecks. Oobleck was green goo from a Dr Suess book. New to New York City, she and Ellen had hung out together with a group of friends, gone to the same bars, lingered around the art world fringes. 'Who are *we*?' someone had said. 'Just Ooblecks.'

She had some money in the bank, inherited from her mother, but it wasn't enough to live on for any length of time; it was just for special emergencies. It would be too expensive, too hard to justify, but for a moment she yearned to go hang out with Ellen and all the other Ooblecks again for a few days, as if she could skip all the pain and sorrow and go back to that part of her life where nothing bad had yet happened.

* * *

55

Biker Bill had a black beard and long black hair pulled back in a ponytail. He was way over six feet tall and probably weighed, what? More than two hundred pounds for sure. Biker Bill bowed to Kate. He smiled. His smile was innocent and ingratiating. 'Just yell out if you ladies need anything,' he said. He turned and lumbered away.

'He's probably good,' said Kate, 'in hand to hand combat, but what if the other person has a gun?'

'Rumor has it,' Dakota said, 'he's got an arsenal inside that house.'

Inside Dakota's studio her paintings lined one wall, acrylic on canvas, dreamy stretches of muted desert colors, Agnes Martin-like, punctuated by what looked like clusters of large black ants. Kate and Dakota sipped at cups of Tension Tamer tea with honey made by American, not Chinese, bees.

'You know what really pisses me off?' Kate said. 'Harry's making this big fuss, when I'm almost positive something was going on with him and this graduate student. Anna Marie Romero. She was gorgeous, but that's no excuse.'

'Maybe nothing was going on,' said Dakota, 'but the thing with Rick made you paranoid, you know?'

'God. I remember a couple of times when I stopped in at Rick's studio. Hannah was there. Rick said she was reviewing some of his work. I never thought a thing about it.' She could talk about it to Dakota, but she couldn't really think about it. Her mind slid away. 'How can I ever ever get together with someone again?'

56

'You asking me?' Dakota said. 'Plus, you have to watch yourself once you get into your forties with guys. The ones that look good usually turn out to be alcoholics or addicts, have borderline personalities or intermittent explosive disorder or are taking antidepressants that are about to stop working.'

Kate and Dakota simultaneously took a long sip of tea.

Dakota set her cup down. 'That's what I'm calling this series of paintings.'

'What?'

'Intermittent Explosive Disorder.'

'Ah,' said Kate.

'Widowers,' said Dakota thoughtfully. 'That's what you have to look for, widowers.'

Lights out, Chico lay in his prison cell. It wasn't uncomfortable – he slept on a harder bed when he spent the night in his studio on the Gulch downtown. It wasn't even a test. Chico liked tests, going farther than he had the day before. He could do this okay. Already, he was having some interesting ideas: A Jail Series, he could call them – maybe strip down his palette to just jail colors.

He worried about Lupita though. She was taking it harder than he was. But she didn't have her art to focus on. That was what he planned to do, focus on his art.

His biggest problem now was his memory. He remembered being in the St Elmo Bar, early, because it was Brewery Gulch Days and people started drinking around noon, and there was this blonde woman, but after that – nothing. And where had the gun come from? He owned a gun, a little .22, not the Smith and Wesson, model something or other, he'd been told he was holding. Maybe he'd slipped into a parallel universe? Wasn't that possible? Or maybe this wasn't even happening but was just an idea planted in his brain. That was what that movie *Inception* was about.

Except where was Ellen Page, the actress in the movie? He really liked her. She reminded him of those smart girls in high school that he got crushes on, even though they weren't supposed to be hot. Where was she now, Ellen Page? Not coming to visit him in jail, throwing him little kisses through the plate glass.

He thought of his life the day before the gun and the murders – his sister Lupita's face laughing, dancing around the living room with his Nana, to an old Jose Hernandez CD. He could remember far back too: his father coming home drunk, and he and Lupita hiding in the closet. His father had shouted and thrown things, and once he'd hit their Nana. His father had been really really sorry afterwards, but Chico could never forget the sound of his angry voice and Nana screaming.

Maybe he had done it after all. Maybe he was just like his father underneath but couldn't face it so he'd blacked out. Maybe he *had* killed those tourists. Even though he was raised Catholic, Chico hadn't gone to church in years, but he still believed firmly in hell.

Art, focus on my art.

Three days later, a grand jury indicted Chico Flores on two counts of negligent homicide.

Ten

A van from KOLD-TV Channel Thirteen, Tucson, was parked by the side of the courthouse on the day of the hearing to modify conditions of release for Chico Flores. The bailiff was just coming out of the Division Two courtroom into the lobby as Malcolm ascended the stairs.

'Division Two is now in session! The honorable Judge Collins presiding!'

Malcolm stayed outside for a moment, chatting up the security guard Hector Rodriguez to get the lay of the land inside.

'Mesa PD, huh?' Hector said. 'Must be pretty lively up there.'

'Lively it is,' Malcolm said. 'Anyone inside for the defendant?'

'Some hippy-looking types went in, probably there for him, him being an artist and all.' Hector grinned. 'That's about it.'

No Lupita? Malcolm wondered. He was here because she'd begged him to be there. 'How about anyone for the victims?' he asked.

Victims – in the case of homicides, their relatives – had the right to make a statement to the judge concerning any releases. And in Malcolm's experience they invariably opposed it.

'One guy,' said Hector. 'A doctor.'

59

'Oh, yeah?'

'A Dr Paul Sanger. Not a relative, he said, just a friend. He's the guy with the Buddy Holly glasses.' Hector grinned. 'Can't miss him.'

Malcolm entered and sat.

Chico, in traditional prison garb: orange jumpsuit, white socks, brown rubber sandals, was at a table next to his attorney, Stuart Ross. The prosecutor, Stan Freeman, sat at the other table. A couple of TV cameramen were set up in the front, near a woman in a blue suit and carefully coiffed hair. The reporter from the local paper sat slouched near the back.

Malcolm scanned the courtroom. There was a cluster of arty types in one corner, those friends of Chico's. He spotted the man who must be Doctor Sanger in one corner by the door, a man in his forties, sitting stiffly, the big black glasses almost cartoonish.

Photographs of former judges lined one wall. The high windows looked out on the big Arizona cypress trees that surrounded the courthouse. One of the windows was open; it got musty sometimes in courtrooms. A breeze swayed the cypress tree, littered with grackles that were kicking up a rumpus.

Stuart Ross stood, about to speak. Where was Lupita?

Then he saw her, in a long purple top, boots from another era, stumbling through the door, radiating angst. She was carrying a brown accordion file. But she smiled when she saw Malcolm and sat down next to him.

'Thanks for coming,' she whispered. 'I brought you the files.'

'Great,' Malcolm whispered.

'Your honor,' Stuart Ross was saying, 'we approach seeking a reduction in the one-million-dollar bond presently set for the defendant. His community connections and reputation are totally at odds with such an amount. Also, it might appear to the enlightened observer that law enforcement's quote-unquote rapid investigation and lightning fast arrest were entirely motivated by the Dudley Chamber of Commerce's concern to signal to the tourist crowd that the coast was clear for their return to Brewery Gulch and the many fine restaurants of Dudley.'

'Your honor—' Stan Freeman protested.

Malcolm stood up and took the files Lupita had given him and left the courtroom.

Outside, it was a breezy day, Arizona cypress trees blowing in the wind, clouds racing over the sun. Malcolm sat on one of the stone benches and opened the files.

Right on top, as if as a reminder, were the victims themselves – a printout of photos taken by Carrie Cooper's cellphone. One of a pleasant-looking man who must be Wes, standing in front of the Copper Queen Hotel, wearing a polo shirt and khaki shorts, and smiling the way you do when you say 'cheese', and another was presumably of Carrie, an attractive blonde, in the same pose in front of the hotel. Her clothes were almost identical to Wes's, but her smile was bright and happy and utterly genuine.

Malcolm felt a pang.

Two more photos: one of a mural somewhere, and the last of Carrie and a dark-haired woman, both smiling. Carrie's smile not so genuine this time, almost strained. The dark-haired woman he recognized. It was Kate Waters, the women he'd spoken to at the Sail Rabbit Arts Collective Gallery. She and Carrie were friends? He'd have to talk to her sometime.

He put the printout aside and began to read the first file.

Chico had been slumped in the alleyway, reeking of alcohol, holding the gun when the police arrived. He'd been arrested immediately. Malcolm didn't know about Dudley PD police work; was it up to par? He stopped reading and did a quick scan through the rest of the files – of course, all the reports weren't in yet, so maybe that was why there weren't results of any drug tests, alcohol tests, a test for gunshot residue.

Hopefully law enforcement hadn't decided all those tests that cost money wouldn't be needed, it was all so obvious.

The medical examiner's report revealed two shots, each shot entering the medulla oblongata: one shot for Carrie, one shot for Wes. Hits to the medulla oblongata bled profusely. It explained all the blood. The medulla oblongata was the best place to aim for if you wanted to kill someone instantly. The accuracy of the shots was uncanny, astounding, unless you knew what you were doing.

A drunk waving a gun around? It was bizarre. Totally bizarre.

God only knew how the legal system worked down here.

In his opinion, the Coopers had been killed by a trained hit man.

All those rumors swirling around seemed to be true; this could easily be drug cartel stuff. Drug cartel stuff? He didn't believe it for a moment. Since when did drug cartels go for nice middle-aged tourists from Pennsylvania? Or *were* they nice middle-aged tourists from Pennsylvania?

But one thing was obvious – he couldn't imagine anything more damaging to a town that relied on the tourist trade than the rumor of a drug cartel killing right in the middle of town. Better to blame a drunk, arrested immediately and safe in jail.

The gun in Chico's hand? For all Malcolm knew it could have been discarded by the killer and then picked up and planted in Chico's hand by law enforcement. It happened, not usually, but for a moment he was filled with disgust at the knowledge that it *did* happen. But not in this case; this struck him more as a kind of panic, blame someone fast.

In his mind right now Chico was either innocent or had an elaborate secret life he'd managed to hide from his own sister.

People were coming down the courthouse steps. Dr Paul Sanger passed close by, loping down the steps, dodging a reporter. Malcolm got up and went back inside. The courtroom was empty except for the bailiff and Lupita, back in a corner, her face sad.

63

'What's wrong?' he asked.

She sniffed. 'The judge denied the motion for release. He said he wanted to wait until it went to the grand jury.'

'Didn't the lawyer tell you that was probably what would happen?'

'Kind of. But it just seems like—' Her lip trembled. 'Like Chico's going to be in jail forever and ever. I miss him so much, and so does our nana.' She began to cry.

Lupita wept and wept. The bailiff got the box of Kleenex always kept conveniently nearby and brought it back to Lupita, who refused it.

Malcolm took it. And now here was Lupita, weeping by his side. He let her cry; she had good reason. In the meantime, he contemplated the framed blown-up photographs of former Cochise County Superior Court judges that lined the wall, one of whom he noticed bore a striking resemblance to Frankenstein's monster.

Lupita's sobs subsided, and she hiccuped.

'It's okay,' he said to her, patting her arm. 'It's okay.'

But of course it wasn't okay at all. It was close to lunchtime. Outside the courtroom, people would be lingering in the halls to chat, cars pulling away down in the parking spaces. Things returning to normal, except there was no such thing as normal, he knew that.

He pulled some Kleenex out of the box and handed it to Lupita.

She took it, blew her nose loudly, then turned her head to look at him. 'It's not okay, and you know it.' Her face was battered, swollen with tears and fatigue, tragic and unbeautiful.

64

He felt a kind of love for her, unconnected to who she was personally.

'It *is* okay,' he said, the words coming out of his mouth as if from a stranger, words he knew perfectly well as he said them he might later regret. 'If it's not okay, I'm going to fix it. I promise.'

Malcolm spent the evening doing some googling, checking out Wes and Carrie Cooper – the drug cartel king pins? – from Millville, Pennsylvania. They'd gotten married, it looked like, five years ago, when Carrie was forty-two and Wes was forty-seven. Wes had sold insurance for State Farm but was retired. Carrie had a crafts store with her sister Rose. Before she married Wes, Carrie went by the last name of Murrah.

No mention of a previous husband or husbands for Carrie, so Murrah must be her maiden name. Married for the first time at forty-two? Well, nowadays people didn't always marry.

Wes had a previous marriage to Nancy who had died of cancer. He had a daughter Polly Hampton of Phoenix, Arizona. Phoenix wasn't all that far, a three and a half hour drive, but Polly Hampton hadn't come to the release hearing. In his experience, the relatives of murdered people usually tended to show up at all the hearings when they lived within driving distance. So that was interesting, kind of, maybe. Maybe the Dr Sanger guy was sitting in for her.

Malcolm delved into the public records, found no criminal record for either Wes or Carrie

65

Cooper, none for Carrie Murrah either, not even one single major drug bust.

Well, he hadn't expected any. If they had any drug involvement at all it would be as amateurs, not really players.

He googled Kate Waters. And there she was on Facebook, with a picture or he wouldn't have made the connection, running a community arts center in Vermont. A community arts center.

He'd liked the way she'd smiled at him, though they had spoken very briefly, at that gallery where Chico Flores' glittery baby dolls hung. Then she'd gone out to talk to some old guy with a white beard.

He could have stopped her, with some witty comment about art; what exactly the comment would have been he had no idea.

The page hadn't been updated for a while. What was she doing here?

He went to bed and kind of slept.

Eleven

'I hear you,' Stuart Ross, attorney at law, said to Malcolm. 'This must be quite a change from Mesa. Bored out of your gourd.'

Malcolm laughed. 'It's not just that,' he said, wondering as he said it if in fact it *was* just that.

'If you don't mind my asking—'Stuart Ross leaned back in his chair. 'Other than total boredom, what *is* your stake in this?'

'My stake?' Malcolm asked. 'I don't have any stake. I just felt sorry for Lupita.'

'Kind of like Jesus Christ, huh?'

'Just like him. Lupita thinks you're avoiding her.'

'I am.' Stuart Ross sighed. 'I know, I know, but what can I do? All this takes time. She wants him out yesterday, and it ain't going to happen.' He paused. 'Poor old Chico doesn't have a clue about the whole incident. It's all foggy.' Stuart leaned across his desk confidingly. 'You know what I'm thinking?'

'What?'

'Rohypnol.'

'Rohypnol?'

Stuart made his hand into a gun and pointed it at Malcolm. 'You got it. Or something like that. Who needs alcohol any more, huh? Just slip a roofie into your sweetie's drink and you don't have to bother with seduction.'

'Ah.'

'Someone got poor Chico stoned, took him for a walk, killed those tourists, then put the gun in his hand.'

'I'm with you on that,' said Malcolm, 'all the way.'

Stuart sighed. 'The thing is, worst come to worst, and I don't think it will, but let's just say it ends up going to trial – I mean, I'm sure as hell not going to plead it out. Rohypnol would fly with a jury.'

'Ah.'

'It's everywhere now. In books, in movies. People who might never have thought of it in the normal course of things getting these ideas. That ballet movie *Black Swan*? It's even in that.'

'You saw *Black Swan*?' Malcolm said.

'My date wanted to.'

Malcolm had an innate distrust of defense attorneys; he'd seen too many that were sleazy. He wondered now if Stuart had slipped a roofie in his date's drink afterwards.

'Course, we'll never know,' Stuart said, 'since the cops didn't run any drug tests. And there's always the possibility that Chico is in fact a professional hit man and he hasn't shared that information with his sister and his nana. Or his lawyer.'

'And the Coopers were serious drug dealers.'

'Or worse, amateurs.'

'This whole investigation is being weirdly bungled,' Malcolm said and added, 'even for cops.' This last not because he believed cops were that bad, but for Stuart.

Stuart harrumphed. 'Chamber of Commerce, like the crazy locals are saying. I don't always agree with them, but I do in this case. So you're seriously up for being my investigator? I got someone I usually use, pretty good, but a Mesa PD detective? Golden.'

'I went online for a while last night,' Malcolm said. 'Wes Cooper has a daughter in Phoenix.'

'Ah, let me remind you of something that, as a cop, you already know,' Stuart said, 'about talking to the designated victims – in this case the relatives of the deceased. Legally, they have no obligation to talk to the defense.'

'The defense,' Malcolm said. 'Who's that? Never heard of them.'

'Tell you what – I still got to pick up some more disclosure files at the County Attorney's. I'll have my secretary make copies of everything and hand it over to you, say, by late this afternoon.'

'Sounds good. I can do some stuff today, like maybe talk to that woman, Kate Waters – the one in the photograph with Carrie Cooper.'

And cards, thought Malcolm, riding a little wave of psychic energy. He would get some cards printed up – just 'Malcolm MacGregor, investigator' and his cell number and email address.

Ryan, the current Co-op manager, and Kate were sitting in the deli area with coffee, going over the list of items customers had written down on the big piece of poster board that asked in block letters, 'WHAT WOULD YOU LIKE TO SEE AT THE CO-OP?'

'Amanita muscaria,' Ryan read out loud. 'Sensimilla.' He rotated his eyebrows. 'Well, not up front anyway, maybe round the back.' He glanced at Kate to see if she got the joke.

She laughed.

'More coffee?' he offered.

'Sure.'

Ryan got up with both their cups and went over to the urn, and as he did so Kate saw a silver gray Hyundai pulling into a parking space outside. A man in a black shirt, black jeans got out. Kate's heart gave a little jump in her chest. *It was Harry*. How could it be. God. How had he—?

Her shoulders tensed up. Then she saw it wasn't him. Didn't even look like him really, except for the black clothes.

'You okay?' Ryan said, putting down a cup in front of her and sitting.

'Fine.'

'You look – I don't know—'

'No, I am fine, really.'

'I was wondering,' Ryan said. 'We've got an order coming into the Sierra Vista Co-op – it should be there five thirty or six, and we need someone to pick it up. Not the regular order, like *crates* and stuff, just those strawberries that everyone's so crazy about. You up for that? We'd pay your gas.'

'No problem.'

'Ryan!' someone called from the back. 'We need some help back here.'

'Shit!' Ryan stood up.

After a moment Kate stood up too and stretched. She took a walk, past an elderly couple buying some supplements that promised to restore them to youthful vigor, past the cash register, and outside to the vista of red mountains, tiny quaint shacks. She felt tired; she didn't sleep as well at Dakota's. Where am I, she wondered. Where the hell am I? Another planet, outer space?

'Hey,' someone said beside her.

She turned her head, and there was that guy, Malcolm MacGregor, who she'd met at the gallery. Who was he, anyway?

'What?' she said flatly.

'You okay?' he said, with what sounded like genuine concern in his voice.

70

There was something vulnerable in his eyes that Kate wanted nothing at all to do with.

'Just fine. Excuse me.' She turned and walked to the back of the Co-op, past the sign that said 'Employees only'.

'Wait,' he called, 'Kate Waters, wait,' but she was gone.

Around four, Malcolm stopped by Stuart's office and got the disclosure files. Something was going on with that Kate, Malcolm thought as he drove home. He dumped the files on the dining-room table, then put some cat food into a bowl and took it outside to the back yard.

'Hey, Buddy,' he called. 'Here, Buddy, Buddy.' Then he went inside to give Buddy some space.

Buddy was the closest thing Malcolm had to a pet. He'd just shown up one day, a big orange tom, scars on his face, ears ragged from fighting. Buddy was always hanging around, but every time Malcolm came near him, he hissed and ran under the porch. So he went to Safeway, bought some cat food and set it out. That first time, the cat ate the food in big noisy bites like it was starving.

Kate. She'd smiled at him at the gallery, but today she'd acted like she didn't want to have anything to do with him, like she was mad at him or something. He'd just wanted to ask her a few questions about Carrie Cooper. *What the fuck did I do?* he thought.

He opened the refrigerator, took out a bottle of Blue Moon beer. He usually went for Sam Adams, but he thought he'd try this, after that cop from

71

Boston drank it at the White House. His shoulder had been aching all day. He rubbed it, trying to get the blood flowing.

Kate's rudeness bothered him; she'd seemed edgy, stressed out. Maybe Carrie *had* said something disturbing to her and the local law had told her to keep it a secret. He could tell by the way she'd looked at him when he'd asked if she was okay that she thought he was a loser. Why?

The problem was, what was he supposed to do? He'd tried, tried hard to change his life, take it easy, take this time off, hopefully temporary time off, to relax, recharge his batteries, learn to live in the moment, etc etc.

He hated that jargon.

Malcolm took a swig of beer. The beer was okay, but he liked Sam Adams better.

He would have saved Cindy if he could, but he didn't see how. He'd tried really hard at first, always being there for her, encouraging her to see all those doctors, never getting mad when she was particularly difficult. And there was always hope every time some new pill came along. She would take it, and for a few weeks, sometimes months, it would work, like a miracle, then suddenly it wouldn't. It would be back to the beginning. Even now when an ad came on TV for a new kind of antidepressant – and there was always something new, half the people this country must be depressed – he found himself thinking, even though she was gone, *maybe this is it*.

But nothing had worked. Nothing.

72

Maybe he was kidding himself, helping Lupita like he was; maybe he was going to turn into one of those old guys without a life that hung around courtrooms. Circling back to the expression on Kate's face when he'd asked if she was okay, suddenly a thought struck him.

Kate was crazy. She was crazy, just like Cindy. He didn't know exactly why he thought this, what it was based on, and why this infuriated him so much, but it did. He looked down at the bottle of Blue Moon he was holding. Then he threw it hard as he could against the wall. Pain like a knife blade went through his shoulder.

The funny thing was, he thought as he swept the shards of glass in a dustpan, mopped up the beer from the kitchen floor, when Cindy was happy, she was happier than anyone he'd ever seen. Her happiness flowed around her, filling up all the empty spaces between them, and she was beautiful.

Twelve

It was still light as Kate drove back through Sierra Vista with the load of strawberries from the Sierra Vista Co-op. There were dark clouds overhead but no rain. She passed the Walmart, turned on to Highway 80 past Target and Fry's. Then the town petered out after a couple more stop lights and the long stretch of desert began. It ran pretty straight, dipping at the San Pedro River, where giant cottonwood trees brooded, then up again. On her iPod shuffle, Neko Case sang 'Prison Girls'.

It was fifteen miles or so to the stop sign and the turn to Dudley.

On the left, the Mule Mountains were dark purple in the distance, lit suddenly from time to time by jagged lightning. The car swerved slightly; bump in the road? Wind? She accelerated a bit to keep herself awake and alert. Oddly, just then in her mind, Harry, in one of his tantrums, ice-cold tantrums, sneered at her.

No cars in front, one behind. Tailgating. How fast was she going? Only sixty. The old Honda Civic didn't have much power or pickup. She accelerated to sixty-five, but on a long empty stretch the car behind passed her, little red taillights receding. Then she was alone on the highway again, up ahead the stop sign where she would make the right-hand turn that would take her to Dudley. The summer rains had brought out all the vegetation: grasses lined the road's edge, a big clump of mesquite on her right, but on her left the highway was clear.

She accelerated a little more, then out of nowhere came a bang. Loud, over Neko Case singing 'The Pharaohs'. *What!*

She stopped the iPod just as there was another bang, the tires of the car made a funny grinding noise on the blacktop, and suddenly she wasn't even on the road, how the hell did she – shit – she'd driven right off the road and up the mountain slope behind.

The car bounced and jounced up the rocky

hill, its undercarriage banging and grinding as it scraped on the rocks, her purse flying, a stray pen hitting the windshield. Then the car hit something, pretty hard, stopped, and for a split second there was an unearthly silence. The car engine ticked, ticked, winding down. Crickets chirped.

Smell of strawberries.

Sirens whined in the distance.

Finally, it began to rain.

Thirteen

Malcolm heard the raindrops ping-pinging on the tin roof as he was cooking up a bunch of hamburger with Beef Stroganoff Hamburger Helper in his big frying pan. Ah, rain. He went outside. The air smelled clean and fresh. He breathed it in for a moment, then went back inside and threw some frozen peas in with the hamburger. He stirred it around until the peas had thawed and heated up, then he took the pan into the living room and ate dinner in front of the TV news.

Maybe it was oncoming rain that had been making his shoulder act up more than usual. It couldn't be throwing that bottle of beer, oh, no, no way.

He finished eating, put what was left of it in the fridge and washed up. Then cleared the kitchen table of its usual debris: old bills, dead newspapers, envelopes containing important and exciting offers he had not even opened, catalogs, and circulars of supermarket specials – Fry's, Safeway and Food City from two months ago.

He brought the files Stuart had given to him over to the table, sat down and began to read. It still all fit the hit man theory. The gun in Chico's hand was a six-inch Smith and Wesson, model 686. Forensics had determined that the 357 Magnum caliber bullets in the gun matched the bullets that had killed the couple. Smith and Wesson 686 model was a good gun, not a Saturday special type. A professional's gun, the serial numbers filed off. He started to make notes on a legal pad – things to ask Lupita.

He began to read through the files systematically, from beginning to end: the initial report, the follow-ups, the interviews, the forensic material. He read the police reports extra carefully, looking for the kind of things that showed up in police reports that were considered irrelevant so not followed through on. Then there was additional information not included in the police report itself because the investigator making the report considered it irrelevant . . . or even possibly pointing suspicion elsewhere, when what was wanted was a quick and easy suspect, locked up, and the tourist town of Dudley safe and sound. He'd like to talk to the detective with Dudley PD who was the official investigator. He checked the name – Luna, Ben Luna – and wrote it down.

Go to the scene, check it out, hunt down

witnesses, not only Mrs Acuna, who'd heard the shots and called the police, but what about other nearby residents, any of them interviewed? Not in the files. What about the bartender at the St Elmo Bar – the bar Chico presumably staggered out of just before he went down the alleyway? Had Chico been with anyone there? And the Coopers, what was their stay like at the Copper Queen Hotel? Were they nervous, apprehensive? Talk to the staff there.

And talk to Chico himself, of course.

He would do everything in a systematic way from scratch, as if he were the detective in charge, starting an investigation.

He sat back in his chair, closed his eyes and let it simmer for a while. Theory of the case. There was always the theory of the case. Sometimes it helped to have one, sometimes it blinded you to the evidence. In this case the theory was a drug cartel hit, or, more to his liking, a hit man hired by an unknown person, disguised as a drunken accident. Want to kill someone close to the border? Blame the drug cartels.

How would it have happened, exactly?

The most logical was that Chico was at the wrong place at the wrong time and the shooter took advantage of that – put the gun in Chico's hand and split. According to the report where Chico was interviewed, he didn't remember anything. *He needed to talk to Chico.*

No one involved in investigating the crime had spoken to the relatives of the victims. Anyone they knew had a vendetta against Wes and Carrie? After all, if someone other than Chico had killed

Wes and Carrie, surely they would want the truth to come out.

Unless one of them had done it.

A family feud?

Then there was Kate, who he kind of had a hankering for. Why? Because he was an asshole.

He yawned, stretched. His shoulder pain had settled down, wasn't too bad. He stood up, aware he was feeling just a little more up than he had for a while. His cellphone chimed.

Lupita.

'Malcolm here,' he said.

'Remember Kate? You said you were going to talk to her?'

'Haven't done that yet,' Malcolm said.

'Well,' Lupita said, 'I hope it's not too late.'

'What does *that* mean?'

'She was in a bad car wreck.'

'*Kate*?' said Malcolm. 'Kate was in a bad car wreck? You're kidding. When? Is she okay?'

'Like, maybe an hour or so ago. She missed the turn from Sierra Vista. My cousin Reynaldo told me. His girlfriend was coming back from Sierra Vista, and—'

'Wait.' For a moment he was stunned, didn't know what he was even thinking. 'I mean, is she *alive*?'

'What I told you is all I know,' said Lupita. 'If I find out any more I'll call you.'

Malcolm opened his laptop, scanning the news, looking for reports of a fatal accident on Highway 80 and had a memory from a couple of years ago. Cindy, his dead wife, one morning, very sad, very down; whatever she'd been taking had

78

stopped working, and he knew they were in for another bout of deep depression. It seemed like things with Cindy went on and on forever, changing all the time, yet nothing ever really changed.

He had thought about this while driving to work back then, through the city traffic. Thought about his biggest fear, that she would eventually give up, kill herself. On that drive long ago in Phoenix, thinking about Cindy maybe killing herself had filled him with exhaustion. The truth was the next thought he'd had was, *God damn, why doesn't she just go ahead and do it?* That was months and months before it happened. He hadn't meant it at all.

Rain was spattering on the car windshield. The smell of strawberries was all pervasive. Kate had called the Co-op first thing and talked to Windsong, but someone on the road must have called the highway patrol because a police car showed up right away. Kate was sitting in her car, and a highway patrolman was pacing around it, when Windsong showed up in his old Crown Vic that he'd bought years ago at a city auction.

'Jesus, you could be dead,' Windsong said. 'What happened?'

'A tire blew.'

'Jeez,' said Windsong. 'Why is it women never notice when their tires are low?'

'My tires weren't low.' Kate got up, almost fell.

'Hey, hey,' Windsong said, 'take it easy.'

Kate steadied herself. 'They were almost new,

79

goddamn it! I bought them in California. Three months ago I had everything checked out when I knew I was leaving Harry. It's not my fault, Windsong, don't you try to make it that way. Something weird happened. I don't know what. I heard these bangs.' Kate started to cry.

'Now, now. Sorry.'

'Windsong,' she cried, 'do you ever feel sometimes like you've done things that don't make sense, like you don't even know why you did them?'

Windsong looked thoughtful, standing there in his drawstring yoga pants, his sandals with red socks, his yard sale black T-shirt with the slogan 'Insufficient Memory'. 'Sometimes.'

'I need some time off,' Kate said. 'I'm going to go see my friend Ellen in New Jersey.'

Late, late that night, Malcolm browsed his computer and discovered Kate was in fact alive. He had a few things he wanted to investigate first, but he'd talk to her pretty soon. After all, she wasn't going anywhere.

Fourteen

Kate put her purse on the scanner belt – her small backpack with its three ounce containers, a magazine and a book, her iPod shuffle and ear buds. She took off her black with white trim Converse sneakers, put them on the scanner belt, then walked through security. She held her arms up as the woman guard ran the sensor over her body. Kate didn't mind the sensor, but she hated to fly.

'Not to worry,' Dakota had said. 'I've got something—'

'Not sublingual vitamin B,' Kate said. 'That stuff doesn't work. I'm tired of people giving me organic solutions that don't work.'

'This will. Ativan. A *pharmaceutical*. Take one an hour before you get on the plane, no problem. Here – I'll give you two. One for the plane, and one for upcoming stresses.'

I'm thrilled, thrilled, Ellen had written in response to Kate's email. *I'll try to get there before you, but I could get tied up. Just in case, there's a key under the rock by the door. Oh, and here's my phone number so we can text.*

Kate bought some water in a plastic bottle at the restaurant and sat on a vinyl chair to wait, listening to the sound of planes landing, taking off, the screams of inanimate objects. On CNN they were reporting the story of a little girl missing.

'*I know she's alive*,' said her mother, '*I can feel it.*'

Dead, thought Kate, she's most likely dead. She reached in her purse, found her little pillbox with the two Ativans Dakota had given her and took one.

The plane flew over puffs of bright trees, then she could see the Atlantic Ocean, like beaten silver and in the distance, the towers of New

York City. Final descent, she imagined Ellen and the old friends, whoever they were, all taking the train into the city, maybe spending the night, traipsing around Manhattan, reliving their youth. Besides, wasn't forty the new thirty?

And then they were on the ground.

Newark, New Jersey.

Waiting to get off, Kate texted Ellen that she had landed. Then she texted Dakota, because she'd promised she would: *Landed!* She exited the plane, wheeled her carry-on to the car rental place and got herself a blue Toyota Tercel. It was chillier here, middle afternoon, than it was in Arizona. She got a sweater out of her carry-on and put it on.

It was an easy trip to the freeway, and Kate figured it was about a twenty to thirty minute drive to Ellen's aunt's house in the vast sea of suburbs. MapQuest said thirty-five minutes, and it was usually pessimistic. She had the printout in a pocket on her backpack, and she pulled it out and put it on the seat. Too poor, she was, for a smartphone with a GPS.

Kate had last seen Ellen more than ten years ago. She and Rick had gone into the City. They used to go regularly – it was only a couple of hours from where they lived in Vermont. Ellen was a documentary film-maker. Now that Kate was thinking about her with a little more focus, she remembered that Ellen had a raucous laugh that went on and on a little longer than it should have, but back then everyone Kate knew was a little nuts and proud of it.

Kate merged on to the freeway, driving more cautiously since the accident than she used to. She still saw, in her mind, the stop sign coming up at her out of the darkness. Although she wasn't feeling nervous; kind of relaxed, actually – in fact, all things considered, quite relaxed. Maybe she was getting over it. In fact, at that moment she felt as though she was finally getting over every bad thing that had ever happened to her. Even new bad stuff, she could handle easily.

Ooops. The *Ativan*. It actually worked.

Miles later, she exited the freeway on to a suburban plaza: a couple of motels, a gas station, Radio Shack, Jack in the Box, Burger King, McDonald's, Kentucky Colonel, Wendy's and Kroger's. She pulled into the Kroger's, got out, stood in the parking lot for a moment in a kind of jet-lagged daze. Then she went inside. It was Senior Day, said a sign by the door. The aisles were full of elderly couples.

Kate found the florist department and bought a bouquet of pink and white alstroemeria and, after a moment's consideration, a bottle of red wine. Ellen (she hoped) would appreciate it. Back in the car she checked her map and turned right coming out of the plaza.

The house, 350 Roscommon Drive, was at the end of a curving street that was off another bigger street, off a third street in an older development, lush with trees beginning to turn and green green grass. She passed several houses that were in foreclosure. The house next to 350 had a foreclosure sign in front and so did the one across from it. Behind 350 Roscommon was a patch of woods.

In front of 350 there was a 'For Sale' sign hanging crookedly from an iron stake, as though whoever had posted it had given up halfway through.

The driveway was empty, so presumably Ellen hadn't arrived yet. Kate pulled in, feeling a little disappointed. By the front door a climbing rose grew over a trellis, full of yellow roses. Kate immediately regretted the alstroemeria, which had probably been injected with who knew what to keep it looking fresh and flown thousands of miles from Chile or Argentina or someplace.

The sun was getting lower now, hitting one of the windows and winking at her. Just in case, Kate pulled back the brass knocker on the door: bam, bam.

'Ellen,' she called. 'Ellen, I'm here.' Bam. bam.

No one came. Kate found the rock by the door and lifted it. There was the key. She opened the door, then got her stuff from the car, including the flowers, and went in, down a short hall, past a living room bare except for a couch, looking for the kitchen and water to put the flowers in.

The kitchen was at the end of the hall, facing west and flooded with light from the sinking sun. An older kitchen, quite big, with a linoleum floor, avocado green appliances. A dead plant stood on the window sill, possibly an African violet. Kate dropped her stuff on the chrome and Formica table in the center of the room and opened cabinets still stocked with a few dishes and pans, until she found a glass pitcher that would do for the flowers.

She turned on the faucet.

There was no water.

Shit. Experimentally, she clicked the light switch. There was no electricity. God damn it. Had Ellen actually invited her to visit in a place with no electricity and no water?

She hadn't gotten a text from Ellen about her arrival time, but just in case she'd missed the blip she checked her phone. No text from Ellen. Her cell was running low so she turned it off. She opened her laptop, to check her email, but, *of course*, just her luck, there wasn't any Wi-Fi connection.

She had Ellen's email address and Ellen's cell-phone number, but she had no idea where Ellen actually lived, just somewhere in New York, outside of the city.

But she still felt quite calm.

'I'm as calm as the waters that fill up Lake Michigan, calm as the waters that fill up the sea.'

A line from Lisa Strange, an indie country singer Kate particularly liked. What did she mean by that song, anyway?

Ellen probably planned to turn everything on as soon as she got here. In fact, maybe that was where she was now, getting the utilities turned on.

But, just in case, Kate went back out to the car, got in and drove to Kroger's. This time she bought three gallon jugs of water, and then she stopped at Kentucky Colonel and got a three-piece meal: dark meat with coleslaw, mashed potatoes and gravy.

Back at the house she put the flowers in water and set the pitcher on a table in the dining room. It was still light enough to reconnoiter and see the rest of the place. Since there would be no light soon she tried to memorize where everything was – besides the dining room, a big den with no furniture in it at all, a couch in the living room and a coffee table, and two bedrooms, both with beds, thank God.

In the second bedroom, there was a bedside table and on it, as if forgotten in haste, was a framed photograph: a woman in sunglasses, a bikini and a big straw hat, smiling on a beach. Was this Ellen's aunt? Her aunt who had died? For a moment Kate stared at the picture in the dimming light.

Things were getting to be a little weird, but so what? She was actually still amazingly relaxed. The Ativan, she thought. It's probably horribly addictive.

Practical. What was practical? She should have bought more water; she would need it to flush the toilet. She went back to the darkening kitchen, opened some drawers and found, hallelujah, some matches and a couple of big fat lilac colored candles. She lit one of them; it smelled of lavender. *Lavender*, she imagined Posey at the Co-op saying excitedly, *it's so soothing*.

She ate the Kentucky Colonel dinner at the chrome and red Formica table. She turned on her cell again, but there were no calls. It was getting late. Where was Ellen? What if, she thought suddenly, Ellen had been in an accident?

Alone without any working devices except a dying cellphone, beneath the quiet pharmaceutical ease of the Ativan, Kate started to worry. To stop the worrying she went outside to the little portico at the front door and stood there, listening to the night.

It was remarkably quiet, not even the chirp of a cricket, and somehow fragrant, not from the yellow roses, which seemed to have no smell, but with ozone from all the green grass. Where were the people? To one side of the house was an empty lot, to the other the house that was in foreclosure. The house across the street was dark.

She walked down the driveway, and from there she could see around the curve. Lights were on in a couple of houses, a silver SUV parked in front of one of them. Dimly, she could see someone opening the back door of the SUV and removing what was probably bags of groceries. It looked so normal, so reassuring.

Then, for some reason, standing alone in the evening at the end of a driveway in this suburban development, with the green trees and the green grass, with nothing between herself and her own company, Kate felt a nostalgia, a longing, so keen that it almost made her want to cry.

My life, where did it go? she thought. My job, I loved my job, and it just went away. And then Rick. Usually, when she thought of him it was with rage, but now, all at once, the rage had turned to grief. All those years they had seemed to be in love, done everything together. How could he? *How could he?*

She went back inside, walked round the house in the dark, looking out all the windows. She went from dining room to kitchen, to bathroom to the first bedroom, the second. Kate was tired now, from the travel and, she suspected, from the Ativan. She found a dish for under the candle, lit the candle, took it into the living room and sat on the couch to wait for Ellen.

Her cellphone beeped battery low, a gentle warning. She hadn't turned it off the last time she checked it for messages. She did now. Outside, the green lawns were dimmed, the trees, shadows. In the second bedroom a woman in a big hat and a bathing suit smiled and smiled.

Fifteen

The Cochise County jail is located in a complex of buildings that also includes the justice court, a mile or so outside the city limits of Dudley in an area of hilly desert.

Malcolm MacGregor, formerly of Mesa PD, parked and went in.

'Hi there, how they treating you?' he said, when he was face to face with Chico Flores, only some plate glass between them.

'Okay.' Chico's voice was so low that Malcolm could barely hear him. He was a handsome young man, or would be if it weren't for the orange jumpsuit that reduced him to one perp among many. 'Thanks for coming, man.'

Next to Malcolm, a perp's mother was weeping, dabbing at her eyes with a handkerchief. He needed to stop thinking of the guys in here as perps, at least temporarily.

'I guess your lawyer mentioned the Rohypnol.'

'It makes sense, I guess.' Chico smiled suddenly, a flash of humor. 'But so what? I was pretty drunk. Could have just been the alcohol, you know.'

'You get drunk a lot?'

'Hardly ever. That's probably why it hit me so hard. Want to know about my cocaine habit?'

'Want to tell me?'

'Cocaine's a little passé,' Chico said. 'Or so I hear. I don't mind a little—' his hands made quotation marks – '"mary jane" when I'm musing in my studio.'

Malcolm looked at him with interest. A smart kid, maybe too smart?

'I have all these images,' Chico said, 'but they're all jumbled up in my brain. Like, I could say to you right now somebody shoved that gun in my hand, but to tell the truth I just plain don't remember.'

'So who was tending bar at the St Elmo that night?'

'Sid.'

'You were so drunk, I'm wondering how come Sid didn't cut you off?'

'Too busy, I guess. Or maybe you're right. Maybe someone put something my drink. Like the blonde lady.'

'The blonde lady?'

'She was buying me drinks.'

'A blonde lady? Name? You got a name?'

Chico shook his head. 'Just some blonde lady. Older, but pretending she wasn't.'

'Just some older blonde lady, no name,' Malcolm said. 'Attractive?'

'Actually, no, not really. But trying to be, you know? Lots of make-up.'

There was a pause.

'Anything else?'

'Hey, man, I was so out of it. But talk to Sid. He was probably the only one in the bar that day that was sober. And it was still daylight. That's how these big weekends play, you know? This town knows how to party.'

'Anything else you can think of I should know that's not in any reports?'

'Naw. Mr Ross asked me that too when we were going over the reports. Everything I can think of I already told him.' He grinned. 'You know what Lupita used to call you?'

'What?'

'The lonely man.'

'Ah,' said Malcolm. 'The lonely man.'

'Hey,' Chico said, 'no offense.'

'None taken, I guess,' Malcolm said.

'It's a cool name, actually, like maybe for an avatar action hero.' Chico leaned closer. 'Guy goes around with this semi-transparent mask like a veil, no one can quite see his face, and he's always, always alone, except, you know, when he's saving people.'

* * *

90

In the parking lot, Malcolm called Lupita.

'How is he doing?' Lupita asked, her voice rising at the end of the sentence.

'He's okay,' Malcolm said, 'a survivor,' still smarting a little from Chico's remarks about lonely men and avatars. 'Listen, help me out here. Know anyone who works at the Copper Queen Hotel?'

'Sure, a couple of people.'

'Well, try to find out who might have had contact with the Coopers when they were staying there. I'd like to talk to them. Call me back as soon as you find out anything.'

He clicked off his cell, got in his car and drove back to town.

Malcolm stood at the top of a flight of stairs in Old Dudley: quaint stairs, in other words kind of crumbly, and looked down halfway to where the bullets had hit Wes and Carrie Cooper. It was getting on in the afternoon, close to the time when they'd been killed. Doves cooed in the Arizona cypress trees nearby, and bees buzzed in the pink valerian. It would have been noisier, of course, the evening they were killed – it was a holiday weekend, lots of people around down on the Gulch.

Behind him were more stairs leading up to High Road, where little wooden houses clung quaintly to the hillsides. The stairs went straight down, passing tiny houses, some close enough to look into their windows – Wes and Carrie's bodies had fallen on a straight stretch maybe ten feet before the next flight. Even from here he could see the darker stains on the old concrete, concrete stamped WPA at regular intervals.

Malcolm's old man had hated Roosevelt with a passion – a hatred Malcolm's father had inherited from his father. Their hero was Lewis Douglas, a true conservative through and through, who came from an old Arizona family and had even lived in Dudley. But it seemed to Malcolm right now they could use another WPA to rebuild the stairs.

He went up three steps, opened a metal gate and went into Mrs Acuna's yard.

Norteño music came faintly from inside. The door was open, the screen door shut. He knocked on the door frame. A big black dog showed up and began to bark. It barked and barked and barked.

'Buster! You be quiet!' A woman, gray-haired, with a cane came to the screen door and peered out at him. 'He gets out all the time,' she muttered. 'Gets out and runs up the hill, and I don't see him for days.'

'Mrs Acuna?' Malcolm said heartily.

'Who are you?'

'Name's Malcolm McGregor, ma'am. I was wondering if we could—'

'I mean, *who* are you?' Her eyes, behind her glasses and the tiny squares of the screen, were sharp. 'A reporter, a lawyer, a policeman, which?'

'An investigator.'

'An investigator?'

'Yes.'

'And you want the story. You know how many

times I've told it? Pretty soon I'll be telling the story, instead of what happened.'

'Wait,' said Malcolm. 'It's not the same thing?' But he knew just what she meant.

'No. You try, but you forget,' she said. 'I heard the shots, at first I thought thunder, but no, better check. I went out, walked over to the gate where I could see better. What I saw, it was terrible, it wasn't like when someone gets shot on TV.' She took a breath. She had a little gold cross around her neck, Jesus hanging – he rose and fell.

'So very very sad,' she went on. 'This poor woman with blood all over her. Pretty, I think, her hair. I'll never forget it. And I saw the man a little way away – there was lots of blood on him too.'

She paused and looked past Malcolm. 'I thought of children, I don't know why, how precious they are and you never want them to be harmed. Then I looked over and I saw Chico with a gun. I know Chico from when he was little, so I wish I hadn't seen him, but I did. I can't help what I saw.'

For a moment Malcolm was silent. Her words seemed to call for it, a moment of silence.

'And no one else?' he said finally. 'You didn't see anyone else?'

'No. How much can you see?' Her voice rose. 'How much can you take in? I didn't see anyone else. Go away now.'

'Wait,' said Malcolm. 'My card. In case—'
But she closed the door in his face.

Okay. He stuck his card in the space between

93

the door and the door jamb, went back out the iron gate, down the three steps, sniffed a hint of marijuana from somewhere, mingling with the smell of urine, heard a woman singing a song he half recognized but not quite, singing it off key. From the steps it appeared that the alleyway dead ended, but when he walked down it he saw that it turned.

In front of him was a house with a 'For Sale' sign on it. It didn't look too saleable – the porch was sagging at one end, and two of the windows had cardboard instead of glass. The yard was full of weeds. In the weeds something glittered. Malcolm went into the yard to see what it was, bent over to pick it up. The tinfoil from a pack of cigarettes. He straightened up and saw directly ahead of him, between a gap in two mesquite trees, the stairs where Wes and Carrie Cooper had been shot – exactly where they had been shot. He could see the bloodstains.

Aha.

This was where a shooter might have stood, a short walk to where Chico had been in the alleyway. Using a revolver, no pesky shell casings, possibly fingerprinted, to pick up. A revolver with the serial numbers filed off. The kind of gun a hit man might use.

Malcolm took a picture of the opening between the bushes with his camera phone. Then he walked as quickly as he could back to where Chico had been found slumped over, gun in his hand. It took no time at all really. The noise of the gunshots would have stunned whoever heard them, Mrs Acuna included, and for them time would have stood still for that moment.

It was a plausible scenario, as likely to be true as the current official story. More likely, in fact.

His cellphone chimed.

'I got a name for you,' Lupita said. 'Diane. She's a waitress there, and she's working today. She gets off at eight. She'll be happy to talk to you.'

So, eight o'clock at the Copper Queen, then after that Sid the bartender at the St Elmo Bar. Time for Malcolm to go home now and have dinner, what was left of the Beef Stroganoff Hamburger Helper he'd made last night.

'Carrie and Wes were sitting out on this bench by the steps, just like now, the way I am with you, when I came on at eleven in the morning,' said Diane.

She was eighteen or nineteen, petite, no more than five one or two, with a cute little nose and an inordinate amount of eyeliner. 'I noticed them 'cause they were holding hands.' She giggled. 'Like, you know, *teenagers*. It was so cute.'

Her voice was breathy. Malcolm couldn't tell if it was from nervousness or just the way she usually talked. 'What day was that?'

'The first day they got here. The day before—' Diane shrugged. She sighed. 'You know.'

It was just after eight in the evening, balmy and relatively quiet, a weekday. Down the steps was the street where, under the street lights, tourists strolled, blocking the road for the cars of the residents. Across was the grassy park and the dark bricks of the back of the Mining Museum, one window lit up near the top, as if someone was working late, researching mines.

'The thing is,' Diane went on, 'she was so *pretty*, but you could tell Wes really loved her, not just, you know, *sex*. I mean, some guys, like my stepfather for instance, old – I mean—' she glanced at Malcolm – '*older* guys, to them things that women say are, like, ohmygod totally uninteresting. But he was really listening to her.'

'Ah,' said Malcolm.

'Anyway,' Diane went on, 'I have a good view of the front steps from my waitressing station. Around, oh, maybe six thirty or so that evening, I noticed Carrie going down the steps alone. She looked all bouncy and happy, you know?'

'Sure,' said Malcolm, remembering her bright smile in the printout from her cellphone camera.

'Then, when I got off work at eight, she was back, sitting outside on this same bench. She didn't look bouncy and happy any more. I sat down across from her 'cause I was waiting for Nick – that's my boyfriend – to pick me up. We started talking, you know, and I could see right away how nervous she was. Her voice was all shaky. I asked her if she was okay. And she said, "I hope so."'

There was a pause.

'I hope so,' said Malcolm.

'Yeah. Kind of a strange thing to say, I thought.'

'Did she say where she'd been?' Malcolm asked.

'The High Desert Market – she showed me this

darling Mexican painted frog that she'd just bought there.'

'And?'

'And nothing. My boyfriend showed up, and that was about it for our conversation. And now she's dead. It doesn't seem real. It just makes me so sad. She reminded me of my mom, if my mom had been a little more lucky with guys.'

'Umm,' said Malcolm.

'Oh yeah, I forgot – one more thing.'

'What's that?'

'She wasn't alone.'

'What? What do you mean?'

'She wasn't alone when she got back. I didn't see who it was, but right before she came up the steps, I saw her waving, like, bye, at someone.'

Waving at someone?

Malcolm took a stroll to the High Desert Market from the Copper Queen Hotel, checking out the route Carrie must have taken to return to the hotel with her Mexican painted frog. She'd been upset, shaky when Diane talked to her. Had something happened to her at the High Desert Market? Or on her way back? What had she seen or encountered during that relatively brief period of time between six thirty and a little before eight?

Under the street lights in the park by the Mining Museum a bunch of teenagers hung out on the benches, a whiff of marijuana coming Malcolm's way. Up and down Main Street the shops were all closed now; here and there was an alleyway where people sold crafts, the stalls shut down for the night. Only a restaurant, Cafe Roka, was open; a couple at a window table stared out at him without interest as he passed. And when he got to the High Desert Market it was closed too, the red umbrellas on its patio furled, a night light on inside and the rest full of shadows.

He'd come back tomorrow, talk to the help. *Who had been with Carrie that night?*

Malcolm walked into the St Elmo Bar. Three depressed-looking regulars sat at the far end, and sitting closest to the door was a couple, arms around each other, maybe not depressed. Malcolm eased into a seat in the middle. Behind the bar was a display of guns and old watches, sheriff's badges, and china figurines of happy drunks.

The bartender came over, a muscular biker type with a shaved head and a big moustache.

'Got Sam Adams?' Malcolm asked.

'Yes, sir, we got Sam Adams.' He pulled one from a cooler and set it in front of Malcolm.

'Sid around?' Malcolm asked.

'Nope.' The bartender grinned. 'I'm Sid all right, but I'm a square.'

'Ho, ho, ho.' Malcolm took a swig of his Sam Adams.

Sid leaned on the bar. 'You know, sometimes I'll wait three or four weeks before someone asks that question. And I know who you are. You're that cop that's helping out Lupita.'

'Small town,' Malcolm said.

'Very. Look, she's a good kid, Lupita. Chico too. They had a drunk for a dad. Chico's not much of a drinker, but every now and then he'll binge. Like, on these big weekends. Doesn't hold his liquor too well. He was so drunk, I wouldn't have kept on serving him, to tell you the truth. Drinking tea.' He winked at Malcolm.

'Tea. Huh.' Long Island iced tea, a lethal combination of five different spirits. 'So why did you?'

'Why did I what?'

'Keep on serving him.'

'I didn't. It was the blonde. She kept on ordering drinks.'

'Chico mentioned a blonde, but he didn't know her. I was hoping you might.'

Sid shrugged. 'Not a clue. The bar was packed. Full of out-of-towners. She kind of glommed on to Chico.'

'So, she an out-of-towner?'

'I'd bet on it. Never saw her before. It looked like she was from Tucson. No—' He snapped his fingers. 'Actually, more like Phoenix, you know what I mean?'

'Phoenix?' Malcolm said. 'Why do you say that?'

'Straight, with a touch of Republican. Tucsonans look more human. She wasn't that good-looking, but her hair had that salon look, not hip. The ladies here, they're *au naturel*.'

'*Au naturel*?'

He looked apologetic. 'My ex was a hairdresser.'

'So, did she and Chico leave together?'

'Not a clue. I didn't notice Chico leaving or

99

the blonde either. But you know what? The whole thing is a set-up. That kid, drunk as he was, he couldn't have killed nobody, you ask me. But hey, you know what? No one did.'

'Well, here I am,' said Malcolm, 'asking.'

''Preciate it,' said Sid. 'Chico's a good kid. I'll ask around for you, see if anyone else has a better memory.'

'That'd be great. I'll check back.' Malcolm finished his beer, stood up, added a dollar and his card to the change on the bar. 'Thanks,' he said.

Outside on the street, he thought, *Phoenix*. And there was the daughter of Wes Cooper's, a Polly Hampton who lived in Phoenix. Interesting. He'd like to know a little more about this Polly. And about other friends and relatives too. He'd like to ask them, for instance, *did* those nice Coopers do drugs?

Tomorrow, he thought, he'd go find Kate, Kate who had risen from the dead. She'd acted so cool that last time he'd tried, but maybe this time she'd give him a chance to explain, a chance to persuade her. *Why the hell not?* Thinking of persuading Kate, he walked a little taller, strolling down the Gulch in the cool night air.

Sixteen

Kate was in the supermarket wheeling her cart past rows and rows of brightly colored produce

– it looked really good, but she knew if she bought it some would turn out to be tasteless. She kept going and going, but the produce section seemed to have no end – she was so tired, but she couldn't find the store exit either. She wheeled the cart faster and faster, afraid if she didn't find the exit pretty soon she would pass out.

She was so tired, finally she lay down on the floor. The other shoppers wheeled their carts around her except for one – a man was pushing a cart right towards her. Then she realized the man was Harry Light, his face red with anger.

'*No! Stop!*' she said.

But he kept coming.

Kate opened her eyes. She was filled with dread. She had no idea where she was, lying in utter darkness. Then her vision adjusted, and dimly she saw she was lying on a couch in a place she had never been before. Something had woken her – what? – and she was certain suddenly it was Harry. Harry was hiding somewhere.

Outside, a dog barked and barked and barked.

Someone was shouting – she couldn't make out the words, they were too far away.

Kate sat up, her heart beating faster. It hadn't been Harry that woke her; it was the dog. She looked at her watch. Four a.m. She'd been asleep for hours. She hadn't meant to go to sleep – it was the Ativan. Why had she taken it when she needed to be alert? Because she'd expected to come to this house, to hang out with Ellen and relax.

Ellen. She reached for her cell on the coffee table. She'd been afraid to turn it off in case Ellen called, but it wouldn't have mattered – it was completely dead. She got up and went to the window.

Abruptly, the dog stopped barking.

Then she heard the whine of a police siren.

The sound was reassuring. She went outside, down the driveway where she'd stood earlier. Around the curve, a couple of houses were all lit up, and a cluster of people stood on the sidewalk in front of the one with the silver SUV. The lights were on there and in another house further down.

'Max!' a man shouted. He wore pajamas and was holding on to the collar of a dog, some kind of lab, and the dog was growling. 'Max, calm down!'

A woman said something she couldn't decipher.

Kate walked a little closer to where the people were.

The police siren whined in the distance, getting louder, until a patrol car pulled up to the cluster of people and a cop got out.

People were talking, but she still couldn't really hear. Then someone laughed. Everyone seemed to be laughing, full of good cheer. The cop was laughing too. He walked back to his patrol car, got in, said something out the window and drove away. People waved, then they went into their houses, they closed the doors. The lights in the houses went out. Up and down the street, the street lights made circles of light on the road, the sidewalks.

Kate walked back into the house and closed the door.

The lavender candle she had lit last night was on the floor by the couch – some time during the night it had gone out. The Ativan had made her careless; she could have burnt the house down. She lit it again and made a tour of the house, looking for what? Who? Ellen? The only car in the driveway was the rental. She checked the bedrooms anyway, but no Ellen was sleeping off a late arrival.

Where was she?

But she might have called or texted last night, called or texted Kate's dead cellphone. Or emailed her useless laptop.

Kate figured she must have fallen asleep around eight thirty last night. By now it was almost five. She'd had close to eight hours of sleep, and anxiety buzzed in her head – there was no way she'd be able to sleep again. What had been going on with the police car, so early this morning? Too early to find out. Too early to buy a cellphone charger for the car, too early – wait, didn't McDonald's have Wi-Fi?

There was a McDonald's back at the plaza where she'd exited from the freeway. She was pretty sure they were open twenty-four hours a day. Not only that, but she remembered a Radio Shack there too where she could buy a cellphone charger for the rented car.

She went into the kitchen, rinsed her face in the kitchen sink with the water she'd bought, brushed her teeth, changed her underwear and put back on her black jeans, black T-shirt, black with white trim Converse sneakers. She left the house, locking the door behind her, put the key under the rock just in case Ellen showed up, got back in the rental car.

She wanted breakfast, real breakfast: eggy and bacony and hot.

Comfort food.

Back at the shopping center she cruised by the Radio Shack. It opened at ten. She pulled into the McDonald's and went inside. She bought coffee and a bacon and egg McMuffin, then sat on a hard little seat at a hard little table and turned on her laptop. No email from Ellen. She emailed Ellen just in case. *Where are you? My cell's dead so I can't get texts till after ten a.m.*

She had no idea where Ellen lived except it was a New York City suburb.

Don't worry, she told herself. Your cellphone died. Ellen's probably texted you, called you. Ten o'clock, and then she could buy a charger at Radio Shack. She ate slowly, dawdling while she watched it get light outside, sun shining off the windows of the cars and trucks on the freeway, anxiety still buzzing in her head.

Malcolm played around with his computer, made a printout of the Carrie picture in front of the Copper Queen from the file and enlarged it. It wasn't great but it was okay. Then he headed for the High Desert Market. The red umbrellas were unfurled now, and people were sitting out under them. Malcolm went inside and ordered a coffee.

'I'd like to talk to whoever works the evening shift,' he said to the young man behind the counter. 'When do they come on?'

He grinned, a young man still spotted with adolescence. 'Around noon. Why?'

'This has to do with the night before the tourists were murdered.'

'You a reporter?'

'No. Investigator. Working for Chico Flores.'

'Chico. Oh, wow. Whatever anyone can do to help around here, they will. That was Brewery Gulch Days weekend? Man, that weekend ended up a bust,' he said. 'Elton was working. Elton Savory.'

'Just him?'

'Dunno.'

'And is he working tonight?'

'Naw.'

'Know how I can reach him?'

'Naw. He's out of town right now, camping.'

'Owen.' A young woman came up from behind the kid and batted his head. '*What*? You never learned how to talk?' She looked at Malcolm. Her face was round and bright and pleasant. 'I overheard what you saying. I was working that night.'

'This would be around six thirty or seven.'

'Yes?'

Malcolm showed her the picture of Carrie. 'Do you remember seeing her that night?'

'That's her, isn't it? The woman who was killed.'

'Yes.'

'I thought so. She bought a ceramic frog. I

don't know why but it makes it seem sadder – she really liked the frog.'

'Did anything about her behavior seem unusual to you?'

'You know what?' the young woman said. 'Just the fact I remember her is pretty amazing. We were packed that night. It was one of the biggest tourist weekends of the year.'

He gave her his card. 'If anyone else remembers anything, they can contact me. I'd really appreciate it.'

And that's it, he thought as he left the High Desert Market. And maybe that *was* it. Maybe he would never know who she said goodbye to at the Copper Queen Hotel. You followed up on everything, and some of it led nowhere. Maybe it meant nothing in terms of the murders. Or maybe it did.

The Co-op was busy when Malcolm walked in, a line of people at the two registers: an old guy in a red bandanna at one and a skinny young woman with multiple piercings at the other. He cruised the store, past rows of more kinds of tea than anyone could ever drink, past bins of bulk nuts and grains, past cereals he had never heard of. *Spelt*? *Kamut*? Past pesticide-free organic produce. At the back was an open door that said 'Employees only'. A man sat at a desk, head bent. No Kate that he could see anywhere.

He meandered to the front again. The line had eased up.

'Can I help you find something?' the old guy asked.

'I'm looking for Kate, actually. Is she working today?'

'No.'

'When is she working?'

The man regarded him with suspicion. 'Who are you, anyway? Why do you want to know?'

'My name's Malcolm MacGregor. I'm helping Lupita?'

'The cop! Of course, from Phoenix. It's just great that you're helping her out. Sorry for the paranoia. I'm Windsong. Pleased to meet you. Look, I'm about to go on break. Let's go outside, we can talk.'

Outside, Windsong sat on a wooden bench by the door. Malcolm sat beside him.

'What's the paranoia about?' Malcolm asked.

'Got it from Kate. She's been paranoid since that newspaper article mentioned her talking to Carrie.'

'Oh? And why is that?'

'Maybe 'cause the killer might think she knew stuff and come after her?'

'Yeah? You don't sound too sure about that.'

Windsong snorted. 'Whatever transpired between Carrie and Kate, it wasn't much of a conversation.'

'You were there?'

'I took that picture, the one that got the cops to come and talk to Kate. Between you and me, that's not why Kate was nervous about the newspaper article.'

'Oh?'

'She's got this ex in California who's mad at her. She doesn't want him to know where she is, and if he googles her now, her name'll probably

107

come up in that article. Then there was the accident. You heard about that?'

'Yeah.'

'It kind of put her over the edge in terms of paranoia. She went to New Jersey.'

'*New Jersey*?'

'Yep. To see an old friend. Look, maybe it was kind of weird. Her tire blew out, and she told me she'd had them all replaced before she left California. But hey, man, it can happen. You encounter something on the road, etcetera, etcetera.'

'Yeah.'

There was a pause.

'Yeah,' Windsong said. 'Really. Or maybe she was right to be paranoid. I don't know a damn thing about this ex.'

'California,' Malcolm said. 'I thought she was from Vermont. You said she'd replaced her tires recently?'

'Oh, man,' said Windsong. 'There's places sometimes you don't even want to go to. Listen, you need to talk to Dakota, she's Kate's best friend here. Don't have her cell number, but she lives on twenty-three Yucca Street, down the gulch a way. She's usually home 'cause she works out of her studio.'

Seventeen

Ten o'clock on the dot Kate went into the Radio Shack and bought a cellphone charger. She plugged it in and drove around waiting for it to charge up. Half an hour, she would wait a whole half an hour, before she checked for a message. She drove back to the house on Roscommon Drive, parked on the street, letting the engine keep running. A woman in a floppy hat came towards her, walking a dog, a dachshund.

'Hello,' Kate called out the window.

'Hi!' The woman stopped. She was wearing big sunglasses. 'I saw your car arrive yesterday. You're staying at the house?'

'Kind of. I'm supposed to meet my friend here, Ellen Wilson?'

The woman looked blank.

'She inherited the house from her aunt.'

'My goodness. We're pretty new in the neighborhood. I never met the woman who lived here; she died a few months ago. That must be when your friend inherited.'

'The problem is, Ellen was supposed to be here yesterday, but she never showed up.'

'Really?'

'She probably tried to get in touch, but my cellphone died.'

'Well! I hope that to-do last night didn't wake you. The neighbor's dog Max stays inside usually, but he got out and he wouldn't stop barking. There was a prowler or something.'

'Really?'

'No one *saw* a prowler, but when the policeman came he said to Jim, Max's owner, just keep that dog outside till morning. So he did. But the dog didn't bark after that, so maybe someone *had* been out there prowling. We all laughed and laughed.' She paused. 'We get so dependent on these cellphones, and then when they go out, we're just lost. I'm sure your friend will contact you.'

Kate turned on her cell. A tiny yellow envelope showed on the little bar at the bottom. Her whole body flooded with relief. 'I think she already has.'

'See. You have a good day. C'mon, Felix,' the woman said to the dog. They crossed the street.

Kate opened the message. A text, from Dakota. *Hi. Hope you're having fun.*

That was it? Just a text from Dakota, and nothing, nothing at all from Ellen?

She called Ellen's number from her contact list. It rang and rang. All she had was Ellen's email and her cellphone, no home phone number, no address either. Damn.

What the hell am I supposed to do now, Kate wondered. *What?*

The 'For Sale' sign was right in front of her with the realtor's name, Evan Bright Realty, and a number. She punched in the number.

'Evan Bright Realty, this is Marci speaking!'

Kate introduced herself. She explained.

'Well, for heaven's sake,' said Marci. 'That's Steve's listing. He's not here right now, but let me see what I can find out.'

Kate waited, it seemed like forever, until finally Marci came back. 'I couldn't locate an address for the owner,' she said, 'but I've got a phone number. A cell, I think.'

It wasn't the same number as the one she

had for Ellen. Kate wrote it down, thanked Marci. She punched in the number immediately. It rang and rang and rang and rang. No one picked up, no voicemail, nothing. It just kept on ringing.

There was no way Ellen would not have made contact by now unless something was seriously wrong.

Time to go to the police.

The woman looked friendly, and she smiled when she saw Kate come up to the big glass window. 'I'd like to speak to an officer about a missing person,' Kate said.

'This an adult?'

'Yes.'

'How long?'

'How long—?'

'How long have they been missing? More than forty-eight hours?'

'No – I mean, I'm not— Look, it's pretty complicated—' Her lip trembled. 'Couldn't I just talk to someone and explain?'

The women looked sympathetic. 'Sure, honey. Hold on.'

A few minutes later a uniformed officer in his late twenties, early thirties, round cheeked and blonde, strolled out to the lobby, eating a stalk of celery. 'Excuse this.' He waved the celery. 'Didn't get breakfast. I'm Officer Matt Dodds.'

Kate introduced herself.

'So what's going on?'

Kate told him the story.

He nodded and nodded throughout.

'Look,' she said when she finished, 'I know about the forty-eight hours wait, but this is really strange.'

'I don't recall seeing reports of any crime against a person by that name. You call the local hospital?'

'No,' said Kate.

'Course, if she was traveling here something could have happened along the way. Look here, let me run back to my office and double-check.'

He came back in a few minutes, shaking his head. 'Nothing. Checked the hospitals farther away too. Checked for crimes against unidentified women too.' He paused. 'How'd you get in the house?'

'The key was under a rock. She told me about it.'

'Everything looked normal inside?'

'*Normal*?' There was a little pause. 'I don't know what normal would be,' said Kate. 'It's pretty bare, but then no one actually lives there. There wasn't any overturned furniture or—' she giggled little shakily – 'pools of blood.'

'Now, now,' said Officer Dodds. 'People go missing all the time, and most of the time they turn up safe and sound.'

'Yes,' said Kate.

'Three fifty Roscommon, huh? We had a call on that street there last night – barking dog.' He chuckled. 'Guess it's turning into a high-crime area. Tell you what, we usually wait a while longer on a missing persons, but I'll take a run over there, meet you outside.'

'Why? I mean, who will that help?' Kate asked.
'Just like to take a look, is all.'

At 350 Roscommon Drive, Officer Dodds got out of his police car, rubbing his hands together. 'God damn technology's taking over the world,' he said. 'People think it makes them smarter, but just look at this – you've been in touch with this Ellen, but you don't know a damn thing about her, not really, not like knowing someone with your *instincts*.'

'I knew her fifteen years ago,' said Kate. 'She said all the right things in her emails and her texts.'

The officer didn't respond, as if she hadn't spoken. Maybe she hadn't. She was beginning to feel a little unreal. She watched as the officer walked slowly around the outside of the house, disappearing around the back then reappearing on the other side.

'Let's check it out inside,' he said.

She unlocked the door and followed him in. He walked through all the rooms of the house, opening closet doors and closing them, Kate following at a polite distance. They ended up in the kitchen.

'Basement door?' he said.

'Basement door—' Kate paused. 'There's a basement?'

'Well—' Officer Dodds paced the kitchen. 'I don't know what the hell else those windows I saw outside, down at the foundation, are for.' He turned a corner near where the back door was. 'Aha, here it is.'

Kate heard a door open. She'd seen the door, thought it was a closet.

'I'll be back in a jiffy,' Officer Dodds said. 'I got a mag-light in my car.'

He left, came back with the flashlight.

Kate heard his steps on the stairs going down to the basement, but she didn't feel like following him any more. She sat down abruptly on a kitchen chair and closed her eyes as the realization rushed over her that that was why he had driven over here. What he was looking for was a body, Ellen's body. She might have spent the night in a house with Ellen's body down in the basement. Or, even worse, when she arrived Ellen could have been down in the basement unconscious, dying, and now it was too late.

She felt herself start to shake, imagining Ellen laying down on a cold basement floor, covered in blood and too weak to call out to her, while she, Kate, slept upstairs on the couch. Anyone could be dead just like that; it happened really fast sometimes, you were gone.

'Ma'am? You okay?'

Kate opened her eyes. 'Did you—?'

'Nothing down there but old magazines, bunch of canning jars and spider webs.' He grinned. 'Most likely she'll show up with an excuse. Shame when you flew in here for a vacation. Where you fly in from?'

'Arizona.'

He raised his eyebrows. 'High-crime state I hear, what with the battling drug cartels killing people and the illegals coming across day and night, killing people and getting tortured and

114

murdered themselves if the banditos rob the coyotes.' His voice was cheery, as if relating the latest episode of *CSI:Arizona*. 'And then if that don't happen, I hear the coyotes take the illegals to a house somewhere, hold 'em hostage and call their families in Mexico for ransom money.'

He smiled at her reassuringly. 'You give me a call when this Ellen shows up, OK?'

Malcolm parked his big truck on the Gulch; God knows what the parking would be like on Yucca Street. He walked to the address, twenty-three Yucca. At the house next door a hulking giant of a man, black bearded and dressed in black leather with silver studs, was just coming down the porch steps.

'Hey, man, how's it going?' he said. 'Can I help you?'

'I'm looking for Dakota.'

'She's home. Just walk on in.'

'Thanks.' Malcolm walked through a small gate, aware of the giant, watching him. The yard was lined with bright flowering gazania. There was a house and what must be Dakota's studio next to it. The door to the studio was open.

He went over, poked his head in. 'Hello?'

A woman stood in front of a big canvas, her hair a blaze of fake red, wearing a big apron and black sweatpants. 'Hello?' she said back.

'I'm looking for Kate Waters. Windsong told me about you,' Malcolm said. 'I'm a detective on leave from Mesa PD. I'm helping out Chico's attorney with the investigation.' And he explained.

'Ohh,' said Dakota, her face brightening considerably. 'I don't think I've ever in my entire life met a detective.' She smiled. 'I remember seeing you at Chico's show at Sail Rabbit. Don't know how I can help you. All I know really is Kate's gone to New Jersey.'

'I'd like to take a look at that tire,' Malcolm said, 'the one that blew out. If possible.'

'Her car's at Ernie Roger's garage. I gave her a ride to the airport,' Dakota said. 'They came out and put on her spare, and someone drove it there. Kate didn't feel up to driving it herself.' She dabbed something on the canvas she was working on, stood back, frowned, then put the brush in a jar of water.

'I don't mean to disturb you,' Malcolm said.

'It's okay. Come on in. I'm done, anyway.' She removed the paint splotched apron she was wearing. 'Sit down.'

Malcolm came in and sat down on a leather couch with stuffing leaking from a tear in one of the cushions. He had a good view from there of the painting she was working on; it looked like a sunset with a lot of bugs crawling across it.

'So who's this ex of Kate's?' he asked.

'What?' Dakota looked startled. 'I thought you were here about Chico and the tourists. I mean, to ask me if Carrie said anything to Kate at the Co-op. Which she did not. So first you ask me about that tire, then you want to know about Kate's ex.'

116

'I know, I know. There might be a connection. I'm trying to look at all the angles. From what Windsong says nothing much transpired between Kate and Carrie, but the killer might think something did. I'd like to talk to her,' Malcolm said. 'Sometimes people don't know what they know. The tire thing, I need to check that out.'

'Her ex, Harry, sounds like a real jerk. But I don't know about Kate's paranoia. I mean – I know she got new tires in California, but you never know if you're getting ripped off nowadays. They could have been retreads or whatever.'

'I thought she was from back east. What was she doing in California?'

'God!' Dakota ran her hands through her red red hair and sighed. 'Kate's had such a hard time. She lost her job in Vermont, or rather her job vanished along with the economy, and at the same time her long-term relationship fell apart. She ran off to California to be with this Harry Light guy. She never would have done that if she hadn't been so vulnerable. Then she realized it was a mistake, so she left him and came here.'

'Tough,' Malcolm said. 'It does sound like she's had a hard time.'

'Harry's a poet if you can believe that. Harry Light. Does that sound like a phoney name or what?'

'A real jerk, you said,' Malcolm repeated. 'Why is that?'

'He had these sort of out-of-control tantrums.

And even after almost three months he's still emailing her these nasty comments.'

'No kidding,' Malcolm said. 'What do they say?'

'She wouldn't tell me. Just that they were nasty.'

'Harry Light,' Malcolm said. 'As in light bulb?'

Dakota laughed. 'Or maybe dim bulb, is more like it. Anyway, like I said, now she's in New Jersey.'

'New Jersey. Of course,' said Malcolm, 'that makes sense.'

Dakota laughed. 'Doesn't it. Oh, and by the way.'

'What?'

'Harry owned a gun.'

'A gun? What kind of gun?'

'I have no idea, and neither does Kate.'

Malcolm drove over to Ernie Roger's garage, outside of town near the Safeway. He saw what he figured might be Kate's car, a Honda Civic parked over by the chain link fence that surrounded the back of the property. The right back tire was one of those inflatable ones that get you a few miles to the nearest gas station.

A young guy came out, wiping his hands on an old rag. 'Help you, sir?'

'Is that Kate Waters' car over there?' Malcolm asked, pointing.

'Sure is.'

'What's going on with it?'

'Not a goddamn thing.'

'What do you mean?'

118

'The owner left it here for us to see if we could fix the tire, but she went out of town for a week, and we're real backed up here. We haven't gotten to it yet.'

'Well, thanks,' Malcolm said. 'When do you think you might get to it?'

'Try back, say, day after tomorrow.'

Malcolm went home and got his gun, not his service revolver but his sport gun, a Ruger Mark III .22 caliber pistol with a bull barrel. He got five magazines and a brick of ammunition from the back of the bedroom closet, a big cardboard box and three or four paper targets. He hadn't used his gun or practiced for a while now; he figured he was getting pretty rusty. He drove out through the Mule Mountains, made the turn to Sierra Vista, down that same road, Highway 80, where Kate had driven not so long ago.

Just desert, mesquite and jack rabbits and prickle poppies, framed by blue mountains. A few miles down was a shooting range. He parked, got out. No one else was there. Overhead, a hawk floated in the cloudless Arizona sky.

He set the big cardboard box some twenty to thirty feet away and taped on the paper target, white with a big black bullseye in the center. Then he loaded up the first magazine, ten rounds of ammunition, and began to shoot. He shot slow and steady, but he hadn't shot in a while and his aim was off.

He shot and shot and shot, the whole magazine, then loaded up the next one and shot some more. After a while his aim started getting better, and then a while after that, he was in the groove, he couldn't miss. *Zen and the art of shooting*, he thought, aiming and shooting, aiming and shooting. Stopping from time to time to replace the paper target.

He kept going until he was clean out of ammunition and his mind was clean out of any thoughts at all. Not one single thought.

Cindy had turned, smiled, walked away.

But she'd be back.

Eighteen

There was no way Kate was going to spend another night in that house. She packed up everything, put it in the rental car. She took a walk through the house in case she'd forgotten something, opening and closing drawers, looking into closets, just in case there was something, somewhere – paperwork, maybe, that would give her a clue as to Ellen's home address – but found nothing.

It was amazing how featureless the house was, not even the sparse furniture (a lot of it must have been sold) told you anything about the person who had lived here. Only the photograph in the second bedroom gave any hints. A woman in sunglasses, a bikini and a big straw hat smiled back at her – where was she, when was it taken, was it Ellen's dead aunt? What was Ellen's dead aunt's name, anyway?

120

Or was it some other relative? It was impossible to tell in what decade the picture had been taken, but it was the only personal thing in the house. On an impulse Kate slipped the snapshot out of the frame. On the back of the photo it said 'Tall Pine Lake, 2005'. But no name. If something bad had happened to Ellen, the picture could get lost in the shuffle. Kate put it back in the frame and into her backpack. Then, just in case, she left a note for Ellen on the kitchen table, anchored by one of the gallon water bottles.

I showed up, where were you? Kate

Then she left the house, locking the door behind her, putting the key under the rock. She got back in the rental car and sat for a moment looking at the green lawn, the yellow roses blooming on the trellis by the front door. It looked so normal, but this was absurd.

Ellen had been delayed in some weird way, in a dead zone, maybe, like in that TV commercial. A dead zone where technology didn't work. But somehow Kate thought of a dead zone as a place where only technology worked, where flowers didn't bloom and no birds sang.

She drove around aimlessly for a while just to listen to Lisa Strange sing on her iPod. Next to Neko Case she loved Lisa Strange the most – had almost all the songs on her last two albums. *Winter* and *Never*. Out of time, no place she had to be.

Then she drove to a motel near the Krogers, the Wendy's, the McDonald's, the Kentucky Colonel, the Burger King, the Taco Bell. She checked in after making sure they had Wi-Fi.

The room looked like all the motels rooms she had ever stayed in. She took a long shower, checked her cell for a call or a text from Ellen, and then opened her laptop and checked her email once again – still nothing from Ellen. Just in case, she fircd off another email and a text to Ellen, then went back to her Ellen folder and reread all the emails Ellen had ever sent her. There was nothing in them that would tell her why Ellen hadn't shown up.

She googled Ellen Wilson to see if she'd been in an accident somewhere but found nothing. Then she googled film maker and Ellen Wilson together. There was a film-making Ellen Wilson in Seattle, Washington and one in Detroit. None in New York or Connecticut or Jersey though. After a while she gave up.

What about Karen and Sandy, the other two Ooblecks? But Karen had married and Kate didn't know her new last name, and she'd forgotten Sandy's last name entirely.

Rick. Rick her ex. They'd liked to go into the city from time to time, and in the last few years she'd been so involved with the arts center that he usually went alone, spent the night. He would still be in touch with people she'd lost track of. But she could hardly bear to think of contacting him – they hadn't parted as friends. Was he still with Hannah? Would Hannah answer his phone, read his emails and texts? What if she called his cell and he saw it was her calling and didn't answer?

She could maybe go to Rustic, stalk Rick, make

sure he was alone, then confront him. She giggled, playing with the laptop, going to MapQuest to see how far Rustic, Vermont was from this motel.

Five to six hours.

Stupid to go that far, for what?

Because she needed to.

She lay back on the bed and closed her eyes, but she didn't sleep.

Malcolm went home. The orange cat was lurking by the door.

'Hey there, kitty,' he said.

It backed away and hissed at him. He dumped some cat food in the dish out by the porch, then went inside, googled the name Harry Light. See how real this guy really was. Wow. Wikipedia, he had a Wikipedia page. He clicked on it, and there was Harry Light, balding a bit – hah! – wearing a black shirt unbuttoned a couple of buttons more than was necessary and smirking in a knowing, superior kind of way. He already disliked the guy.

Wikipedia informed him that Harry Light was an award-winning poet who lived in California, in the Los Angeles area, and did a lot of workshops and poetry readings throughout the country, including Boston and Vermont but mainly in the Southwest.

He'd written a lot of poetry books. Malcolm scrolled down a list, with weird names like *Causal Geography*, *A Mote of Indifference* and *Hamburger of Desire*.

Hamburger of Desire?

Malcolm exited Wikipedia and scrolled down more listings.

Blah, blah, blah, blah. Then an entry made him pause. *English Professor-Poet Harry Light Questioned.*

He clicked on it.

English Professor-Poet Harry Light Questioned in Grad Student's Disappearance.

What?

He scanned it for the real information.

Hours before her disappearance, missing grad student Anna Marie Romero had gone to one of Professor Harry Light's popular workshops. Her car was later found parked by a tennis court near where Professor Light lives. Her mother, Cecilia Romero, notified law enforcement when she failed to come home.

Professor Light denied any rumors that there was more to their relationship than teacher-student.

And Harry Light had been sending nasty emails to Kate.

He searched for more articles about Anna Marie Romero, found just one – *Graduate Student Still Missing* – with no mention of Harry Light, and that was it. It struck him as strange, this petering out. He had a sense of things being covered over, hushed up. Why?

He'd like to talk to the investigating officer on the case, probably could through his Mesa PD connections. But he was investigating the Cooper murders for Lupita and Chico; how did he get so far afield? But he didn't care.

He searched a little more and discovered at one

site that Harry was doing a reading in Phoenix at some place called the Poetry Barn. Tomorrow night. He'd been planning on going to Phoenix at some point, anyway.

Polly Hampton, Wes Cooper's daughter, lived in Phoenix. There was the blonde lady, the one the bartender thought was from Phoenix – he'd like to get a good look at Polly Hampton. He googled her without really expecting anything, and there she was – the owner of a store called Polly's Collectibles in a little mall in Tempe. He could spend the night at his brother Ian's. He had an open invitation to dinner anytime he was in town.

Well, at least if this Harry Light guy was any kind of danger, Kate was safe and sound back east in New Jersey.

Kate slept finally, then woke, not knowing where she was, and in fact she could be anywhere, from the blandness of the motel room. A dim light shone through a small gap between the double curtains. She looked at her watch: close to nine p.m. She'd slept longer than she'd intended, her internal clock all askew. It was time for a delicious fast food dinner. She got up, brushed her hair, put on some lip gloss. Her laptop was on the meager desk. Time to check for messages from Ellen, yeah right.

First her cell – and sure enough, a text had come in while she was asleep. She opened it. Dakota. *Guy came 2 c me, name of—*

No time for that now. She opened the laptop and went to her email. Messages of no consequence were piling up, and then she saw it, a message from Ellen, Subject: *please help me out.*

Of course! Thank God. She opened it.

Hello, I am sorry I didn't inform you about my travel to Europe for a program called Empowering the Youth to Fight Racism, HIV/AIDS, and the Lack of Education, the program is taking place in three major countries which are Belgium, Spain, England. But I am presently in England, London to be precise. Unfortunately all my money and traveling documents were stolen in my hotel room during a robbery incident in the hotel where I lodged. I am so confused now: I don't know what to do. Please could you urgently assist me with a soft loan of $1,800 pounds—

Damn it! Kate hit delete. A scam. A stupid scam. And that meant that Ellen's email was probably compromised too. Kate kicked the leg of the desk hard and hurt her foot.

Vermont, she thought. First thing in the morning. If she left at eight she would be there by early afternoon. Suddenly, she remembered Dakota's text that she hadn't bothered to read. She read it now. Something about Malcolm, the guy she'd met at the gallery, needing to talk to her. It even included his cell number. Yeah, right. This was hardly the time. No way she was going to call him. But she'd promised Dakota she would kind of stay in touch. She texted her: *GOING 2 VERMONT* ☺

Migas, Chico was thinking as he rested, for no reason other than boredom, in his cell. The guy

126

who'd had the bunk below him was gone, and no doubt a new guy would appear very soon, but right now Chico was alone lying on his back, thinking *migas*. Corn tortillas fried in a skillet with eggs. He was thinking *Lupita's migas*. They were special – she added a can of those Ro-tel tomatoes, that had the green chilies in them and something else he wasn't sure what, but the result was, in Chico's opinion, the very best thing on earth you could eat for breakfast. You could eat *migas* for lunch too and maybe even as a light supper.

He'd never really liked bologna, one of the jailhouse staples, and now the thought of it, compared to the spiciness of the chili and tomato next to the earthy flavor of the corn tortillas and the bland deliciousness of the eggs, made him feel slightly sick, or would if he weren't so hungry most of the time that he would eat anything.

Lupita came to see him regularly, and so did his nana, but they just cried and made him even more depressed. His lawyer kept saying, 'Be patient, be patient, it's going to work out,' but how did he know, really? He was just a lawyer. Besides, look at all those people that got convicted on no evidence at all, especially in Texas, only one state away, and besides, this was Arizona, home of SB1070, a totally racist law directed, in his opinion, not only at illegals but also perfectly innocent Hispanic citizens like him.

Anything could happen.

Right now he didn't have it so bad, really, the

guards trusted him with little tasks, wheeling the cart from the library, that kind of thing, but there was nothing, nothing to look at that wasn't industrial, bland, nothing except the faces of the guards and the other inmates

The really bad crazy guys, of which there at this moment two, were kept separately. He wished he could see them – the faces of the really bad guys might be interesting.

Migas, he thought, *migas*.

Nineteen

A few miles away from Rustic, Vermont, Kate stopped at a little tourist store and bought a big straw hat and some bottled water. She put the hat on the passenger seat and drove the winding road through the mountains she and Rick had traveled frequently so long ago. The closer she got, the more nervous she felt. She passed the sign: *Rustic, 3 miles*.

Where would she sleep tonight? Then, just before town, she remembered there was the ancient Shady Grove Motel, little wooden attached cabins all in a row, office with a peaked roof at one end, tall trees all around. And, sure enough, there it was. She parked in front and went in to make sure they had a room.

Inside, a punkish-looking kid with bright red streaks in his hair was at the desk. She didn't know him.

'Afternoon,' he said, looking bored.

'Afternoon.'

She checked in, paid cash, on impulse signed her name as Ellen Wilson. She didn't bother inspecting the room. She got back in her car. At that point she remembered what everyone used to call that motel. The Bates motel. Oh well. She drove through Rustic, past the little shops selling maple syrup and maple candies, handmade aprons and rag dolls, past the restaurant, Dottie's, where she and Rick went almost every Friday.

Their lives together had had a whole routine, a way they did the same things over and over, that made it seem as though that was the way the world functioned, like spring turning into summer, summer turning into fall.

She took a turn and drove down a short street to the Arts Center, parked in the lot across the street. Every day except Sunday and Monday she'd driven to the big red converted barn. There was a sign in front that said 'Seven Vermont Artists' and a sign on the door that said 'Closed'. A line from a children's poem her mother used to read her came into her head.

They stole little Bridget for seven years long,
And when she came back all her friends were gone.

She felt tired, jet-lag, the terrible house of the dead aunt, the long drive here, everything – so tired. For a moment the earth seemed to whirl around her as if she were on a revolving sphere. She closed her eyes for a few minutes.

Well, she thought, *at least I got away from the*

129

cold. She wanted to giggle, but knew if she did she would lose control.

Time to go.

She started the car and drove just to the far side of town and down a diminishing side street to a house with an old gray pickup parked in the driveway, the same vehicle that frugal Rick had always had. The mailbox was guarded by a seven-foot-tall twig man, one branch raised in greeting, one of Rick's creations. The barn-like structure that was Rick's studio was surrounded by tall twiggy figures, some of whom she already knew, pointing twiggy arms to the sky, as if to say, *God knows.*

The two-story wooden house looked the same, painted a silver green, her choice, the color of spring. If she went inside she would know each room by heart, but would no longer belong. The house had belonged to Rick from the start, but she'd never minded that. They'd never gotten married; she'd never minded that either. *Idiot.* She slowed down, just creeping along. For a brief moment she imagined herself pulling into the driveway, getting of the car, walking to Rick's studio, putting her head in the door.

'I'm home!' she would say.

Then she lost her nerve and drove right past. *What the hell am I doing here?* she wondered. It seemed to her when she left the motel in New Jersey she'd had a plan, but she no longer knew what it was.

She turned around and drove back to the square in the center of town. She parked her car, put on the big straw hat, her Ray-Ban sunglasses and got out. She sat on a bench with her bottled water. It was so peaceful here with no freeway noise, just birds and dogs and people. A couple of benches down was a young woman with a toddler and on another bench an old man, reading a newspaper. Kate was invisible, in her hat and sunglasses.

Invisible like the woman in the photograph, in her big straw hat and sunglasses, the woman in the photograph in the bedroom of Ellen Wilson's deceased aunt's house.

She sat for a long time, eyes closed, listening to her iPod, Lisa Strange singing 'Lost'.

All the days are gone: lost. The houses. Lost. The parks. Lost. The winters. Lost. Every fall we had: lost.

She opened her eyes. Across the street, the door of the drug store opened and a blonde woman in a black tank top and long swirly ethnicy skirt came out. She was laughing, turning her head to look at the man behind her. A bearded man with longish hair in a faded black T-shirt, tattered jeans and work boots.

Rick. It was Rick and his new girlfriend, Hannah.

She'd known Hannah but not well – she wasn't a local. She'd shown up in town one day about a year ago and just stayed. She worked in a clothing store, everything handmade, some of it by Hannah. Hannah would come to the gallery from time to time, dressed in her ethnicy handmade clothes, peruse the show, ask questions. It wasn't till later that Kate realized Hannah was there to make sure Kate was, so she could go see Rick.

She watched as Hannah sashayed over to an old Volkswagen, got in. Rick stood and watched as she drove off. The dizziness Kate had felt at the gallery, swirling in a vortex of anxiety, was back. She suddenly recognized what it was masking. Rage. Rage at Hannah. Hannah could die slowly and painfully of some kind of cancer for all she cared. She would be glad, glad.

Hannah was gone. Rick turned the other way, walking, headed for home most likely. Now was the time to talk to him; she only had to call his name.

Rick!

But she didn't. It was over. She already knew that, but maybe that was why she'd driven all this way – just to make sure. She had a little flash of herself and Rick, back when they lived in the city, dancing in some bar in the Village, in love forever and ever. Then it was gone. She reached into her purse, got out her cellphone and called Bethany, her closest friend in Rustic.

'Kate! Where are you?'

'Arizona,' Kate said, because she felt too vulnerable for old friends and socializing; not here, anyway. 'Listen, this is very important. I need to find an old friend, Ellen Wilson. Rick might know where she is, but I don't want to talk to him.'

'I wouldn't either,' said Bethany. 'I never speak to Hannah, you know. She's just scum. I miss you.'

'Miss you too,' said Kate. 'I really really need to find Ellen.'

'Okay,' said Bethany decisively. 'I'll call Rick right now. I'll get back to you as quick as I can.'

Kate waited. People passed by. The trees would be turning soon. She knew fall and winter here by heart. After an hour or so, Bethany called back.

'I didn't mention you, like you said. He doesn't know where Ellen is, doesn't know anything about her, but he gave me two numbers for a Mandy Foster who might know.'

'Mandy! Of course.'

'She's not Mandy Foster any more; she's Mandy Fleming. She's still in the city, teaching psych at Columbia. Here's the numbers, cell and home.'

Kate added them to her contacts. 'Thanks, Bethany. You're my friend forever and ever.'

'I can't believe you're in Arizona! All those right-wing people with guns.'

'Instead of Vermont, with all those left-wing people with guns, you mean,' said Kate.

Bethany giggled. 'Not left wing, *independents*. We *all* miss you, not just me. We're all on your side.'

'It doesn't matter,' Kate said.

'Anyway, you should come back to Rustic and visit.'

'Maybe I will sometime,' said Kate.

Twenty

Tempe, Arizona, on the outskirts of Phoenix, had grown from a population of twenty thousand to

133

two hundred thousand in fifteen years. Mile after mile of brand new developments lined the freeway: beige stucco houses with red tiled roofs. Malcolm took an exit in Tempe, drove down a street, turned and turned again, and ended up at a little mall, brand new too he'd bet, in spite of the weathered-looking beige stucco shops. Up close Malcolm could tell that the tiny cracks on the stucco had been painted there with a fine brush.

Polly's Collectibles had a bright-red door and a creaky-looking metal sign overhead with the name in old-timey gilt letters. In the window display he recognized a tin and enamel toy train, just like one that had languished in his parents' basement many years ago, and a hideous lamp that looked like a rocket, an item he had once coveted when he was eight.

Ahem. He pushed open the door, which tinkled. Inside it smelled of the past, though he couldn't say just why or even describe what the past smelled like, that past seen in old magazine advertisements of happy couples in convertibles heading into a sunset. He browsed his way to the back where out of the corner of his eye he could see a thin blonde woman: large silver earrings, a bright-blue peasant blouse. He picked up a hefty turquoise ceramic ashtray, oh, speak of the past. A sticker on the bottom said seventy-five dollars. He set it down.

He was almost at the back. His phone was in his shirt pocket, already set to take a picture.

'Good morning,' said the blonde in a pleasantly surprised voice, as if she had only just noticed him.

134

'Good morning. Are you the Polly of Polly's Collectibles?'

Her smile dimmed slightly; he wasn't sure why. 'Yes?' she said.

He looked at her blonde hair – short, with straight across bangs. Was it a salon do or *au naturel*? He wasn't sure what either of those descriptions meant, exactly, but he would probably go with the salon do for her. He took his phone out of his pocket.

'Always liked the name Polly,' he said. 'Reminds me of gentler times, you know? And I love those old collectibles,' he said, holding up the camera and taking a picture of the ceramic ashtray. He turned the camera then, got Polly, just before she realized he was taking her picture and put her hand up to her face.

'What are you doing?' she said indignantly. 'Who are you? I'm tired of these asshole reporters coming round, asking me underhand questions.' She held out her hand like it was a microphone. 'This last one? You know what he asked? How did it make you feel about the Obama administration's immigration policies when you found out your dad had been brutally murdered by a Hispanic?'

'They did *that*?' Malcolm asked, genuinely disgusted.

'Nothing's anything any more around here except politics.' She put her hands on her hips. 'You publish that picture in any kind of media without my permission, I'll sue you.'

Could she? Even if he put it on the Internet? Malcolm didn't know. He didn't care. He just

135

wanted to show it to Sid the bartender. 'Look.' He spread his hands wide. 'I'm not the press. I'm not here to invade your privacy.'

'I think you just did.' Her eyes were the color of blue steel now. Then they wavered. 'You're not the press?'

'Nope. I swear it.'

'Then who are you?'

'My name's Malcolm MacGregor,' he said. 'My wife, my ex-wife now, had the same damn thing happen to her – her father got murdered. She was so upset—' He paused. 'I don't know, I guess I wasn't there for her in the right way. Broke up the marriage. Then I heard about this case and, well, I don't know, it's hard to talk about and all—' He lapsed into silence, exhausted suddenly with his own lies and, even more, a tiny grain of truth he felt might be in them.

Polly looked sympathetic. 'I guess you'll have to learn to live with yourself, so maybe the next time someone needs your help you'll be there for them. My husband's there for me, and I love him for it.' She paused and looked off into the distance. 'You know, we kind of always learn things too late. I've been, well, kind of estranged from my dad. It breaks my heart now.'

'Wow,' said Malcolm. 'I'm real sorry to hear that. Sad. What about your mom? Same thing?'

'My mom? She's been dead for a while.'

'Your mom wasn't Carrie then?' he asked, although he knew the answer.

'Her? Carrie?' She shrugged again. 'No. She was just Carrie. Okay, I guess. Wishy-washy, getting by on her looks.'

136

'This was a first marriage for Carrie, I noticed.'

'Yes.' Polly frowned, two sharp lines appearing between her eyes. 'She doesn't – didn't – have kids, so I guess she didn't have any reason to. She had a couple of kind of long-term things, but I doubt if her last ex gives two hoots that she was murdered. He's been married for a while.'

'You ever been to Dudley?' Malcolm asked.

'No,' said Polly. Her voice was suddenly out and out hostile. 'Why are you asking me these questions? I thought this was all about your wife's murdered father.'

'It is,' Malcolm began, 'but this is—'

'Why don't you just leave?' Polly said.

So he did.

Malcolm was invited to his brother Ian's for dinner, but first he made a side trip to his old neighborhood, just two more stops down the freeway. He drove slowly through the development, which bore a marked similarity to all the places he'd passed on his way to Polly's Collectibles. Beige stucco, red tiled roofs. The sun was high in the sky, draining the color from the lawns – *lawns* of all things, in what was basically desert. Every fifth house or so had sprinklers going full blast.

Then there it was, the 'For Sale' sign hanging on its post, a little dusty, as if the realtor had forgotten about it, which it felt like they had since no offers had been made. Beige stucco, red tiled roof, louvered blinds closed as if to preserve the privacy of the ghosts inside. He drove by slowly.

They'd had gravel for a lawn, red bird of paradise, a palo verde tree in the middle. In spring it used to be full of yellow blossoms. Cindy used to point it out: 'Look, how beautiful, and you just sit inside in front of that TV, you don't even notice.'

Or at least she pointed it out when she was trying whatever new meds she was on and they were working.

Did he spend that much time in front of the TV? It hadn't seemed that way to him. After all, he worked a full-time job. But somehow remembering her saying that now, and remembering that it was probably true – a way of avoiding her – pained him more than usual, a pain that felt as if it had no end, bottomless. He accelerated, driving a little too fast, back to the main road and on to the I10 freeway, headed for his brother's house.

Kate drove back to the Shady Grove Motel, carried her stuff into the room. There was a little porch with a retro cast-iron chair outside the room, so she went back out with her cellphone and sat. The day was winding down, but it was mellow outside, smelling of woodchips and grass. Everywhere there was grass, grass, grass. It calmed her down. For a moment she felt at peace in woody Rustic, Vermont.

Time to go back to work. That was what her little vacation had turned into – work. She called Ellen's number once again, just in case, but, of course, no one answered. Then she called one of the two numbers for Mandy that Rick had given

Bethany. It rang and rang. Waiting for someone to pick up or for voicemail to kick in, Kate suddenly felt weary, as if she'd been running in place all day and had gotten nowhere.

'Hello?' A man's voice, just when she was about to give up.

'Could I speak to Mandy?'

'Not here.'

'Thanks, I'll try her cell.'

'She left it here this morning. Boy, I bet she's pissed. Anyway, this is Phil.'

'Phil.' Kate's voice was flat. She had no idea who Phil was. 'Phil—?'

'Well, never mind, who's this?'

'Kate, I'm an old friend.'

'Kate, hey. The Kate who's with the sculptor – what's his name – Rick? Rick Church?'

'Used to be,' Kate said. 'You've heard of me?'

'Course. You guys are old friends. Saw you in some video that Mandy's having digitized.'

'Really? What kind of video?'

'People goofing off at parties, stuff like that. Listen, Kate, Mandy won't be home till late – she's got a seminar – but she'll be excited to hear from you. Where are you, anyway?'

'In Vermont.'

'Like I said, Mandy would love to see you. You coming into the city? We got a spare room here you can sleep in.'

'You know,' said Kate, suddenly happy, 'I just might. What's the address?' He gave it to her, somewhere on the upper west side, and she wrote it down. 'Phil?'

'Yeah?'

139

'I'm looking for another old friend, Ellen. Ellen Wilson. Does that name ring a bell?'

There was a silence, punctuated by static and blips.

'Hello?' Kate said. 'Phil. Are you still there?'

'Yeah. This connection sucks. Listen, Kate, come into the city, okay? I know Mandy would love to see you.' He was shouting now over the blips and the static. 'You can talk to her about Ellen.'

Kate got off and went out on search of food, complicated by the fact she didn't want to run into anyone she knew. She drove ten miles to the next town over, to a little diner she remembered off a side street, and it was still there. Besides the waitress, there was only a bearded old man sitting at the counter and a young couple at the back. She ordered a bowl of vegetarian chili and watched it get dark outside as she ate, the trees silhouetted against a cobalt, then an indigo sky.

Going out to the car, she saw the moon was just rising behind the darkness of the trees. Tired and a little disoriented, it struck her that it was rising in the wrong place, as if by some cosmic mistake it was not just herself but the entire solar system that had gone off kilter – the moon hurtling ever closer to earth.

'Malcolm! So good to see you.' His sister-in-law Sally advanced towards him, gave him a big hug. Sally was dark and pretty with a Chinese kind of haircut, straight bangs and blunt. She was wearing a white polo top, white shorts, silver jewelry and flip-flops.

140

'Looking good,' Malcolm said, because she was.

'Ian's outside firing up the grill as we speak.'

The house was in a nice part of Tempe, nicer than the house in Mesa where Malcolm had lived with Cindy, nicer as befitted the son who had finished law school as compared to the one who had dropped out early. Beige stucco, red tiled roof, desert plant landscaping – the usual Southwestern look, like the house he'd lived in with Cindy, but a bigger house and airy.

Malcolm followed her through the living room, Southwest art on the walls, Indian pots by the unnecessary fireplace.

Ian came in from the back followed by Shawn, his five year old.

'Hey, hey, hey!' Ian said.

'Uncle Mac!' Shawn ran over and grabbed Malcolm's leg. 'Walk!' he said. 'Walk!'

Malcolm walked, zombie style, with Shawn clinging to his leg and giggling until he fell off. 'You're getting too big,' Malcolm said. 'Bigger every time I see you. So what's for dinner?' Malcolm asked Sally.

'Not chicken,' said Sally. 'It's ready now, come on.'

Dinner was big juicy steaks at the picnic table out on the ceramic tiled patio.

'How's the shoulder?' Ian asked.

'Improving.' Malcolm cut a bite of steak. It was excellent: rare, swimming with red blood. 'Or so the physical therapist tells me,' he lied.

'Good, glad you're getting some help. Those rural health clinics,' Ian said. 'They're fine as long as you're not sick. You might want to consider doing some of that therapy in Phoenix. I mean, we can put you up.'

'It seems to be working out okay down there,' Malcolm said.

'You're not incredibly bored?' Sally asked.

'Actually—' Malcolm cleared his throat. 'I've been working on a little investigation, local thing.'

'Really,' they said in unison, smiling, interested, *happy* for him.

They were both so nice, his brother and sister-in-law, scared to bring up the subject of Cindy at all for fear of reminding him, as if he would have forgotten.

'It's a little hush-hush right now,' Malcolm added and immediately felt stupid – he sounded like one of those cop wannabes he used to look down on.

Shawn giggled. He put his finger to his lips. 'Hush, hush, hush, hush,' he whispered.

'Of course,' Ian said.

'Good steak,' said Malcolm. 'Really good.'

'We get it from this place online.'

'We don't get it too much,' Sally said. 'Just for special times. I mean, it's not the healthiest way to eat.'

'She'd have me on salad and fruit every day if she could,' Ian said. 'Maybe some salmon thrown in for the omega three.'

'It's for your own good,' Sally said.

'We're talking about men here,' Ian said. 'Me and my brother. Real men. Real men eat red meat.' He pounded his chest for emphasis.

Shawn pounded his chest several times too, giggling wildly.

'Shawn. Calm down,' Sally said.

'Red-blooded men,' said Ian. It was an old family joke whenever they had steak when they were kids. 'Right, Malcolm?'

'Right. Red-blooded men.' Malcolm glanced at his watch. 'Oops. Got to be somewhere in half an hour.'

'Where's that?' Sally asked.

'A poetry reading at the Poetry Barn.'

The Poetry Barn was a little detached house, not really a barn at all, near downtown Phoenix, where some alternative art galleries were. Malcolm was a little late due to having to find a place to park. He finally did and hiked back two blocks. Outside the open door, he paused. There was a poster that looked handmade, saying 'Poetry Reading Tonite', and a picture of Harry Light, the same one that was on his website. Inside, someone was strumming a guitar carelessly, as if they were doing it for their own pleasure and didn't care what anyone else thought.

Malcolm stepped inside. The strumming stopped, abruptly. On a table by the door was a big glass of the kind used for wholesale pickles, full of bills. A sign on the jar said 'Donations'. Malcolm dropped in a dollar bill. A woman in black sitting by the inner door smiled at him, her dark-red lipstick inviting, mysterious.

'Hi,' Malcolm said. 'This Harry Light. He's from California, isn't he?'

She nodded. 'Yes.'

'Does he read here often?'

'This year we've been lucky. He's read here several times.'

'Oh? When was the last—'

She put a finger to her lips. 'Shhhh. Not now. Go on in. He's just started.'

He went through the inner door, sat down on the first empty chair he came to and took a deep breath.

The room was half full, maybe twenty people, and dim, with a spotlight at the front that shone on a lectern. A man stood at the lectern in the spotlight.

'—speculative vanishing against the brightness—' he was saying. 'Oh, holy, holy, oh, holy—'

It took a second before Malcolm realized this was Harry Light – he looked different than the photograph, smaller.

'—and extreme, extreme—' Harry Light raised his fist and banged it on the lectern, making Malcolm jump. 'I said—' Pause. 'EXTREME, EXTREME, EXTREME, but – madness. This is madness. No more the tulips, the saguaro, the, the, the, TENNIS BALLS. The balls of tennis, the holy balls of tennis, the balls of holy tennis.'

He stopped. He looked around the room, as if to catch the eyes of everyone there. The silence stretched out.

'But I died,' he said. 'Long ago I was already dead.'

He bowed his head.

There was another silence, then thunderous applause.

'So *powerful*,' Malcolm heard the woman beside him say to her companion as he made his way out.

Kate slept fitfully at the Shady Grove Bates motel, tossing and turning. The headlights of passing cars reflected through the sheer curtains at the window, making patterns on the wall. Close to dawn she finally fell into deeper sleep, full of dreams. Then she found herself back at the house in New Jersey, wandering in the dark from room to room. Lights flickered on and off enough for her to see that every room she came upon was empty, though she was certain that before there'd been some furniture: a bed, a couch, a table. When she got to what must be the last room, she saw there was something on the floor. She bent to pick it up. The framed snapshot of the woman at Tall Pine Lake, 2005.

But she was certain she'd packed that in her carry-on, yet here it was still in the room. She took it over to the window where there was more light and saw in the reflection of a passing car what she should have realized all along: that the snapshot of the woman in the sunglasses, the bikini, the big straw hat, smiling back at her on the beach at Tall Pine Lake in 2005, was a snapshot of herself.

In the night a thought flickered through Malcolm's brain and woke him up with a start. Where the hell was he? A window across the room. Street light shining through frilly curtains. *Holy fucking*

145

tennis balls. His brother Ian's spare bedroom. And what was the thought? Kate. Kate was in trouble. How did he know? Just a feeling, an intuition he'd formed, the man with the radar for angst and depression.

Twenty-One

The next morning before he left Phoenix, Malcolm called up an old friend, Detective Frank Cruz of Mesa PD.

'Mac!' Frank said. 'Hey, Mac, how's it going down there in Dudley? I hear they even got crime. Like, in the two tourists.'

'Exactly. So, I was wondering. I got a little gig there, helping the defense on that—'

'Helping the defense! Good Lord, you always was a mite liberal. You know what though, I forgive you.'

'In my opinion the whole thing's a rush job by the Chamber of Commerce.'

'I hear you.'

'Anyway, I'm curious if there's anything hinky with the daughter of the male victim, Wes Cooper. Polly Hampton – Polly's Collectibles – right here in Tempe.'

'I'll see what I can do.'

'And listen, just one more thing, there's this case in Ocean Front, California? Missing persons, Anna Marie Romero?'

'Yeah?'

'I'd like to talk to the lead investigator. I was wondering if you could assist me in that.'

'What? What? Asking for special favors?'

'Yup.'

'There is no way, no way at all that I won't assist you in any way I can. I'll see what I can do. The number you're calling from—'

'My cell. It's good.'

Harry Light – no, *Hairy Lite*, thought Malcolm as he drove the boring truck-riddled stretch of freeway between Phoenix and Tucson. It was hard to imagine it ever rained here, ever, ever, ever. What had Kate seen in that guy anyway? What kind of emails were those nasty emails Dakota had mentioned? Actively threatening or just underhand and snide? Probably, Hairy Lite was just an ordinary jerk and you could leave it at that.

But for Anna Marie Romero.

Back in Dudley he drove straight to Ernie Roger's garage. Was it his imagination or had the Honda moved over two spaces? It looked like the tire hadn't been fixed yet. He went inside to the office. The same guy he'd talked before looked up.

'Remember me?' Malcolm said.

'Sure do.'

'You gotten to that Honda yet?'

'What's your interest, exactly?'

'Friend of the owner,' Malcolm lied. 'She told me she had a funny feeling about it so I told her I'd check it out.'

The guy pulled a pack of cigarettes out of his

pocket. Ed, said the name stitched on it in red letters. 'Let's go outside,' Ed said.

Over by the Honda, Ed lit up. Past the chain link fence, the desert stretched on and on to the mountains and Mexico.

'That tire?' Ed said.

'Yeah.'

'It looked almost new. It wasn't your average blowout.' He paused, as if for effect. 'Some son of a bitch shot the goddamn thing, that's why it blew. There was a goddamn bullet in that tire.'

'No fucking shit. You call law enforcement?'

'The cops?'

'Yeah, the cops!' Malcolm was almost shouting.

'No, sir, I didn't.'

'Why not? Somebody shooting at someone's tires is a criminal offense.'

'Hey!' Ed backed away, arms raised high. 'Cool it, man, I just found this out myself. I'll do it, okay.'

'And not Dudley PD. It happened outside city limits. It would be the County Sheriff's jurisdiction. Never mind. I'll do it myself.'

'Mesa PD, huh,' said Officer Brad Holmes. He stretched out his hand, 'Pleased to meet you, sir.' He scratched his head. 'DES, the department of public safety, would have gone out on the original call. I'll get their report ASAP. Man, oh man – hope we don't have some random shooter out there.'

'I see your point,' said Malcolm, 'but I doubt

148

if Miss Waters would be happy to find out it wasn't a random shooter.'

'Haw, haw,' said Officer Holmes. 'I see your point too. This a pissed off ex or what?'

'Dunno.'

'Well, I'll be needing to interview her.'

'She's out of town at the moment.'

'Maybe that's for the best, huh?'

Did Hairy Lite know how use a gun? Would Hairy Lite have traveled all the way to Cochise County to take a pot shot at Kate's car? Maybe not, but a new thought occurred to Malcolm, a good one. All those writers who did workshops and stuff in prisons so they'd have juicy material for hopefully best-selling novels. Maybe Hairy was one of those guys, did the prison circuit – if so, he'd have some criminal connections. He could have hired someone.

Why exactly had Kate left Hairy Lite? Just because he was a jerk? Women had been staying with jerks instead of leaving them for centuries now. Dakota had said out of control temper tantrums. If the Anna Marie Romero thing did turn out to involve Hairy Lite, then Kate, having lived with Hairy, might have some useful information about a possible motive for him to want Anna Marie dead, which in turn would give Hairy a motive for going after Kate.

Though some guys, all the motive they needed was for the woman to leave them.

Might, maybe, what if. At least Kate was safe back east for now.

He drove to Dakota's studio. She was outside watering the gazanias.

'You're in touch with Kate, right,' Malcolm said.

'Right. She's in Vermont.'

'Vermont? I thought she was in New Jersey.'

'All I know is she texted me she was going to Vermont. We haven't actually talked. She's probably having too good a time, seeing old friends and stuff – she deserves to have some fun.'

'I talked to the guy at the garage where her car is. Her tire blew because someone shot at it.'

'What!' Dakota dropped the hose, and it twisted and wiggled, a stream of water hitting Malcolm in the leg. 'Oh my God. Do they know who?'

'No. It could have been a random shooting.'

'Great,' said Dakota. 'Just great. I'll think about that next time I drive to Sierra Vista, if I do ever ever again.'

'I talked to law enforcement. They're investigating it.'

'Call me when they find anything out, okay? I'll give you my cell number, and you give me yours too.'

'Better yet. I got a card.'

'Should I tell Kate?' Dakota asked. 'It will totally freak her out.'

'Maybe not yet.'

Sid wasn't at the St Elmo Bar for Malcolm to show him the photograph of Polly Hampton. A tired-looking blonde bartender said wearily, 'He's out of town, camping in the White Mountains. Back in a few days.'

Camping, everyone was camping. Maybe Sid was camping with Elton Savory, the night-shift guy at the High Desert Market.

Malcolm went home.

Inside the house it was hot. He opened all the windows. Then he looked in the fridge to see if he had to go to the store, which he was not in the mood to do at all. There was still some hamburger meat left – it smelled a little funny, but it had aged, that was all. People had been eating aged beef for centuries. Out on the porch the orange cat lurked by the empty bowl. Malcolm filled it.

The sister. There was still Carrie Cooper's sister, far away in Millville, Pennsylvania, running a crafts store. Far away back east in Millville, Pennsylvania, which wasn't that far from Vermont or New Jersey, probably. Not that that had anything to do with anything. If he wanted to do this right, he should go to Millville himself and talk to Carrie's sister. What was her name? Rose Kelly. Why the hell not? The defense would have some money to pay for expenses.

Surely they would. He called Stuart Ross's cell.

'Ross here.'

Malcolm explained.

'Sure, sure,' said Stuart. 'Why the hell not? It's a murder case, after all.'

He sounded distracted, like he was thinking about something else. Malcolm hoped this wasn't going to turn out to be a conversation that Stuart Ross conveniently forgot. His own brother was an attorney, and he'd gone to law school for a year himself, but he thought, once again, he never trusted lawyers, especially lawyers for the defense. But what the hell.

Suddenly seized by a sense of urgency he went online, looked up the closest airport to Millville, Pennsylvania. He booked the earliest flight, ouch, very early.

Nothing left to do right now. It was too soon to cook up the aged hamburger so he took a Sam Adams out of the fridge and went out on to the porch. A curve billed thrasher flew up on a branch, and a big black crow was carrying on. It was getting cooler now, and the light slanted through the branches of the trees in a way that for some reason reminded him of being ten years old.

All of a sudden here he was working a case, or maybe even two, if in fact Hairy Lite had something to do with Kate's tire getting shot out. He was feeling a little better, a lot better in fact, looking forward to tomorrow for the first time in months and months.

Chico wasn't looking forward to anything much, except in his dreams. He pushed the cart loaded with worn-out paperback books slowly in front of him – a little job he had as a trustee. Pretty ironic that everyone seemed to trust him here, him, the double murderer, though of course he'd gone to high school with two of the other inmates and one of the guards, and another of the guards had been married briefly to one of Chico's aunts.

He pushed the cart slowly down the bleak hall and left it by the door to the prison library.

From somewhere down the hall, came a shrill scream and then another – 'Mothafucah!!' – one of the inmates going over the edge. It happened all the time. He heard the sound of guards coming from somewhere. Chico sauntered past the front lobby, going slow, not wanting to get involved in any kind of melee. Manny, the guard he'd gone to high school with, was usually on duty at the front lobby this time of day, getting on in the evening, but Manny was nowhere to be seen.

In fact, no one at this one small second of time was anywhere to be seen, all attending to the screaming inmate. The doors to the outside were just to Chico's left, past the security checkpoint. Chico stopped thinking. His body, longing for *migas*, a decent bed and a good violent action movie, took over and strolled to the security checkpoint. Then he hesitated, but just for a moment.

Then, suddenly, he was past the checkpoint, was out the door and into the evening.

He saw no one. He ran fast, as fast as he could ever run, past the cluster of buildings that made up the complex and into the desert. It was still light enough to see, dark enough that he might not be seen by someone approaching the complex. Under a small moon just rising, he ran over rocks, dodging cholla cactus and prickly pear, mesquite and tamarisk. He knew where he was going, knew the area well, not like some of the inmates.

Panting, he stopped to catch his breath, resting against a large rock. But he hadn't much time; someone would notice he was missing, alarms would sound off. He needed to get to the outskirts of town where he would be one of many, not a lone runner out in the desert under the moon, the stars. He started up again, climbing this time, up and over. Then all of Dudley lay below him, just beginning to twinkle in the dusk. He started down the mountain to the first house on the edge of town.

He knew the house, half rotting wood, half adobe – it had been abandoned for years. Back when he was in high school he would go there with a bunch of other guys, get high. For a moment he considered hiding there, but it was too obvious – he kept going further down, tired by now, stumbling. He heard the sound of television somewhere, the warmth of laughter, *phoney*. He was really tired, out of shape after being in jail, but he kept going, down some crumbling cement steps, through someone's yard, the Rodriguezes', yeah, sure, but no one was home.

Where the hell am I going, he thought, and the thought distracted him. He stopped noticing where to put his feet, tripped on a rock and fell, hitting his head on another rock.

A bright light exploded in his brain as he lay there, then things got dark as he lapsed into unconsciousness.

And in another part of town, Lupita was just setting the table for dinner – she'd made *chili rellenos*, nana's favorite, as a special treat – when her nana suddenly sat upright and screamed.

Twenty-Two

Mandy lived on the Upper West Side, and it took Kate forever to find a parking place, and when she did it was three blocks away. It was getting on towards evening and raining, just a slight drizzle. She didn't have an umbrella, but that was okay. The moisture felt refreshing. Cars swooshed by, lights reflected on the street, the smell of the rain and the closeness of people, people everywhere. A couple passed her by, laughing under an umbrella, speaking Russian?

Kate breathed it all in. She'd forgotten what it felt like being in the city – the energy, the privacy of being just one in many.

And here she was at the apartment building where Mandy lived, a nice building. Doorman.

'Mandy and Phil,' she said to the doorman.

He smiled a big smile, hustled her over to the elevator, and up they went to the fourth floor. She walked down a short hall and stopped. The sound of a party in full swing came from behind Mandy's door.

No. No, no, no.

She'd woken up still tired, and the energy she'd summoned up for the drive from Vermont to New York, the energy the rain had given her, was that false second wind that comes just after total exhaustion.

All she wanted was to go to sleep in a safe place.

Her mind seemed to fog up, and she couldn't trust her own thoughts. Maybe she'd simply gone to the wrong address to meet Ellen, to the wrong state, and Ellen was waiting impatiently for her arrival somewhere in Pennsylvania or Connecticut or Kansas. She knocked on the door.

A man answered it, a big man, balding, with a kind face.

'You must be Kate,' he said. 'Phil. Come in, come in.'

She followed him through a foyer into a large living room. Seven or eight people were sitting around, on chairs and the couch. There was music coming from somewhere, but it was drowned out by people talking, chattering, it seemed to Kate, like the monkey house in a zoo. A woman close by, brown-haired with tiny pink framed glasses, looked over at her, face distorted by a smile.

Somewhere someone laughed loudly, braying like a donkey. The air in the room felt close, full of too many bodies.

Kate felt dizzy. She steadied herself on the back of an armchair.

'Hey. Hey, you okay?' Phil asked.

'Tired.' Kate said. She heard herself say it from a distance as if someone else were saying it instead.

'Kate?'

Kate turned. It was Mandy in long black leggings and a blousy print tunic top. Dark hair, olive skin, very thin. They hugged.

156

Mandy stepped back. 'It's wonderful to see you again. I was so excited when Phil told me you'd called.' She paused. 'How are you?' She asked it as if she were a little worried and really wanted to know.

'Tired,' Kate said. 'But other than that I'm fine.' She felt as though she'd been saying *I'm fine* for weeks and weeks and it hadn't been true for a while. 'I mean—' Her lower lip trembled involuntarily. 'I guess.'

Mandy gave her a look. 'Not so fine, huh? Let's go somewhere quiet and talk.'

The rain pitter-pattered on the bedroom window pane. The curtains were half drawn, and Kate could see the glimmer of lights that lit up the private lives and the public places in the city outside. Kate and Mandy sat on the bed in the guest bedroom where Kate would be sleeping.

'Phil said you were asking about Ellen Wilson.'

'I was,' Kate said.

'Were you guys close? I mean, I know you knew her, but I wasn't sure how well.'

'Don't you remember? You and me and Ellen and Sandy and Karen, fifteen years ago by now. We called ourselves the Ooblecks?'

Mandy smiled. 'I do remember. Of course. I'll send you a JPEG file of this DVD I'm putting together. Or maybe I'll just make a bunch of DVDs. It's kind of a mishmash of various events from the old days. You guys are in it, you and Rick. You before Rick. Tom Litmus, remember him? He got really rich, something to do with Wall Street, and now he's poor.'

'Ha ha,' said Kate.

'Yes, ha ha. And Buzzie? Didn't you go out with Buzzie?'

'Once,' said Kate. 'It was boring.'

Mandy giggled. 'You know what? He joined the military after nine-eleven. He got really hyped up over the whole thing.'

'Wow,' said Kate.

'And of course Ellen's on it too.' She smiled. 'All of us Ooblecks, being silly. So, anyway, what was it you wanted to know about Ellen?'

Kate took a deep breath. 'Ellen emailed out of the blue and told me about this house she'd inherited in New Jersey. To make a long story short, we were supposed to meet there, me and Ellen, and maybe some other people. I flew in from Arizona and drove to the house, but she never showed up. There I was waiting in this empty house, no electricity, no water, nothing.'

'Wait,' Mandy said. 'The time frame is a little skewed here – I'm not sure when you're talking about. Phil didn't explain very well. She wasn't Ellen Wilson any more, you know.'

'No?'

'I'm surprised she didn't tell you.'

'Not as surprised as I am.'

'Wilson was her married name from one of those early doomed marriages, and she kept it out of inertia she always said. But she'd changed it back. It was Ellen Wallace. I gather this empty house stuff was quite some time ago.'

'Not really. The last email I got was right before I left Dudley. I guess it was four days ago.'

Mandy looked at Kate strangely.

'*What?*' said Kate. 'Why are you looking at me like that? I went to the house where we were supposed to meet, and she never showed up. That's that, basically.'

'Kate,' said Mandy. 'Ellen's dead.'

'No.' Kate stared at her. 'What happened? Oh, *no*, I was afraid something had happened to her. Was she in an accident?'

'She died of pancreatic cancer.'

'Cancer? She didn't mention being sick.'

'Eight months ago. She died eight months ago, Kate. Someone's playing tricks on you.'

There was a silence. Kate didn't know what to say. She got up and went over to the window. The cars swooshed by. Somewhere out there was her rental car, three blocks over, or was it four?

'I bought a plane ticket and everything,' she said finally. 'I went to the address she'd given me and waited. Who would do that to me, trick me like that?'

'Some people never grow up. Maybe it was one of the guys we used to know,' said Mandy. 'But that's hard to believe. It would be *so* lame.'

'Too lame. No. I don't buy that idea.' Kate covered her eyes. 'She mentioned the Ooblecks, so I never doubted it was her. God, I'm such an idiot.'

'No, you're not.' Mandy reached out, touched Kate's arm. 'It's not so bad. Look what happened. You're here. In the city. So where's the tragedy? I bet you wouldn't be here if it weren't for this Ellen thing. I'm having a little party. Come on out and meet some people.'

159

Kate lay back on the bed and closed her eyes. 'Or not,' Mandy said. 'Whatever.'

Later, Kate woke up. The party sounds were gone. Outside cars were still going by, but it wasn't raining any more. Her watch said 12:03. She sat up and texted Dakota that she was in New York City. Then she lay down again, but she couldn't go back to sleep. Thoughts kept running through her mind; she couldn't stop them. Maybe take that last Ativan? She decided not. Who would have sent her those emails, played such an elaborate trick? Someone who knew something of her past, it had to be – but who? Harry? Had she mentioned Ellen and the Ooblecks to Harry?

She didn't think so.

And would he have come all the way from California, found a vacant house to lure her to? Or maybe he had an aunt who had died and left him the house? She hadn't had a nasty email from him in a while. She'd thought it was a good sign, but maybe he was moving to the next level.

She got up and went to the window. It was after midnight, and there were still people out, shadowy as they passed beneath the street lights, the sidewalks still rain slick. Maybe, she thought, when I'm very old, I could come back here and end my days looking out a window on to New York City. She thought she'd be peaceful then, faraway from the life she had been leading.

Her return flight was the day after tomorrow. *I have to find out who did this*, she thought. *I have to go back to New Jersey.*

Twenty-Three

'What!' said Stuart Ross, all righteous indignation. 'You don't have a warrant? Since when do you guys come in like Nazis and think you can search the home of two perfectly innocent and vulnerable women without a warrant? Luckily, Lupita is well informed about her rights and thought to call me before letting you into the sanctuary of the home she shares with her elderly nana.' Stuart gestured at Lupita and at Ariana.

Oh, cool it, Lupita thought. What a windbag. 'She's not *elderly*,' she said out loud.

They stood, all of them – Officer Debbie Hannigan, and Detective Sergeant Ben Luna, and Lupita, Ariana and Stuart – in Ariana's crowded kitchen. It was after ten p.m., and Ariana wore an attractive negligee and fuzzy slippers, Lupita, an old black sweatshirt of Chico's and gray sweatpants.

'We were only inquiring, Counselor,' said Officer Hannigan, with dignity. 'Not to mention it's against the law to harbor a fugitive.'

'We're not harboring anyone!' Lupita cried.

Ariana put her hand on her heart and closed her eyes.

'It wasn't a smart move on Chico's part, and you know it,' Officer Debbie Hannigan said to Stuart Ross. To Lupita she said, 'He should know

161

he's a lot better off in the safety of the county jail than he is if he's gone across the line.'

'That's a matter of opinion,' said Stuart Ross. 'All this brouhaha about crime along the border is all Republican bullshit and you know it.'

Officer Hannigan's face got bright pink. 'Not when there's drugs involved,' she said.

'There isn't. Chico's an artist not a doper, for Christ's sake.'

'Anyway, he hasn't gone across the line!' cried Lupita. 'I mean, I hope not.'

'I can assure you as an officer of the court,' Stuart Ross said to Sergeant Ben Luna and Officer Hannigan, 'that if Chico shows up here you will be duly informed.' He looked meaningfully at Lupita and Ariana.

'Of course you will be!' lied Lupita.

'And now I'd like to talk to my clients alone if you don't mind,' said Stuart.

Lupita, Ariana and Stuart watched as Officer Hannigan and Sergeant Luna walked away and down the steps from the house.

Stuart turned to the two women. 'I cannot believe,' he said through his teeth, 'that Chico absconded like that. It's about the dumbest thing he could possibly have done.'

'He's an artist!' Lupita cried. 'Not like other people.'

Stuart ignored the remark. 'Do you know that if this goes to trial, the judge can instruct the jury to take into account as a factor that he absconded, when they consider his guilt or innocence?'

'Absconded, absconded,' cried Lupita. 'Speak

162

English, please. You said it wasn't going to trial, you said he'd be out long before that, that we just had to be patient.'

'Not only that,' Stuart said, with just a touch of sadist glee, 'this is a man who's charged with a double homicide. That means, technically, he could be considered armed and dangerous.'

'Armed and dangerous!' said Lupita. 'That's nonsense.'

'Technically. I said, technically. He could get shot, killed. It just takes one trigger-happy idiot, which, believe me, includes several Cochise County law enforcement officers that I can think of right off the top of my head, or the Border Patrol, for that matter.'

'Malcolm,' Lupita said suddenly. 'We need to tell Malcolm.' She reached for her cellphone.

His cell rang and rang, but no one answered, and his voicemail box was full. She texted him, *Call me. Urgent. Urgent.* That should do it.

She turned to Stuart. 'Malcolm can fix this,' she said. 'I know it.'

Twenty-Four

Jet-lagged but valiant, Malcolm parked his rental car outside the Jack in the Box in an undistinguished sort of shopping mall, in the suburb of Millville, Pa. Suburb was what it was: middle-class tract houses, going on and on, though for some reason Malcolm had imagined a fantasy small town, tree-lined streets. Still, it was certainly green around here, green green green, obscenely green.

Inside the Jack in the Box he ordered a Sourdough Jack and ate it sitting on a plastic seat next to the big plate-glass window that looked out on to the Crafty Woman Arts and Crafts store.

What the hell did I just do? he wondered. *Hopped on a plane and flew to Pennsylvania? What the hell am I doing here? I must be crazy. But a good kind of crazy.*

He took out his cellphone, still switched off for the flight, and turned it on. A text from Lupita. *Call Me. Urgent. Urgent.*

Such drama. It would have to wait.

The window of the Crafty Woman was draped in black and garnished with black artificial roses. On a stand in the center place of honor was a framed photograph, a head and shoulder shot of a smiling blonde woman. Carrie Cooper. Malcolm opened the door, and a bell tinkled. He walked inside. A blonde woman who resembled Carrie Cooper was sitting on a big wicker chair near the back, knitting. She wore jeans and a pink T-shirt with spangles on it. Beside her was a small wicker table that held a stack of books.

'Rose Kelly?' Malcolm asked.

She smiled: pretty, dimples on both cheeks. 'That's me.'

'Malcolm MacGregor. I'm an investigator.'

'Yes?'

'I flew in this morning from Tucson.'

164

'Are you with the media?' she asked suspiciously.

'No. I'm an investigator, like I said.'

'Good,' said Rose. 'They twist things around and don't even listen sometimes. One of them even got in to see my mom, and my poor mom isn't even clear that Carrie's dead, she's so confused. I had to close up my shop to hide for three or four days 'cause of these photographers, and then this woman from the newspaper – this local weekly – came in and asked a bunch of questions, but she didn't use my answers, just made some up. This *is* about Carrie, I assume.'

'Yes.'

'Personally, you know what I think? She and Wes should never have gone to Arizona. I've been reading up on it online, and it's full of people waving guns around just about everywhere, on the streets, in bars, on college campuses.' Her voice rose. 'Then they have these drug cartels, shooting across the border at people, then more people from Iowa and Wisconsin come down and they shoot at all those illegal immigrants. Plus—'

'Wait,' Malcolm said.

She stopped, in mid sentence.

'It's not as bad as all that, trust me.'

'Whatever,' she said. 'Listen, Carrie called me and texted me the day she was killed, did you know that?'

'No,' said Malcolm, 'I didn't.'

'She texted me three times. *Call me*, it said, and she called me twice, and I was really busy so I just never got back to her.' She covered her

165

face for a moment. 'I'm so sorry. I just think about it all the time, over and over. It's like I can't stop. I'll never, never know what she had to say to me.'

'You have no idea what it might have been?'

'None.' She sighed. 'Please. Sit down. You can ask me about Carrie all you want. Except for the media, you'd be surprised how many of the people who come in here – regular customers, I mean, who take our classes – will do anything to avoid even mentioning her name.' She paused. 'Wait,' she said. 'Who are you investigating *for*?'

'The defense.'

'Oh.' Her face fell. 'Oh. Then maybe I shouldn't talk to you.'

'Look,' said Malcolm. 'Legally you have the right not to. But I'm sure you want to find out the truth, don't you?'

Rose stared at him. 'The truth?'

'Yes, hear me out – I'm with law enforcement, but I've been taking a break. Then Chico's sister Lupita persuaded me to look into this, and now I have.'

'His sister,' breathed Rose. 'She must be going through hell too, in her own way, but at least her brother's *alive*.'

'I don't think Chico killed your sister and Wes. The shots were too accurate.'

She blinked. 'What do you mean – too accurate?'

'Really accurate. Like a hired hit man.'

'No,' said Rose. 'A hired hit man?'

'Chico's just an arty kind of kid.'

166

'Then why would they arrest this Chico?'

'They needed to arrest someone right away. It's a tourist town. Assuming your sister and Wes weren't involved in serious drug dealing—'

'Of course not! She didn't even like to take Tylenol, for heaven's sake. But a hired hit man?' She looked bemused. 'Well, then, I guess I'd say Polly. It could have been Polly—'

'Wes's daughter?'

'Yes. She hated Carrie.'

'Oh, really?'

'Polly's mom, Nancy, died of breast cancer four years ago, not all that long after Wes left her for Carrie. So she blamed Carrie. And Polly hated Wes too – for leaving her mom for Carrie. But Wes and Carrie, they were in unhappy relationships. No one was happy. Who wants that? Carrie's ex went off and got married to someone else, and Polly's mom would have done the same probably if she hadn't . . . um . . . *died*.'

There was a small silence.

'Anything else you can think of that might be helpful?' Malcolm asked. 'Anyone else mad at them?'

'I don't think so, for heaven's sake, I mean not really, *really* mad – who goes around killing people, anyway?'

'Okay, then what *about* Polly Hampton? She's married, I take it? What's her husband like?'

'She *is* married, but her husband? He's a mouse.' She paused. 'You could talk to Paul Sanger. He's close to Polly still, I think.'

'Paul Sanger?' The name was familiar. Malcolm snapped his fingers. '*Dr* Paul Sanger?'

'Yes. You've met him?'

'Not really. But he was pointed out to me, in the courtroom at the release hearing.'

Rose smiled. 'Really? I haven't seen him in years. He's a pediatrician in Tucson. He's an old friend, went to the same high school as Wes and Carrie and Nancy.'

'Really? Wes and Carrie went to high school together?'

'They did. They even went to grade school together. And you know what? I think Wes and Carrie always, always loved each other, from the minute they met in second grade, in Mrs Mueller's class. But somewhere along the way they got sidetracked with their lives. Carrie went off to college. Then Wes got Nancy pregnant and, well, you know.' She shrugged. 'But as for Paul, he kind of sided with Polly rather than Wes on things, you know.'

'Ah.' He paused. 'So putting rage and hatred aside, who benefits financially from these deaths?'

'Just me and my mom for Carrie – but she didn't really have much, just the shop with me – but Wes, he was pretty well off, I think, but actually right now I can hardly think at all. I just remember. That's not the same as thinking, do you know that? Like—'

She reached for the stack of books beside her, took one off the top. Malcolm saw then that it was a photo album. She opened it and pointed to a snapshot. Two little girls on tricycles. 'That's me and Carrie when we were six and seven. And this one—' she pointed – 'is Carrie in her Halloween costume. It's a cat. She made it herself. Those whiskers? They're drinking straws!' She turned more pages. 'Here's Carrie at her prom, isn't she pretty? I remember going with her to get the dress. It was so—' She stopped, sniffed. 'So silly. We were so silly.'

'I'm sorry,' Malcolm said. 'I'm so sorry.'

'We'll never remember anything again, me and Carrie.' She looked up at him eagerly. 'Would you like to see their house? I can close up shop for a bit.'

'Yes,' said Malcolm. 'As a matter of fact, yes, I would.'

Kate pulled into the parking lot near the Kroger's, the Wendy's, the Kentucky Colonel, the McDonald's and all the motels. Home at last. She had what was left of today and all of the next day. She was due to fly back to Arizona the day after that. She could check into a motel right now or go look at the house first. She opted for the house – just a quick drive by.

The tree-lined street was deserted, and the house looked the same: the whitewashed brick maybe slightly flakier,the trellised climbing rose bush by the front door still full of yellow roses, except it wasn't the same since it was no longer a house belonging to Ellen Wilson's aunt. Yellow roses stood for something, Kate remembered, all roses did. What was yellow?

Was the key still under the rock? But it would feel like breaking and entering to go inside now – better to do things as legally as possible. Besides, what was there to learn by going inside? The 'For Sale' sign still hung crookedly from the iron stake. 'Evan Bright Realty' and a phone number.

Sitting in her car, she called the number.

'Hi! No one's in right now but leave a message for the realtor of your choice and they'll get back to you. Or stop in tomorrow, we open at nine. Have a good day!'

Kate left a message – 'I'd like to speak to a realtor regarding the property on three fifty Roscommon Drive' – along with her name and cell number. It seemed like the best place to start.

Yellow roses stood for jealousy.

But so what?

She drove back to the shopping mall, parked at the same motel she had stayed in before and went inside.

The clerk looked like a high-school kid with a part-time job after school – nerdy glasses, big grin, favorite film-maker: Jude Apatow, favorite actor: Jonah Hill. He grinned at her as he took her credit card. His nameplate said 'John'. Kate leaned against the counter, looking out at the cars parked row after row after row in the motel parking lot, in the Kroger's parking lot, at McDonald's, Wendy's and Kentucky Colonel.

'Kate Waters.' The clerk snapped his fingers. '*Aha.*'

She turned to face him. 'Aha, what?'

'Now I remember. Your husband called.'

'What husband?'

The clerk looked taken aback. 'You're not married?'

'No, I'm not married. Tell me,' said Kate gently, 'exactly what you're talking about.'

'This guy called, he said his name was Roger Waters, his wife was Kate Waters and she was supposed to check in here, but he hadn't heard from her and he was worried.'

'So what did you do?'

'I checked our records and told him a Kate Waters had checked in here three days ago but she'd checked out the next day.'

The cellphone pinged in Kate's purse – someone texting her. She ignored it.

'Are you aware,' she said to the clerk, 'that it's probably illegal to give out information like that?'

'He sounded worried,' the clerk said. He paused. 'That's not true about illegal. If someone calls and wants to talk to someone who's here, we patch them through to the room.'

Patch them through? 'What if I were a domestic violence victim,' Kate said, 'escaping from an abusive husband?'

'But you said you weren't even married.'

'Never mind.' Suddenly, Kate had a headache. 'If anyone calls looking for me, don't tell them I'm checked in here, okay? Tell them nothing. Please, it's important. It's not my husband, it's an abusive boyfriend. He could be very dangerous.'

John's eyes widened. 'Sure. Sure thing.'

'If I want to talk to someone I have a cellphone.' She stretched out her hand. 'Key, please.'

She went out to the rental car and got her carry-on. Someone was looking for her? *Who? Why?* Maybe it was a mistake to have come here. She walked with her back straight, one step, two step, three step, but her knees were trembling.

The Cooper's house was two story, painted blue gray with two different shades of trim, white and navy. There were roses everywhere, along one side of the house, in the front and a rose garden in the back.

'Carrie loved roses,' said Rose. 'We used to joke about it, 'cause of my name.'

She unlocked the door to the house, and Malcolm followed her in, down a hallway to a big den. There Rose stopped; the room was dim, curtains drawn. She flicked on a light, which only served to yellow the dimness. Malcolm saw a big flat-screen television, two leather recliners facing the TV.

He and Rose stood together. Rose seemed suddenly very close. Her hair smelled of sweet shampoo, and he was aware of the roundness of her body under the pink spangled T-shirt.

Malcolm stepped away. 'So what was their life like?' he asked.

'Well, they went out to eat and to social events, but they spent lots of their time here,' Rose said. 'The TV's pretty new.'

Lots and lots of their time here, Malcolm thought. There was a router, so they had Wi-Fi, and a Roku box too. He looked around and spotted a Big Mouth Billy Bass hanging on the far wall. His brother Ian had bought one as a joke a couple of years ago – three year old Shawn had screamed in terror the first time Big Mouth Billy had turned his head and sung 'Take Me to the River'.

'Ahem,' Malcolm said. 'So. You said they had no enemies – not really. So you can't think of a

172

single one?' The question seemed unreal to him, by rote. How pretty Rose was, like a rose herself, in her pink spangly T-shirt.

'Don't all of us at times have enemies?' she said, face a little flushed. 'But no, not really. Wes played golf a lot. He retired a couple of years ago, early retirement – he got some kind of package deal to do it, so he took it. He and Carrie played bridge once a week with some other couples. Carrie and I ran the shop. They liked to travel.'

'Carrie never married before Wes?'

'That's right. She had long-term boyfriends; they would last maybe four or five years, with some short-term guys in between.' Rose flushed even deeper. 'It makes her sound awful. She was just always so attractive to men.'

'Any of them, um, abusive?'

'Not that I know of. Carrie wouldn't tell me if they were; she had a lot of pride.'

'Local guys?'

'No. That's the thing, I never really knew any of them. Carrie moved away after she graduated from high school. She went to college at Penn State, then she spent some time in Pittsburgh. Pittsburgh was the closest she got to home. Then New York City. But I think unconsciously she was kind of saving herself for Wes. I think both of them were in love from the day they met, and they never stopped.' Rose sniffed. 'I guess if they had to die in such a horrible way at least they were together. And now—' She sniffed again. 'Pretty soon I'll have to start dealing with all their stuff. It's kind of like them dying all over again, you know?'

They stood together. Malcolm and Rose, in the den. Rose looked forlorn, needy, as if she might burst into tears. Good god, thought Malcolm, what if she did? He imagined the scene, Rose weeping, him holding her, comforting. He would feel obliged to comfort her; he was just that sort of man.

And then what?

'Umm,' said Rose, her face reddening even more, as if she'd had the same thought. 'There's nothing really here. Let's go back out.'

Outside, bees buzzed round the roses. He could smell the grass, so much grass back east. At the end they traded cellphone numbers.

'I'll keep you updated,' he told Rose. He handed her his card. 'And if you think of anything, anything at all that might be helpful, give me a call.'

Twenty-Five

Malcolm was lying on top of an overly floral print bedspread watching the news with the sound off. It didn't really matter; the news repeated itself over and over until you knew what they were going to say before they said it, and just in case you didn't they told you again in the banner that slid across the bottom of the screen.

His cellphone chimed. No number he recognized.

'Malcolm here.'

'Hello. Malcolm MacGregor?' A man's voice.
'Yeah?'

'This is Dan Piper, Oceanside PD. Frank Cruz of Mesa PD gave me your number. Concerning Anna Marie Romero?'

'Right.' Malcolm got up and walked over to the tiny refrigerator, opened it. 'Hey, thanks for getting in touch.' He took out a Sam Adams. 'What can you tell me?'

'Anna Marie left her parents' house where she was still living and drove to the tennis court at a local high school in her mom's car, parked it there and was basically never seen again.'

'I read that article,' Malcolm said. 'Wasn't there some workshop she'd gone to?'

'That was hours earlier.' Dan sighed. 'Beautiful girl. What's your interest?'

'One of the suspects was a professor, Harry Light? He ran the workshop.'

'The poet guy.' Dan Piper laughed. 'Yeah. Well, I wouldn't call him a suspect. Not exactly, anyway. I mean, he'd dated her a couple of times, so we checked him out, is all.'

'Dated her? She break it off, do you know?'

'According to him, even though she wasn't technically a student when they dated, she took workshops from him and he felt uncomfortable about it, so he broke it off.'

'Aw,' said Malcolm, 'a saint.' He began to pace from the tiny kitchen to the bed and back again.

'He's got a misdemeanor charge from a while back, criminal damage.' Dan laughed. 'It was dismissed. But as far as being a suspect in the

175

Romero case, he was down the list. It got some attention 'cause he was pretty well-known locally. But I didn't really consider him a contender, if you know what I mean. Though at least one person did.'

'Yeah?'

'Another poet. I'm not kidding. A colleague. Name of Gregory, Michael Gregory. There was some kind of rivalry going on there. Said he saw them together at a local restaurant later than Harry Light admitted to.'

'And?'

'And nothing. It was a restaurant out of town, but we couldn't confirm it. Crab Heaven was the name of the place – down on the beach. We talked to the staff, but it was a busy night, no one remembered. No credit card receipt or anything like that. It didn't go anywhere.'

'You said Harry Light was down on the list of suspects. So who was on top?'

'I exaggerated. She had a couple of other boyfriends – I mean, she was gorgeous – but I wasn't really looking at the boyfriends.'

'Who were you looking at then?'

'Anna Marie's dad.'

'Her dad? No kidding.' Malcolm paced back to the kitchen.

'Name of Raymond Romero. He scared off her last boyfriend. He had a long history of domestic violence. His wife was scared of him, and Anna Marie was too, from what I understand. She's twenty-four years old and still living at home with a jealous dad; I figured maybe she was talking about moving out and he got mad.'

One of the problems, Malcolm thought, with having a strong suspect like the dad, in a case like that: it meant nobody followed up on anyone else. But he had no reason to point that out. 'So what's going on with the mom and dad now?' he asked.

'The dad calls us up every once in a while with tips that never go anywhere. Then he gets mad and says we're not really trying. He could be playing a role, covering up or he could be for real, for all I know. What can you do?'

'What about the mom?'

'Cecilia is her name. The whole situation put a big stress on the marriage, but they struggled through it. Best thing that can happen right now is for the body to turn up. Then we'll have something to go on. You know, come to think of it, Cecilia has family in Phoenix. Visits them sometimes.'

'*Really*,' Malcolm said. 'Where in Phoenix? You got names of the relatives? I'd sure like to talk to the mom, without, you know, the angry dad.'

'Let me see what I can do, okay?'

Lupita, he thought after he got off the phone with Dan Piper. Lupita had texted him a couple of times now and he hadn't gotten back to her. He called her now, but got no answer. He didn't bother with her voicemail.

In the motel room Kate tried to reassure herself – so someone had called the motel looking for her, claiming to be her husband? The motel guy had told him she'd checked out. He wouldn't know she'd come back. How could he? At least it sounded as though it wasn't a woman, eliminating fifty percent of the world's population from suspicion.

Then she remembered she'd gotten a text while she was talking to the clerk. She opened her cell, checked the message. It was from Dakota. Suddenly, she felt lonely, lonelier than she had before. Lonely for Arizona.

Where r u now? Let's talk. Malcolm was looking 4 u.

Malcolm? Who—? Ah, the guy at the gallery, the one who'd tried to talk to her at the Co-op later. What was that Malcolm guy doing, talking to Dakota? Why was he looking for her? Could he be nuttier than she realized, could he have something to do with all this? But she couldn't imagine how. She needed to talk directly to Dakota, hear the nuances of her actual voice. She called her.

'Kate, wow, how are you? Are you having fun in New Jersey? Why did you leave New York City, anyway? I wouldn't have.'

'Dakota, stop. Why are you talking to this Malcolm guy? I don't trust him.'

'Kate, no, it's okay. He's a detective. From Phoenix, Mesa actually. He's a cop, and he's investigating the tourist murders.'

'He *says*.'

'He's really a nice person, Kate.' She paused and added significantly, 'That's probably why you don't trust him, if you know what I mean.'

'Oh, please. Look—' Kate took a deep breath. 'All these things have been happening to me.'

178

And she told Dakota the whole story, the empty house, Ellen being dead, everything.

'Kate,' Dakota said afterwards, 'I think you should come back home right away.'

'Home?' said Kate flatly. 'Home? And where is that?'

Malcolm was sound asleep on the motel bed, in a room with the TV on and the sound off. A room whose air conditioning was cold enough to preserve the dead, dreaming about one of them, Cindy, who wasn't really dead; she was telling him this, that she wasn't really dead, as they sat side by side on the swings in the playground where he'd gone to in first, second and third grades.

'At least not yet,' she said, and just as she said that he heard a noise, kind of musical.

He opened his eyes. His cellphone chimed again from the end table next to the bed. He reached for it, saw it was Dakota, then it slipped from his grip and fell to the floor. He leaned to over to pick it up, but it had stopped ringing. Lupita, Lupita had texted him earlier too, but he hadn't gotten back to her. If she called him now, he would be too tired to talk to her.

He turned off his cell and fell asleep again.

Twenty-Six

The big plate-glass window of Evan Bright Realty displayed photographs of houses, remarkably similar in architecture, big McMansions on little lots. A lot of the snapshots had little banners across saying, 'Marked Down!!' And the words 'motivated seller'. Kate paused for a moment looking for 350 Roscommon Drive but didn't see it. She gave up and pushed open the door; a bell tinkled. Three women seated at desks looked up at her hopefully. All of them were smiling.

'Hi!' said the one closest to her, whose name on her desk said 'Marci'. 'I see you're admiring our trophy case.'

Their what? Then Kate saw it, across from the door, a big wooden case with a glass front, full of shiny trophies. 'Yes,' she said politely. 'My goodness, so many.'

'Most of them are Evan Bright's. He was a big local basketball star, all state in high school. He was the owner – he passed. His widow keeps everything the same. We're encouraged to bring our trophies in—' she giggled – 'if we have any. Alice—' she gestured somewhere behind her – 'has one for *golf*.'

'Ah,' said Kate.

'I'm sorry, I didn't mean to go on and on. May I help you?'

'I had some questions about three fifty Roscommon Drive?' said Kate.

Maybe it was just an impression, but it seemed to Kate that everyone's smile dimmed, just slightly, and the room got just a little chillier.

A woman near the back, a plump blonde in a blue suit, came to the front. 'I'm handling that for now.' She held out her hand. 'Abbie Flintstone. And you're—?'

'Kate. Kate Waters.'

'*Kate*?'

'Yes.'

'I'm so pleased to meet you, Kate.' Abbie's smile was big and shiny bright and somehow irrelevant and wrong.

'I just had some questions—' Kate began.

'I have some questions myself, Kate.' She reached in her purse, jingled some car keys. 'Why don't we meet at the house? We can talk there.'

'It's okay,' Kate began, 'I—'

But Abbie was gone, headed presumably for her car.

Kate pulled in the driveway, and Abbie parked her car on the street. They met by the door. A woman – the same woman, in fact, that Kate had spoken to the last time she was here – was out walking her dog again. Kate had no idea what the woman's name was, but she remembered the dog's name was Felix.

'Jane?' Abbie called. 'Is it a yes or a no?'

'It's a yes,' the woman called back.

Abbie turned back to Kate. Her expression was no longer cheery. 'So,' she said. 'Now Jane has identified you.'

'What?'

'You showed up at this house, spent the night like it was a motel, called our office, talked to Marci, told her some kind of ridiculous story, which you also told to Jane over there. Want to tell me what's really going on here?'

'What's really going on?' Kate's voice rose.

181

'What's really going on? I have absolutely no idea. What I *thought* was going on was that I was meeting an old friend, Ellen Wilson. We were emailing back and forth discussing it. I flew all the way here from Arizona, and she never showed up.'

'The people who own this house live in Minnesota. The Parkers. They inherited it from Emily Madigan, who died a year ago. This Ellen person? You'd mentioned the name to Marci, so I called the owners. They've never heard of her.'

'Ellen's been dead for eight months,' Kate said. 'I just found out, day before yesterday. Someone, I don't know who, got me to come here, pretending to be her.'

There was a long silence. Birds twittered, and somewhere a dog barked and barked, but not like he really meant it.

'Well, I don't know what to think.' Abbie whooshed out a breath. 'I really don't.' She paused. 'How did you get in, anyway?'

'The key,' Kate said. 'It's under that rock by the door.'

'We're not in the habit of leaving keys under rocks at Evan Bright Realty,' Abbie said formally. She went over, lifted the rock. There was nothing there.

'I left a note,' said Kate. 'Inside on the kitchen table.'

She followed Abbie inside to the kitchen. The note was gone too.

Kate remembered something else: she peeked into the dining room. 'The flowers,' she said. 'I brought them for Ellen, but they're not here either. I even talked to the police. You can check on that. A man from law enforcement came over and went through the house.'

'No kidding.' Abbie's face softened a bit. 'You talked to the police, and they actually came to the house?'

'Yes. Officer Matt Dodds. You can check it out. He was looking for—' Kate began to giggle, a little hysterically. 'Ellen's body.'

'Wow. I didn't realize you'd called the police. Well.' Abbie looked as Kate as if seeing her for the first time. 'Somebody was really mad at you. Let me guess. An ex.'

'Maybe.'

'Oh my god!' said Abbie suddenly.

'Oh my god what?'

'I just remembered something. Now it's all coming together.' She sat down heavily at the kitchen table. 'I need a drink.' She stood up again. 'Water, I mean. Got some bottled in my car. Want one?'

'Yes, please,' Kate said.

Abbie handed Kate a bottle of water and sat down across from her.

'We're not showing this house at the moment,' she said. 'The owners want us to sit on it till the housing market improves. But up to a couple of weeks or so ago we – I should say Steve, he's handling it, but he's out of town right now – Steve was showing it from time to time.'

She paused, took a swig of water. 'Not that anyone was lining up to see it. As a matter of

183

fact, right now Steve's at a conference for realtors: How to Improve Sales in a Tanking Economy.' She sighed.

'It's tough,' Kate said.

'Oh, yes, it is. Anyway, there used to be a spare key on one of those hooks over there by the door. Then one day Steve noticed it was gone.'

'Ah,' Kate said.

'He tried to remember the last time he'd actually noticed the key. It was maybe a month before – during which time he'd shown the house three times, once to a young couple, and twice to men. One he didn't remember much about, but the other one, the last one to look at the house, was maybe late thirties, early forties, and Steve didn't like him.'

'Oh,' said Kate. 'Why is that?'

'He felt uncomfortable. He thought he was maybe some kind of real-estate scammer. Remembering this guy was kind of an aha moment for him.'

'Really?' Kate said.

'Steve was pretty stoked about it, you know? What I think is—' She paused significantly. 'It could be the person who pretended to be your friend. Anyway, we debated getting the locks changed, but we never did.'

'Why not?'

'Partially inertia on Steve's part, to be honest. But there's nothing in this house of any value. The relatives came here from Minnesota, auctioned off any furniture that was of value and either threw away or took everything left that was personal. What's here now comes with the house.'

'Names? Do you have names for any of these people who might have taken the key?'

'Steve should. I don't have his card.' She reached in her purse. 'Here, take mine. Call me later—' she glanced at her watch – 'tomorrow and I'll give you his cell number. He'll have names – but of course there's no telling if they're real.' She locked the door, started down the driveway. At the end she paused. 'Honey, I'm sorry.'

'Not your fault,' Kate said.

Abbie's car was blocking the driveway. Funny, Kate thought as she watched her pull away. Abbie had said all the personal stuff had been taken away by the relatives, and it was true, there'd been nothing personal in the house anywhere that Kate could tell, except for the photograph of the woman in the bikini at Tall Pines Lake.

Tired from her night in the motel keeping vigil, too tired to think any more, Kate, the scourge of decent neighborhoods everywhere, got slowly into the rental car. She drove slowly back to the motel, which was a nondescript building, she thought wearily, painted in bright colors, surrounded by many other nondescript buildings in similar bright colors and a freeway full of fast-moving cars and trucks and vans, going quickly from one nondescript place to another.

She was so tired that she went back to her motel room, put the sliding chain on the door and lay down on the bed. Her flight tomorrow was at seven in the morning, which meant she should leave for the airport around five. Why had she made it so early? Then, suddenly, she began to weep, but fell asleep almost at once.

When she woke it was dark outside. What time was it? Nearly eight o'clock. She got up, still groggy, and splashed cold water on her face, checked her cellphone. She'd missed a call from Dakota, no message. Why hadn't Dakota texted her? Oh, well. Time for dinner. She picked up her purse from the dresser.

There was a Subway not too far, a couple of parking lots away. Kate decided to walk; it would wake her up. The freeway was humming, but in a subdued way, and the Subway restaurant was empty, just a clerk yawning behind the counter. Kate scanned the menu above her and ordered a Diet Coke and a seafood sandwich. She ate it there, staring out at the parking lots and the brightly lit plate-glass windows of Kroger's.

Then she walked back, dodging the parked cars, past the office and down to her room. A few doors down from her room a hallway led to the interior of the motel, where there was, Kate had checked earlier, a mangy-looking swimming pool. As she walked by the hallway someone just inside coughed, a deep cough.

An alarm bell went off in her mind.

She walked a little faster, scrabbling in her purse for her room key with her free hand, fingers slipping off the slick plastic. She could feel someone right behind her now, right behind her as if he had been waiting for her all along.

'Wait!' a man's voice said. 'Kate, *wait!*'

She didn't turn, just tightened her grip on the plastic card. She reached her room, tried to insert the plastic card key, but her hands were shaking and it wouldn't go in.

Maybe she shouldn't go inside, anyway – he might push in behind her. She should try to get around him, go the office. She stepped back from the door and turned to make a wide berth around him. Then she saw his face.

'*You,*' she said. 'What are *you* doing here?'

Twenty-Seven

It was Malcolm, the supposed detective. He was wearing jeans and a rumpled blue denim shirt, and he looked tired.

'I came here to find you,' he said. 'Dakota told me where you were.'

'Right,' Kate said. 'Thanks, Dakota.' She stepped around him, closer to the office. 'Are you the man that called the motel looking for me, who said I was his wife?'

Malcolm looked surprised. 'No. That happened?'

Should she believe him? Had he been stalking her all this time? She had a sudden thought – was he the man lurking in the neighborhood, the one the dog was barking at, the night she'd slept at the house at Roscommon Drive? But he couldn't possibly know about Ellen Wilson, *could he*? She didn't see how, and the sane part of her brain told her all these thoughts were paranoid and totally irrational, but just in case she moved even further away from him until she was out in the parking lot.

'Yes,' Kate said. 'That happened.'

She could see the office out of the corner of her eye. She walked towards the office lights, noticing thing she hadn't noticed before. For instance, the blue Toyota Camry parked a couple of spaces down from her room. It hadn't been there earlier.

'Wait,' he said. 'We need to talk.'

Kate began to laugh, a little out of control laugh. She walked a little faster. 'Why?' she asked over her shoulder. 'Are we breaking up?'

'Not just yet,' he called out to her. 'Go to the office, sit inside. It's a safe place. I'll meet you there.'

John the desk clerk looked up from a book he was reading. *Outliers*, Malcolm Gladwell. 'Some guy was looking for you,' he told her, 'but it's okay, I told him you weren't registered here.'

He straightened his nerd glasses.

'He found me anyway,' Kate said. The office was chilly, overdone on the air conditioning. John the clerk, she noticed, was wearing a thick brown sweater. She sat down on the only chair, an uncomfortable one, so close to the desk that John would probably be able to hear any conversation that might take place.

She bet he'd listen, too – he looked like that kind of person.

Malcolm walked in.

John looked over at Kate nervously. 'It's not my fault,' he said. 'I told him there was no one here by your name, I swear.'

'I believe you,' Kate said.

'You did right,' Malcolm told the desk clerk. 'I could have been an abusive husband or, even worse, a stalker or a serial rapist.'

'Okay, okay.' The desk clerk looked disgusted. 'I get the message. *Whatever.*'

'Dakota told me everything,' Malcolm said to Kate. 'Your friend who's dead, the empty house all of it. Look, I'm with law enforcement – I'm just on leave at the moment.'

'So I heard.'

'And—'

'This isn't going to work,' Kate said. 'Let's go to one of the fast food places to talk.' She stood up. 'You've seen him now,' she said over her shoulder to the clerk, though by now her fear had dissipated. 'If I turn up missing, it was him.'

'Wait!' John, the desk clerk, held up his cell-phone. 'I'll take his picture.'

Malcolm mugged briefly for the camera.

They walked outside. It was cool but warmer than the chilly office, and lights sparkled and glimmered from the cars and the fast food chains and the Kroger's, giving the impression that they were in a place that was interesting and exciting – and maybe they were.

'Nothing,' Kate said. 'Carrie said nothing to me. I'm so tired of thinking about it, okay?'

They sat in a booth at the McDonald's with

hard orange seats that said *eat up, hurry, hurry, customers are waiting*. Kate got a Diet Coke and Malcolm a Coke and three quarter-pounders with cheese and fries. It took him one of the quarter-pounders to explain to Kate how he had ended up in New Jersey, sitting across from her.

'Okay,' he said. 'And now I have to ask why you took it at face value – that it was this Ellen who was emailing you?'

'It never occurred to me, really, that it might not be her.'

'Why not?'

'I guess it was the Ooblecks.'

'Ah, the Ooblecks.'

'Green slime from a Dr Suess book. *Bartholomew and the Oobleck.*'

'Ah.'

Kate reached for one of his fries. 'Do you mind?'

'Go ahead. Ketchup?'

'*Yes.*' Kate opened a packet and squeezed a little mound beside the fries. 'That's what we called ourselves, a group of us in New York City.' She dipped a fry in the ketchup and ate it. 'It's too hard to explain.'

'That's it? That's what made you trust whoever it was? That they knew about the Ooblecks?'

'Yes. I guess I *wanted* to trust her, him, it, whatever.' She paused. 'I really needed to trust somebody so, as usual, I guess I chose the wrong person.'

'As usual?'

'Never mind.'

'So maybe we can narrow down who might

190

have done it,' Malcolm said. 'Someone from your past who knew about the Ooblecks stuff. Or – this old boyfriend of yours, Harry Light?'

'What! Dakota told you about him too?'

'Dakota's your true friend,' said Malcolm, 'and don't you forget that. Did he know about the Ooblecks?'

'No.' She frowned. 'That's one of the reasons I was hot to go see Ellen – New Jersey's so far away from California.'

'So you spent the night in the house. Ellen never showed, and then you left the next morning. Doesn't make much sense – just a really stupid joke. Anything unusual happen during the night?'

'There was a dog. It kept barking. It woke me up.' She smiled. 'It woke up the whole neighborhood, and the police came.'

'Aha.'

'What?'

'Harry ever do workshops and the like within the prison system?'

'I don't know. I mean, not that I know of. Why?'

'Anna Marie Romero. That name mean anything to you?'

'She was one of his students at a workshop he did.' Kate shrugged. 'Actually, I kind of suspected something might be going on between her and Harry. By then, though, Harry had turned out to be such a jerk I was basically thinking to myself, *leave*.'

'She's gone missing.'

'*What?*'

191

'She's gone missing. Harry was questioned.'

'And?'

'And nothing. He wasn't charged or anything.' Malcolm polished off the last quarter-pounder and wiped his mouth with three napkins. He looked over at Kate. She seemed pale, weary. Should he mention the fact he might be talking to Anna Marie's mother soon? No. Too much right now. Wait. See how it played out. 'But he does have a criminal record.'

'What!'

'Misdemeanor criminal damage.'

'What does that mean, exactly?'

'Hard to tell. Got mad, broke something that belonged to someone else. In the end it was dismissed.'

'Great.' She put her head in her hands. 'I don't even want to think about it right now, okay?' Her voice was tense, high with anxiety. Familiar.

'You take any medication?' he asked.

'What do you mean?'

'Like, for anxiety. You seem a little high-strung.' Plus he could imagine how she'd be once he told her what he was going to tell her next.

'Don't I have a right to be anxious and high-strung? And I've hardly slept at all for days. Dakota gave me two Ativan before I left. I took one for the plane, and I have one more, okay? But I don't want to take it and lose my edge.'

'I'm here. Relax. You don't need an edge now. You have an Ativan on you right now?'

'Yes.'

'Well, then take it, okay?'

'Tell me something first.'

'What?'

'You were a cop in Mesa; now you're on some kind of leave?'

'Right, some kind of leave.'

'Why?'

'My wife Cindy killed herself about nine months ago. I had a little trouble dealing with that.'

'Oh!' Kate put her hand over her mouth. 'Oh, I'm so sorry. How could I be this horrible self-centered person? Look—' She reached into her purse and took out a gold metal pillbox. She opened it and took out a small white pill. 'I'm taking this Ativan, okay?'

'Okay. Good.'

'There,' she said after a moment. 'Your wife? Do you want to talk about it?'

'No.' Malcolm avoided her eyes.

Outside, a car pulled into a parking slot near them. Bugs batted futilely at the street lights. Kate and Malcolm rested.

'The tire blowing out on your car?' Malcolm said after a while. 'It wasn't an accident. Someone shot out the tires.'

'Someone did *what*?'

'Shot out your tires. It's being investigated right now. In fact, you're going need to talk to the investigator – Brad Holmes. He's with the sheriff's department.'

'No! No!' Kate closed her eyes. 'What's going on? What did I *do*, for God's sake?' She put her head down on the table.

In a way he wished he hadn't told her, but he

had to. He wished she were tougher, then again he didn't.

'God.' Kate's hands began to shake. 'How am I going to feel safe back in Arizona? I don't even feel safe in that motel room now.'

'Tell you what,' he said, like a fool, 'when you go back to your room the Ativan's going to kick in. You can get some sleep. I'll sit outside the door in my car and keep watch.'

They would have to go over everything, both of them knew, but for the moment Malcolm let her rest. He stared out the plate-glass window at the lights of the cars and trucks going by on the freeway, at the Wendy's, the Kroger's, the Kentucky Colonel, waiting till she was able to compose herself.

The shining lights out in the parking lot, the cars going by, the blank night sky with its stars blotted out: how oddly beautiful it all seemed. He'd flown clear across country to this alien place, but already it was beginning to feel like home.

Late that night in his rented car, parked under a street light near the door of Kate's room at the motel, Malcolm searched the web on his laptop. A few entries in he found an article from some obscure paper, *Vermont Art News*. Kate Waters, Director of the Rustic Arts Collective. And a picture of Kate, longer hair, a brighter smile – possibly even happy. *Vivacious Kate Waters*, the article said, *has lived here for the last eight years with her partner, sculptor Rick Church.*

'I hung around the New York City art scene for a few years,' Kate was quoted as saying, 'me and my arty friends, Ellen Wilson, Mandy Foster, Karen and Sandy. We called ourselves the Ooblecks.' And why was that? 'It's a joke.' Kate laughed. 'A long story. To make it short we were all feeling down one day, and someone said how low can you go, and we all decided green slime was pretty low.'

So, not just someone from Kate's past, but anyone – anyone motivated enough to search the web – could have come up with Ellen Wilson and the Oobleck thing. It was quite an elaborate scheme – someone would have to be a highly motivated egomaniac to carry it out. It put Hairy Lite back in the picture. Kate had told him about the man who'd looked at the house and the missing key. No reason once you had a key not to make copies. He wasn't going to really go into it with Kate, but he suspected she was alive today because of a barking dog.

The door to Kate's room opened. Malcolm checked his watch: four forty-five.

Kate came over to the car, fully dressed, wheeling her carry-on.

He opened the window.

'My flight's at seven. Thank you,' she said, 'for keeping me safe. I was thinking maybe this whole thing is one of those events people stage.'

'What people are we talking about?'

'Artists. They stage something, film it, and it's an event.'

'I haven't seen any cameras.'

195

'No,' Kate said. 'Me neither. See you back in Arizona.' She turned away.

'Wait,' said Malcolm. 'Where are you staying when you get back there?'

'With Dakota.'

'Be sure to talk to Officer Holmes right away.'

Kate nodded. 'I put his number in my contacts,' she said. 'That way I'll always have a policeman when I need him. Oh, wait, maybe I already do.' She smiled, and for the first time Malcolm saw her smile without the cloud of anxiety.

She held up her hand, fanned her fingers. 'Bye, bye,' she said.

Twenty-Eight

Malcolm went to his room and managed to get three hours' sleep after Kate left for the airport. Then he went to McDonald's, fueled up on coffee and three steak, egg and cheese McMuffins, then called the number for Abbie of Evan Bright Realty on the card Kate had given him.

'An investigator,' Abbie said, after he'd explained. 'That's wonderful. All of us here in the office have been just freaking out about this whole thing.'

He drove over to Evan Bright Realty, pushed open the glass door, found a line of desks and three women ranging in age from twenties to fifties. Two of them smiled brightly at him, expectantly.

'Hi there,' they said in unison.

'Abbie here?'

One of them nodded her head at a third woman at a desk near the back, partially obscured by a youngish couple. 'Helping a client,' she said. 'Are you Malcolm?'

'Yes.'

'Have a seat. She's expecting you.'

He sat, surveyed the office. Cheery with potted plants, family photos on the empty desks, a trophy case displaying sports trophies. Basketball, it looked like. Then the couple left, and Abbie came towards him, blonde and plump, wearing a red suit.

'So you're with law enforcement in *Arizona*,' she said. 'That must be exciting! Never a dull moment, apparently, in *that* state.'

He considered making some crack about New Jersey and *The Sopranos*, but didn't. 'Right,' he said.

'Here's the house key and also Steve's card. I called him myself, when I got back to the office after talking to Kate. He can answer some of your questions that I can't. But he told me to tell anyone concerned to wait till next week when he's back from the conference and can check his notes.'

Malcolm opened the front door at 350 Roscommon Drive with the key Abbie had given him. He'd stopped at Kroger's and bought a cheap flashlight and a pair of rubber gloves. He didn't want to leave any fingerprints to confuse the issue, if in fact anyone decided there was an issue. Inside, he put the gloves on; they weren't the greatest, but they would have to do. He planned to tell law enforcement the whole story as Kate had told it to him – luckily, she'd notified the police about Ellen's absence – but he wanted to go through the house first.

The scenario, as he envisioned it, was get her out of her element, in a strange place. She would be disoriented, not thinking clearly, wondering where her friend Ellen was. A perfect spot: empty houses on either side, woody fields behind, out of sight of any occupied houses on the street. Plus, from the look of all the 'For Sale' signs, the neighbors wouldn't be as aware of who was who as they might normally be.

Get her in there, then slip in late at night with your key. Except a dog barked and woke up the neighborhood.

Focus.

He walked down the hall, starting with the kitchen, opening all the drawers, the cupboards. He opened the dead refrigerator, its insides smelling faintly of old food, and found nothing – nothing in the freezer part, the vegetable hydrator, the meat keeper. Nothing in the bedrooms, under the beds, the closets, the drawers of the only chest of drawers. Nothing in the living room. He went back to the kitchen, found the door to the basement.

He opened it, got a whiff of old mold and must. The steps looked pretty steep to someone as sleep deprived as he felt. He held on to the railing as he went down. At the bottom, light shone through a couple of high narrow windows, dim with dirt and spiderwebs.

He played the flashlight all around – the floor was beige speckled linoleum tile, the walls cinderblock painted white. Two cardboard boxes were against one wall – he walked over and opened them. One held a stack of *National Geographic*s and a large dead daddy long leg spider, the other a cache of glass jelly jars. There was a sink in one corner, hook-ups for a washer-dryer, and that was about it.

Nothing at all of interest that he could find in the whole house, not even a handkerchief embroidered with the monogram HL. Not only that, there was no sign of any break-in. There was nothing of interest or anything personal in the whole house, which made the snapshot Kate had found in one of the bedrooms maybe more significant than it might normally have been. She'd shown it to him this morning. A woman in a bikini, smiling. *Tall Pines Lake, 2005.*

He'd laughed, though, because in a way it didn't look like a real snapshot, more like those pictures that come in frames when you buy them.

'But it *is* real,' Kate had protested.

'I know, I know, it just has that phoney look. Familiar, somehow.'

He walked outside and around the house – roses bloomed at the side, yellow like the ones in front – looking for something, anything. He checked the borders, the perimeters. The basement windows were half above ground, half submerged. He knelt and peered down through the dirty glass into the basement.

Nothing.

Time to return the key to the realtor.

At the police station Officer Matt Dodds came out from the back, chewing on a carrot. 'You with Mesa PD, huh?' he asked Malcolm. He was a friendly looking guy, young, baby faced and blonde, probably went into law enforcement to keep the peace rather than to chase bad guys, or maybe a little of both.

'Not now,' Malcolm said. 'I'm on leave.'

Officer Dodds laughed. 'But you can't stay away.'

'Just can't.'

'I remember Cindy pretty well; it was just a couple of days ago. It was a little premature to file a missing person report, but I checked out the house, made sure her friend wasn't dead in the basement.'

'*Cindy?*' Malcolm stared at him, feeling as if he'd fallen through some hole in space into another dimension. 'Kate,' he said. 'Her name is Kate.'

'Kate. Yeah. Didn't I say Kate? Sorry. So, what's up? She find her friend?'

Malcolm launched into the whole story.

'Jesus Christ,' said Officer Dodds when he finished. 'What kind of a joke is that?'

'It's a little too screwy, you know what I mean? It looks like a stupid joke, but I have concerns it might have been a set-up. And I understand you guys were called out to Roscommon Drive on that same night Kate stayed there.'

'I hear you. I remember thinking it was kind

of strange, two incidents on that same basically quiet street so close together, but I couldn't see any connection. Let me get Officer Brindle out here – he went on that other call.'

Officer Brindle was as congenial as Officer Dodds, as if they'd both just taken a workshop about community relations.

'I filed a report on that,' he said. 'Suspicion of a prowler. He was gone when I got there; I just put down what the neighbors told me. So many empty houses in that neighborhood; you worry about homeless guys breaking in to sleep.'

'Yeah,' said Officer Dodds. 'Homeless guys, like probably the former owners.'

They both chuckled sadly.

'Anyway,' said Officer Brindle. 'There was nothing specific to indicate that anything of a criminal nature was going on.' He looked over at Officer Dodds.

'You got any sort of description at all of this alleged prowler?' Malcolm asked.

Officer Brindle laughed. 'Male. Height, medium to tall. Wearing a baseball cap.'

'There's a guy, Harry Light. He might be involved in this.'

'An ex, you mean?'

'An ex.'

'An ex. Lures her here. Has nefarious plans for her late late at night, but the big dog chases him away. Justice!'

'Justice.'

'This Harry from around here?'

'Not as far as I can tell. Maybe you can run

201

an APB on him and see if anything turns up locally.'

'Sure thing.'

Malcolm doubted anything would turn up.

While the officers were running an APB, Malcolm went outside for some air. Parking lot. Big office-building across the street, fringed with smokers. Cindy had quit smoking shortly before he met her, had taken it up again, and had quit for the second time a few months before she killed herself. Why had she bothered quitting that second time? Malcolm wondered now. And what was she doing popping up here in this faraway state instead of buried in a graveyard in Mesa, Arizona? Ha ha, joke.

Abruptly, he turned and walked back into the police station, away from a thought of Cindy in a pretty red blouse he'd given her one year for her birthday, laughing at something silly – blonde hair soft, blue eyes smiling, happy. The lighting inside was bland, comfortingly sterile.

Officer Dodds came out the door by the plate-glass sliding window. 'Got nothing on your guy, Harry Light. Sorry.'

'Thanks, anyway,' he said.

'Not a problem.'

As he walked out the door Malcolm realized what was going to happen. No crime had actually been committed, and the police were not going to be investigating anything he had told them. Budgets were being cut all over the country. Nothing was going happen at this end. Nothing at all.

'Hey, wait a sec,' Officer Dodds called to him. Malcolm turned.

'So this all started with an email to your friend?'

Malcolm nodded.

'You trace the IP address?'

'Next on my list,' Malcolm said.

Malcolm drove back towards the motel. He had a friend in Phoenix who could do the IP trace and cellphone too, though by now whoever had sent the fake emails from Ellen had probably covered his – her? – nah, probably not, but maybe – their tracks. He hadn't found out much; wasted his time, if you looked at it a certain way, but another way, he hadn't wasted it at all considering the other options he had for spending his time, so – so what?

He pulled into a fast food place, Kentucky Colonel, and decided to park, go inside and order. They had iron tables and chairs out in front; he could eat dinner to the smell of gas fumes. He went in and came out in a few minutes with a three-piece dinner: dark meat, corn, mashed, biscuit on the side. Coffee to go with it. The sun was beginning to sink in the sky, the light slanted a funny way and as he watched the cars drive by, while sitting at the table, he had some sense of déjà vu, that he'd been in this place before, this very place, eaten this exact same meal in some other life that resembled a paradise.

This is it, he thought. *I've finally gone over the edge.*

His cellphone chimed. Lupita. *Lupita.* That's right; he'd flown back east for Lupita, to talk to Rose, sad pretty Rose. She'd left him messages to call her, and he never had.

'Hi,' he said.

'Malcolm, where are you? I haven't heard from you in days, and you haven't come into the restaurant.'

'I'm in New Jersey,' he said. 'Investigating. I talked to Carrie's Cooper's sister. She—'

'You could still have gotten back to me,' Lupita broke in, her voice accusing, with a hint of tears. 'Chico escaped from the jail.'

'*What?*'

'He escaped. He just walked out. No one knows where he is. His lawyer's really mad.'

'I don't blame him.'

'I think he must have gone across the line. We have some cousins there.' Her voice trembled. 'He was going to be a famous artist some day, and now he'll just be like all those illegals. When are you coming back? Did you find out anything from the sister?'

'I'll be back tomorrow, then we can talk, okay?'

'You come into the restaurant. Frank's got a new recipe, peanut soup.'

'I will, I will.'

He would, he would. Chico had escaped. That was dumb – the dumbest thing Chico could have done. In some obscure way it seemed like his fault – he'd lost track of what he was doing, derailed by Kate.

Twenty-Nine

Kate took the shuttle from the airport back to Dudley. What's the worst that can happen, anyway? she thought as the shuttle made the turn at the Sierra Vista exit. So I'm murdered. Then I'll be dead, no more worries.

I can do it.

It helped that the views here were all unimpeded as they passed through the small dusty towns of Whetstone and Huachuca City. Mountains rose to her right, close, and to her left, further away. It wasn't like coming home, exactly; she didn't know where her home was any more. But should she die prematurely, murdered right here in Arizona, where would she be buried? In the tiny dusty graveyard outside of Dudley, full of miners and their wives?

No way.

Bill. Her stepfather. She hadn't talked to Bill in a while, not since he'd called her the night of the murders. She needed to get in touch, tell him to reserve her a burial plot next to her mom. Or had he done that already?

Back in Dudley, Kate walked up from the shuttle stop to her house. The weeds that lined the driveway had blossomed in the rainy season and gone to seed in the dry. She opened the door. The house smelled musty; she'd closed

205

all the windows before she left, and the house had baked for days in the high desert sun. No dog waited for her in the house, no cat, only the spiders. With fresh eyes from a journey, everything looked drabber. She noted that her one and only house plant, a fern, was now dead.

She went around the house, unlocking all the windows, opening them. Most had screens except in the back bedroom, which was unused but for an ironing board and a pile of unironed clothes. The window in there was already unlocked and open a couple of inches. The lock was old and didn't catch. Had it been closed all the way when she left? She couldn't remember. She'd been in a hurry.

She hardly lived here; how was she to know? Ask the spiders; they never left home.

She called Ernie's garage. Her car was ready. She called Dakota, got a ride over there.

'Chico escaped from jail,' Dakota told her on the way over.

'No! How did he do that?'

'Just walked out the door is what I heard. He had some trustee job 'cause they, haha, trusted him. Rumor has it he went across the line.'

Kate thought of his show at the gallery, the tortured dolls. But then she thought: what if he had actually killed those tourists? Maybe he had. Who knew?

'I know what you're thinking,' Dakota said as she pulled into the gas station, 'but he didn't do it.'

Kate got out, went into the office.

'Hey, you're quite the talk around the garage,' the guy called Ed, according to his name tag, said as he gave her the keys. 'You all take it easy now, you hear!'

She waved goodbye to Dakota, got in her car and immediately called the number Malcolm had given her – Officer Brad Holmes, who was investigating the shot-out tire case.

Kate and Officer Brad Holmes stood by the side of the road, half a mile before the turn to Dudley. Cars and pickup trucks whizzed by. The air smelled of dust and creosote and gas fumes.

'It wasn't dark yet,' Officer Holmes said. 'Do you remember seeing any cars or trucks parked by the side of the road?'

'No. Nothing. I mean, cars were passing me, but none of them were stopped. All I remember is hearing two bangs. I was listening to music during the first bang, but I disconnected it. There might have been three bangs; I just heard two.'

'Someone mad at you?' Officer Holmes asked.

'I don't know,' said Kate. 'Maybe.'

She didn't want to mention Harry Light. They might get in touch with him, ask questions – there was still a chance he wasn't involved in any of this, didn't even know where she lived now. It would be like disturbing a hornet's nest. Besides, Malcolm knew. She was planning to trust Malcolm, at least for a while.

'Couldn't it just have been an accident?' she said.

'Anything's possible, but two or three shots?

207

Probably not. I guess it could have been someone on a dry drunk, just wanting to make someone pay, didn't much care who. Anyway, whoever it was,' he said, 'is a damn good shooter.' He paused. 'Course, that's if they were actually aiming at your tires.'

She started back to her house, but went to the Co-op instead.

'Kate! Ka-Ka-Ka-Katie!' said Windsong at the register, his face red and shiny with delight. 'We missed you, Ka-Ka-Ka-Katie.'

Posey twirled on her toes. 'Raspberries this week,' she bubbled. 'Raspberries! Organic and all!'

'Sensimilla's here too!' Ryan said. 'Big shipment in. Go round the back to collect. Ha ha. Good to have you back! Heard someone shot at your car. Bet it was one of those military survivalists who go around shooting at everyone all the time. This state is full of them!'

'And Chico escaped,' said Posey. 'Good for him too!'

'And don't worry! Even if he did it, which we know he didn't, you're safe with us! Safe from the survivalists too,' said Windsong. 'We'll take a bullet for you, Ka-Ka-Ka-Katie, if we have to.'

And in all that good cheer, for a moment she believed she *was* safe.

Safe and sound.

Dakota and Kate got four basil, mozzarella and Asiago cheese individual pizzas and two eclairs to go from the High Desert Market and went back to Dakota's to eat them in her living room. Then they went online on Dakota's laptop and read all the articles – not that many, really – about Anna Marie Romero's disappearance.

'Do you think Harry killed her?' said Dakota in a hushed voice.

'I don't know. He had that gun in his bedside table drawer. And there was one time when I thought he was going to hit me. We went to the movies, I can't even remember what we saw, but he was already in a bad mood, and afterwards he asked me what I thought of it – kind of aggressively, you know? – and I said, what did *he* think of it, 'cause he was so grouchy I just wanted to agree with him.'

'Out loud? You said that last part about agreeing with him out loud?'

'Yes. His face got red, and he kind of pulled his hand back in a fist, then he stopped himself.'

'That's it? Did he apologize later?'

'No. And Malcolm told me he had some kind of misdemeanor charge from before – criminal damage, he said. But I just can't see how this connects with the New Jersey stuff. It's so far away from Harry.'

'You know what? Maybe it was that what's-her-name, the one that Rick was cheating on you with.'

'Hannah?'

'Sure. Maybe Rick was starting to regret losing you and Hannah got jealous. So she set things up to make you suffer.'

'I don't think she's smart enough for that.'

They talked for a while more, then they rested, eating the eclairs and watching TV: some special on Africa – tragically beautiful black children, bellies swollen from starvation, looked out with enormous eyes in some dusty African village. Seeing the children made Kate cry. She sniffed, blew her nose.

'God, you are so on edge, so stressed,' said Dakota. 'I worry about you.'

'What good does that do, worrying about me?' Kate's voice rose. 'Give me a break. Besides,' she said, giggling, 'I took time off to go to New Jersey to check in with myself, and look at me now!'

Dakota giggled too. After a moment they both began to laugh. They laughed and laughed, egging each other on. Finally, they stopped. Kate wiped her eyes.

'You need to find a – a – *hobby*,' Dakota said.

'That's *it*,' said Kate.

That set them off again.

Exhausted now, Kate and Dakota stared at the TV, where a gorgeous blonde celebrity in a safari outfit was holding one of the African babies and smiling for the camera.

The street light shone directly in on Kate as she tossed and turned in Dakota's spare bedroom. Finally, late, close to morning, she fell asleep and dreamed of Africa, beautiful dark children in dusty villages, long green vistas and brilliant skies, and Windsong and Posey and Ryan were there, cooking up a big barbecue for all the starving children and smiling, but not for any camera.

Thirty

Malcolm got back to Dudley just in time for lunch. He parked at El Serape and called Kate's cellphone, thinking she might like to join him, but just got her voicemail. The restaurant was full of chattering people: lawyers from the court-house across the street, tourists in bright tops and khakis, locals in faded casual clothes.

Lupita looked tired, dark circles under her red-rimmed eyes, but she smiled when she saw Malcolm, the savior, here to fix everything while she worked hard at El Serape for a few bucks and no benefits.

'Any sign of Chico?' he asked her.

Her smile faded, and her lips tightened. 'No.' She looked at him accusingly.

'I'm sorry.' Malcolm sat down at a window table. There was a little pause, as if to honor the missing Chico. 'So, what's good for lunch?'

She recommended the Senegalese peanut soup, one of Frank's experiments – he'd gotten the recipe out of one of his wife's women's magazines.

The restaurant started to empty out and hardly anyone was left when she came back with his soup, so he gave her the run down on what he'd

211

been doing. He left out the Kate stuff – he wasn't sure if it was connected or if it was a separate case. That was the great puzzle right now, he thought.

'So, what next?' she said.

'I got at least one lead. Dr Paul Sanger. An old friend of Wes and Carrie, and a friend of Polly Hampton – that's Wes's daughter. I'll be heading to Tucson to talk to him – probably tomorrow.' He'd looked up Dr Sanger already. He had an office in Tucson at a medical plaza off Oracle Road.

'So how exactly does this Dr Sanger fit in?'

'He was at Chico's release hearing?'

'He was? What did he look like?'

'Anglo guy, mid thirties to mid forties. He wore black framed glasses.'

Lupita shrugged.

'Rose couldn't think of anyone who had it in for Wes and Carrie, but maybe he can.'

Lupita nodded.

'And that's just one aspect of the investigation. Sid, the bartender at the St Elmo, should be back in town now, and I'm going to show him Wes's daughter's picture. There's a chance she was in town the day of the murders, which would be extremely interesting.'

'Good,' said Lupita decisively. 'You did good. Now, eat, eat.'

He swallowed a spoonful of the soup. Then another. It was creamy and spicy – sweet potatoes, peanuts and coconut milk – and startlingly delicious, so good he felt guilty, enjoying it in front of Lupita whose beloved brother was accused of a double homicide and was now missing, all because he hadn't fixed it for her yet.

'By the way, there's another hearing coming up,' she said.

'What kind?'

'Evidence hearing.'

'Evidentiary?'

'I guess. How can they do it without Chico?'

'In absentia. It means in his absence.'

'Oh.' Lupita sat down across from him. 'Is the soup good?'

'It's very, very good. My compliments to the chef.'

'Listen.'

'What?'

'There's something I want you to do for me.'

'What's that?'

'Go across the line to Mexico.'

Malcolm called Kate again on his way out of town – still no answer. He drove the five miles down to the border, passed the dance hall on this side of the line, the houses with their tiny gardens. He parked on the US side and walked across as the border guard waved him through. Suddenly, he was in Mexico. Liquor store on one corner, curio shop on the other. Narrow streets with adobe houses. Everything seemed softer, dustier than on the other side.

He walked past a church, a *maquilladora*. Came to the little plaza, with a statue of Álvaro Obregón, thirty-ninth president of Mexico, born in Sonora on February nineteenth, 1880. A grower of garbanzo beans, commander in the Revolution

213

where he'd lost an arm, and president of the first stable regime since the Revolution began.

A salute to Álvaro Obregón. Where is a man like you now? Malcolm thought.

He turned down a side street, per Lupita's instructions. She'd given him a little gift for Chico, a gold cross. He had it in his pocket.

'To keep him safe,' she said.

At the third house down he knocked on the blue painted wooden door. Knocked again.

After a while the door opened, and an old woman looked out. '*Como?*'

'Pedro?' Malcolm said. '*Sta aqui?*'

'*Si, si.*' She turned her head and bawled out in a surprisingly loud voice in English, as if Malcolm's Spanish had not fooled her for one moment, 'Pedro, someone here for you.'

A man came to the door, younger than the woman, bushy eyebrows, lean build. He held a big napkin, dabbing at his lips. 'Hello, hello. You are—?'

'Malcolm. Lupita sent—'

'*Si, si, si.* Come in. Come in. I am Pedro, and this is Maria Claudia, my mother.'

Malcolm followed him in, through a little living room, Virgin of Guadaloupe on the wall, flat-screen TV, and out to a tiny patio with a wrought-iron table and chairs. He sat, Pedro sat. There was a silence. Into the silence a bird began to sing. Maria Claudia brought coffee, then sat on one of the wrought-iron chairs, a little away from the two men.

'Thank you,' Malcolm said to Maria Claudia. He took a few sips; it was dark and slightly bitter.

214

'So,' Pedro said, as if now they could begin.

Malcolm reached into his pocket and brought out the gold cross. He laid it on the wrought-iron table. 'For Chico,' he said, 'from Lupita.'

Maria Claudia gave a half sob.

Pedro looked stern. He pushed the cross away from him, towards Malcolm. 'I have told Lupita this several times. She doesn't want to believe me. You must make her believe this. Chico is not here. He never came here. I have not seen Chico for several months. No one I have spoken to in Naco or Agua Prieta has seen him either.'

'But she was so sure—' Malcolm began.

'Because she wanted to be,' said Pedro. 'Look, Chico isn't coming here. Chico is not a Mexican. He was never a Mexican. Chico is an American. Do you understand?'

'Yes,' said Malcolm, 'yes, I do.'

Driving back to Dudley, Malcolm was seized with a profound reluctance to go back to El Serape and tell Lupita what Pedro had said. Besides, according to Pedro, he'd already told her the same thing several times. He checked his watch. Only three, so she would definitely still be at the restaurant. He should stop in, tell her. Or maybe just text her. Yes. Texting her would be best.

Coward.

He drove to El Serape. Lupita was working the register, but no one was in line to pay. He told her what Pedro had told him.

'But, listen, I'll keep the cross, since I plan to keep on looking for him until I find him, okay?'

215

This, partly to calm her down. 'Tell me something: who is Chico close to? I mean, in the arts community?'

'Well—' She thought for a moment. 'Maybe the closest is Melody. She runs that Sail Rabbit Gallery.' She lowered her voice. 'We don't get along, me and Melody. She's kind of – I don't know – *phoney*.'

'Horrors,' said Malcolm. 'Well, gotta run.'

Malcolm got back in his car, drove to the Gulch. It was still early, and there was plenty of parking. He could kill two birds with one stone here. The Sail Rabbit Gallery was right down the street in one direction, and in the other direction was the St Elmo Bar and Sid the bartender. He thought he'd hit the Sail Rabbit Gallery first.

He got out of his truck. The air was dense and rich and smelled of licorice and tar and creosote. He walked into the Sail Rabbit Gallery. All along the walls hung Chico's bright crucified dolls. The place was empty except for a pale woman with dense black hair and red-framed glasses at a desk near the back, doing something on a laptop. She didn't look up when Malcolm walked in.

'Afternoon!' he said loudly.

She looked up then. 'Hi! How are you today?' Her voice was surprisingly sweet and archly accented.

'Fine, thanks. Are you Melody, by any chance?'

'I am. And you are—?'

'Name's Malcolm, Malcolm MacGregor. I'm an investigator working for Chico's attorney, Stuart Ross?'

'Oh,' she said. 'Oh, oh.' She stood up and came around the desk. She wore a red and black flowered mini dress, leggings and lace-up gladiator sandals. She held out her hand. 'I'm pleased to meet you.'

They shook.

Behind the red framed glasses, her eyes were warm yet somehow guarded. 'Have they found Chico yet?'

'No, they have not. Lupita said you were close to him, so I was wondering—'

'That Lupita.' Melody sighed. 'I really like her and all, but she's so *bossy*.'

'Be that as it may, I was wondering if you had any idea where he might be.'

'I don't.' Melody shook her head from side to side sadly. 'I wish I did, but I really really don't.'

Malcolm took out his card. 'Well, if you ever do, could you give me a call? I'm on his side, you know.'

Melody smiled dreamily. 'I know,' she said. 'Of course.'

He left the Sail Rabbit Gallery and strolled down Brewery Gulch, headed for the St Elmo Bar. In broad daylight the whole street was somehow faded. The regulars, who always hung out on the sidewalk and the street in front of the St Elmo, looked faded too. He went inside and sat at the end of the bar close to the door.

The sun streamed in through the small front windows in gold streaks but failed to penetrate very far. Eric Church was singing 'Springsteen'

217

on the jukebox, his twangy country voice full of long ago summers.

Sid came moseying down, shaved head agleam, still smiling at something one of the regulars had said to him. 'Sam Adams again?'

'You got it.' Malcolm waited until Sid came back with the beer, then he said, 'You okay about taking a look at something?'

'Sure thing.'

Malcolm had his cellphone out and ready. 'Remember the blonde you told me about, who was talking to Chico that night?'

Sid nodded.

'This her?'

Sid took the phone, held it up for the best light. He looked at it for a moment or so, taking a good look, then he handed it back. 'Nope. Not even close.'

'Damn,' said Malcolm, 'damn, damn, damn.'

He left the bar, called Kate's cellphone again, but got the same old voicemail. In a way the whole trip back east seemed unreal, an illusion that hadn't really happened. Had she stayed with Dakota last night? Was Harry Light really connected to what was going on with Kate? Simple enough, Malcolm was thinking: check and see where Harry Light was the night Kate's tires were blown out, where he was the night Kate arrived in New Jersey. Unless, of course, he'd hired someone to do the dirty work. Maybe an ex-con, like he'd been speculating, or maybe even some former student, who thought Harry Light was a genius and obeyed his every command.

Or Harry had nothing to do with any of this.

But he'd sent out feelers, done what he could for the moment, and as if in answer to his thoughts his cellphone chimed. An unfamiliar number.

'Malcolm here. Hello?'

'Hey, Mac, Dan here.'

'Dan—?'

'Dan Piper. The investigator. Anna Marie Romero.'

'Of course,' Malcolm said. 'Sorry.'

'Thought you'd be interested in knowing this – Anna Marie's mom, Cecilia?'

'Yeah?'

'I spoke with her, and she'll be happy to talk to you. She's coming to see relatives in Phoenix today. She gave me a number where you can call her once she arrives – sometime, say, after seven tonight. A landline, not a cell. She's got a cell, but she doesn't want to get called on it.'

'Interesting,' said Malcolm. 'And why doesn't she want to get called on her cell?'

'Like you said, interesting.'

He got off the phone, stared down the street at nothing. Why *did* Cecilia not want to get called on her cell? Because then there would be a record? What was she afraid of? Or who?

And then Kate called.

Thirty-One

'Cindy and I were married twelve, thirteen years. I met her when I was eighteen and she was seventeen,' Malcolm said. 'We were both freshmen at ASU.'

'ASU?' Kate asked.

'Arizona State University. It's in Mesa. She was from LA, actually. I thought she was wonderful: funny and sophisticated and unavailable. She had lots of guys after her. I was sort of her fallback guy, the one she confided in about her problems, which, back then, weren't especially serious. She'd had one bout of depression in high school, but she talked about it like it was a one-time thing.'

The evening was balmy, and they sat outside at the Copper Queen Hotel eating pasta and meatballs, linguine and clams.

Malcolm picked up the bottle of Merlot. 'More wine?'

'Just a little.'

He poured, poured some for himself.

'So you were college sweethearts,' Kate said.

'No, actually, we weren't. I got involved with someone else, and she got involved with a series of guys. I didn't see much of her after a while except from a distance.' He took a sip of wine. 'She kind of, I don't know – in my mind, when I think of her back then, she kind of glittered. Very animated, very—' He paused. '*Happy*.'

Kate took a very small sip of her wine. She'd already had half a glass to start with, and she didn't want to lose control. 'And—?'

'So we graduated, six, seven years went by, and I saw her again at a bookstore in Scottsdale. We started talking, you know, and it was like the time in between had never happened, except—' He shrugged.

'Except what?'

'We went out to lunch. She was different. That glitter she had seemed diminished. I asked her what was wrong, 'cause, you know, I could tell. She said she'd had a hard time, but she didn't really explain. But we reconnected, and I helped her through the hard time. She came out of it, thanks to me, the white knight, so I married her.'

The waitress came by, took away their empty plates. 'Dessert?'

Malcolm shook his head. 'None for me.'

'No, thank you,' Kate said.

'Just the bill.' Malcolm handed her his credit card.

They waited in silence for a moment, then Malcolm said, 'When I think about it sometimes, I wonder if I didn't marry that memory I had of Cindy when we first met. It stayed with me, all that sparkle, that glitter. That wonderful, wonderful smile. The smile—' He paused. 'It was probably what they call mania.'

'I'm sorry,' Kate said. She paused then went on. 'I guess my story's pretty simple – Hannah

221

showed up, Rick fell in love with her, and bam, it was over between us. No real sadness, no tragedy, you know? Just life.'

'And your job was over too,' Malcolm said. 'I'm sorry for *your* story. By the way, my friend got nowhere with the cellphone and IP trace.'

'Big surprise,' Kate said and shrugged, looked away from him, fiddling with her napkin – folding and unfolding it.

The bill appeared, Malcolm signed, looked at his watch. 'Time to make that phone call to Cecilia.'

Kate planned to stay at Dakota's that night, but they walked up to Kate's house to make the call. Inside, seeing it through Malcolm's eyes, it was obvious that no one really lived there. Nothing hanging on the walls, nothing personal that said Kate.

'It's a dump,' Kate said. 'I think it's the first place I've ever lived where I didn't go overboard fixing it up. It's like I can't settle on anything yet. Including—' she gave a little laugh – 'my life.'

He could just imagine how Cindy would have handled what Kate had gone through. Or maybe she would have been stronger, more able to deal with her life, had he not cushioned her every move.

'Before I call,' Malcolm said, 'I'd like to take a look around. See how secure this place is.'

'Sure.

Malcolm went from room to room, looking at the locks on the windows. At one point he laughed.

'What's so funny?'

'Nothing, nothing.' He checked the front door and the side door and the door to the porch inside and out. Then he came back in.

He started to punch in the number Dan Piper had given him but stopped, went outside where the reception was better. Kate stayed inside.

It rang a few times, then a man answered. Malcolm asked for Cecilia Romero.

'Hold on.'

'Hello?' It was a soft voice, sweet. 'This is Cecilia.'

Malcolm explained who he was.

'Yes. Detective Piper told me all about you. I mean, that you're all right,' she said. 'A man in law enforcement too. Otherwise we wouldn't even be talking. He said it was about Harry Light? Harry and my daughter, Anna Marie?'

'Yes. You've met him, I think Dan said. He and Anna Marie were dating?'

She gave a little sigh, exasperated. 'Like I told the police and everyone else, what they're referring to was a while before Anna Marie disappeared. And, besides, they weren't *dating* exactly. They were good friends, is all.'

'You never saw him as possibly a suspect in her disappearance?'

'No. No, I did not.'

'Why is that?'

'He was a very nice man, a gentleman.'

'That's not what I hear.'

'From who?'

'An old girlfriend. She's scared of him.'

'*Really.*' There was a pause. 'You know, people

223

have bad spells and good spells. Maybe she just knew him at the wrong time.'

'Maybe.'

'Who is this old girlfriend?' Cecilia asked.

'I'm sorry. I just don't feel comfortable saying.'

There was another pause, longer this time. Malcolm wondered if she'd hung up in disgust, but then she said, 'I can't talk to you like this on the phone. Are you far from Phoenix? Could you come here maybe tomorrow or the day after, and we can talk in person.'

'I could do that,' Malcolm said.

'And bring the old girlfriend too,' said Cecilia. 'I could tell her some things in person I can't say on the phone.'

'I'll talk to her about that,' said Malcolm.

'Me? She wants to talk to me? Why?' Kate said. 'You *told* her about me?'

'Not really. I just mentioned an old girlfriend, and she said to bring you, that she could tell you some things in person she couldn't say on the phone.'

'Really? Like what, I wonder?'

'She didn't say. But the two of you can compare notes about Harry.'

'Did she say anything at all about Harry? I mean, does she suspect him of – you know.'

'She said, and I quote – "He was a very nice man, a gentleman."'

'*What?*'

'Maybe someone was listening to the conversation and she was covering up. I'm going up there tomorrow. I think you should come along. She might be more forthcoming with you there.'

Kate nodded, a little doubtfully.

'Mesa is my old stomping grounds, just outside of Phoenix. My brother Ian lives close by in Tempe. We could go up the day before, stay at his place.'

'At your brother's?'

'It's fine. He's an attorney, and so's his wife, Sally. They have a five year old, Shawn.' He spread his hands wide. 'Utterly respectable. You could sleep in the spare bedroom. I'd sleep on the couch. We could go to a nice restaurant. A movie, maybe.'

'Actually,' said Kate, 'it sounds nice.'

'And you could use a vacation.' He paused. 'I mean, a real one. I was a cop in Mesa, so I know the Force—' He waved his arm in a wide sweep, as if by knowing the Force they were all at his command. 'You'll be safe. I have to be honest with you, I don't feel you're safe now. Are you staying at Dakota's again tonight?'

'Yes.'

'Good. At this point anyone can get into your house if they want to. When we come back from Phoenix, we can talk about making it more secure.'

Thirty-Two

The traffic thickened. They'd left Dudley after lunch so Kate could put in some time at the Co-op, and now it was nearly time to start

225

thinking about dinner. It had been a long drive, more than three hours, the I10 to Tucson then on to Phoenix, through a barren landscape of red dust, with giant lumbering trucks to the left and giant lumbering trucks to the right, the sky above bright blue and cloudless.

Malcolm had called Cecilia back last night, and they had arranged to meet her tomorrow morning at ten o'clock at a Denny's in Mesa.

'A Denny's?' Kate had said in surprise.

'Well, why not?'

Now, in the present, Kate turned her neck from side to side and up and down to loosen up.

'Almost there,' Malcolm said. 'Want to stop and stretch?'

'No. Let's just do it.'

The landscape changed; shopping malls appeared, motels, endless developments of low stucco buildings with red tiled roofs and lots of palm trees.

'That's the motel,' Malcolm said suddenly. 'Over on the right.'

'What motel?'

'Where Cindy died.'

'How did you say?' Though he never had.

'She took a bunch of pills.'

Kate stared out the window. It looked like all motels – like the motel where she'd stayed in New Jersey, for instance. Then it was behind them. There had been nothing to distinguish it from all the other motels they had passed on the crowded freeway going into Phoenix.

She tried to imagine Cindy – hadn't Malcolm mentioned once that she was a blonde? – checking into the motel. When you made a decision like Cindy had, what happened to vanity? What would you wear at a time like that – would you care how you looked when your body was found? What about make-up? Would you freshen up a little before you took the pills?

Malcolm took a Tempe exit off the I10, headed for his brother Ian's house. They went down a couple of side roads, turned some more, and they were in a development, but a nice one – upscale beige stucco, the ubiquitous red tiled roofs, desert plant landscaping – the usual Southwestern look, but the houses, at least from the outside, looked big and airy.

They pulled into the driveway of a corner house. A tall sandy-haired man in khakis and a blue polo shirt, accompanied by a little boy in a baseball cap, came out of the front door almost at once, as if they'd been hiding behind the curtains looking out.

Malcolm parked, and they got out of the car.

'Uncle Malcolm, Uncle Malcolm, Uncle Malcolm, Schmalcom, Halcom!' the little boy shouted. He wiggled his body around in a little jiggly dance. Then he suddenly noticed Kate. He stopped, turned to his father. 'Who's she?'

'This is my friend Kate,' Malcolm said. 'Kate, this is my nephew Shawn and my brother Ian.'

'It's a pleasure to meet you,' Ian said to Kate. 'Come inside, come inside.'

Shawn walked next to Kate. They went through a short hall and into the living room, Southwest art, Indian pots, nice kilim rugs.

'Sally, my wife,' Ian said, looking at Kate,

227

'should be back any minute. She's at the grocery store getting something for dinner. You guys are joining us, I assume?'

'Actually,' Malcolm said. 'I thought Kate and I would just go out to eat.'

'Why would you want to do that?' Ian said. 'When you can stay in and eat a home-cooked meal?'

And you can check out Kate, Malcolm thought. He'd told his brother she was just a friend.

'What do you think, Kate?' Ian said.

'A home-cooked meal sounds wonderful,' said Kate dutifully, just as she imagined she was expected to.

'Sit, sit.' Ian gestured at a big white couch.

Kate sat, and Shawn sat down beside her.

'Looks like you've got a fan,' Ian said to Kate.

Shawn grinned and ducked his head.

'Can I get you guys something to drink? Raspberry iced tea, Kate? Beer? Beer for you, Malcolm, right?'

'Iced tea's good,' said Kate.

Ian left the room.

'Be right back,' Malcolm said, following him out.

'Want to see me when I was just a little kid?' Shawn said to Kate.

'Sure.'

'Over here.'

Kate followed Shawn to a table to one side of a white brick fireplace. The fireplace was filled with an arty arrangement of dead branches, the table with silver framed photographs.

228

'Here.' Shawn thrust a frame at her. 'Me and my mom.'

A pretty woman with dark straight bangs held a baby in her arms and smiled triumphantly, as if she just accomplished a major achievement, and maybe she had.

'Very nice,' said Kate. 'Sally? That's your mom's name?'

'Yes.'

She moved closer to the table. More pictures of Sally with the dark bangs and Ian and Shawn, Shawn in different sizes. Birthday parties and Christmas; picnics and barbecues. One of Malcolm grinning at someone and, aha, one of Malcolm with a blonde woman.

Kate picked up the frame. 'And who's this?' she asked, all innocence.

'My aunt Cindy,' Shawn whispered.

Kate held the frame closer: a head shot of Malcolm and Cindy, Malcolm younger looking, Cindy with short blonde hair, well cut, face with classic features, tip of a tennis racket showing by her shoulder. What does a photograph say? – how someone looked at one split second in time, nothing more.

'She got really sad,' Shawn confided. 'My aunt Cindy got sadder and sadder and sadder, and one day she got so sad she went away, and she's never coming back.'

'I'm sorry to hear that,' Kate said.

'So are you and my uncle getting married?'

The front door opened then, and the woman from the photographs came in, carrying a load of groceries. She smiled. 'You must be Kate.'

Kate smiled back. 'And you must be Sally.'

'So, are you?' asked Shawn, in a louder voice. 'Are you? Are you?'

'What are you going on about, Shawn?' Sally said.

'I just want Kate to answer my question.'

'Not now,' his mother said. 'Go find your dad, okay.'

Shawn ran out of the room.

'What was that all about?' Sally asked Kate.

'Nothing.'

It was such a pleasant evening, but then practically every evening in Phoenix was pleasant, once the sun went down. The sky was streaked with orange and blue and indigo, purple mountains in the distance. They ate out back on the patio at a picnic table near the barbecue grill. Along with the steaks, there was roasted corn and roasted portobello mushrooms and roasted eggplant.

'Ian's on a roasting kick,' Sally had explained to Kate. 'But I can make a salad if you like.'

'No, I'm fine.'

Earlier, Sally had asked Kate if she'd rather have steak or salmon. 'I'm so into omega three,' she said.

'Actually,' Kate told her, 'I'd like steak. I haven't had steak in such a long time.'

Malcolm had planned for dinner at a restaurant, some place nice, so Kate could see he had good taste, but he saw now this family dinner had been unavoidable from the start. There was an excitement in the air that made Malcolm uncomfortable – Ian and Sally and Shawn all checking out Kate,

230

wondering what was going on. As for himself, he had no idea. But there they were, his relatives, wondering if Kate was The One – the woman who would replace Cindy and give Malcolm a real life.

They'd never liked Cindy, not really. Their condolences, their sympathy had grown more and more strained with each episode: bored with her pain and what seemed like her endless needy drama.

'So, how's the steak?' Ian asked Kate. 'Rare enough for you?'

'Perfect,' Kate said. 'Everything's perfect, the eggplant, the corn, the mushrooms.'

Malcolm watched as Kate ate her steak. It was quite large steak; he'd offered to split it with her, but she said no, that was okay, she was pretty hungry. A large, rare steak, oozing blood all over her plate. She ate it with verve, with gusto, and finished it off. She also ate an ear of corn, a few slabs of eggplant and several grilled mushrooms.

'I love that you're eating everything,' Sally said. 'It makes the cooks feel worthwhile.'

'Hold still!' Shawn said. 'I'm taking a picture with Malcolm's camera.'

Everyone held very still, grinning: one split second in time, nothing more.

Thirty-Three

'Just coffee for me,' Malcolm told the waitress at Denny's the next morning. 'We had a pretty big breakfast,' he said to Cecilia, 'at my brother's house.'

'I think,' said Kate as she perused the menu, 'I'll have a waffle, just one, with a side of bacon. Oh, and a small orange juice.'

'Coffee?' asked the waitress.

'Yes, please.'

The waitress took the menus and left.

Cecilia smiled at Kate. 'So thin,' she said, 'and such a good appetite. You're a lucky lady.'

'Thank you,' Kate said politely.

Cecilia was plump, ever so slightly, with dark curly hair and skin soft as a crumpled rose. She wore black capri pants and a black T-shirt with a silver moon and silver stars appliquéd on it. She'd already arrived when they got there, sitting in a booth at the back with an English muffin and a cup of tea. She'd waved, as if she had already met them and knew what they looked like.

'Well,' Malcolm said as they waited for their orders. 'Here we are. It's a pleasure to meet you, Cecilia, and I guess we're meeting you here in person because there were things you couldn't say on the phone. What were they, exactly?'

But Cecilia was looking at Kate. 'Malcolm said you were an old girlfriend of Harry's?'

'Yes. Not that old a girlfriend, really; it's only been close to three months since I left. But we weren't together very long.'

'Ah,' said Cecilia. 'Then maybe that explains it.'

'Explains what?'

She sighed. 'Let me start from the beginning. Maybe you've met my Anna Marie? She's known Harry for over a year.'

'No.' Kate flushed, glanced at Malcolm. 'I just knew of her, is all. It struck me she might be more to Harry than just his student. I saw them talking once outside, after one of his workshops.'

'She was maybe more to Harry than just a student,' Cecilia said, 'but not the way you're thinking. His workshops were very good. Or so Anna Marie told me. They helped her see things, she said.'

'Ah,' said Kate. 'I took one of his workshops once in Vermont. I thought it helped me see things too, but in the end it didn't. Not really. Harry's kind of, I don't know – a flimflam man.'

'Yes,' said Cecilia, 'I understand. The relationship you had with him, it was not so good.'

Kate nodded. 'Well, sometimes it was, especially in the beginning. But he started having these rages. He would throw things and yell at people for nothing at all. There didn't seem to be any reason for it. I found myself tensing up all the time, kind of anticipating.'

Cecilia nodded. 'I understand very well. But I've never seen Harry like that. Go on.'

'I was tired of being tense all the time. If I tried to talk about anything with him that he didn't agree with, he would just get mad, so finally one day when he was at a class I packed up everything I had and just drove away.'

'And you didn't tell him you were leaving?'

'No.'

'Really? Why not?'

Kate stared at Cecilia. 'I was afraid of him. When he went into a rage he was a different person, not like the Harry you're talking about.'

'But now you're still thinking about him. This—' She glanced at Malcolm. 'This *detective* here wants to investigate my daughter's disappearance. You're wondering if Harry did something to my daughter.'

'Yes. Look, someone seems to be after me right now. Someone shot at my car, someone— It's a long story. I left Harry so abruptly, and now, with Anna Marie missing, I'm wondering, well, you know . . .'

'I don't know.' Cecilia sat straight up in the booth. 'Let me tell you something – Harry was never ever anything but a gentleman to my girl. He always treated her very lovingly.'

The waitress brought the coffee, the waffle, the side of bacon. Kate pushed the bacon towards Malcolm, towards Cecilia. 'I only want one slice,' she said.

Malcolm took some bacon.

Cecilia did not. She watched as Kate smeared butter on the waffle, a little jam, and took a bite. Cecilia pushed her own plate away – about half the English muffin was uneaten. Everyone sat silently watching Kate eat her waffle.

'They wait,' said Cecilia suddenly, 'until you trust them. This certain kind of man. The man I married, such a temper. Not just with me but with Anna Marie too. And so jealous. For no reason, for nothing. I *know* my husband had something to do with my little girl disappearing, and—'

'I understand he was a suspect,' Malcolm broke in for the first time, 'but nothing ever came of it.'

'Yes. In confidence, in strictest confidence, I talked to Detective Piper.' Cecilia shrugged. 'I still have to live with my husband, you know. We've had *good* things together too. He's a sad man in many ways. And besides, I still love him.'

There was a silence.

'I'm sorry. We can't keep talking about this in such a public place,' Cecilia said. She stood up. 'Look out the window,' she said, 'at the parking lot. I saw you pull in. My car is parked right down from there – the green Toyota Corolla. I'm leaving as soon as I pay, and I want you to follow my car.'

They followed the green Toyota Corolla out of the parking lot at Denny's and down the street to the light just before the freeway. Cecilia signaled then, and they followed on to the ramp and on to the freeway.

'So, what do you think?' Malcolm asked Kate.

'She's a very nice lady who was conned by Harry. Like I said, a flimflam man.'

'My impression,' Malcolm said, 'is that she thinks her husband had something to do with Anna Marie's disappearance, but she's too afraid of him to deal with it properly.'

'Do you think this is smart?' Kate asked. 'Following her?'

'Sure. Why not?' Malcolm slowed and merged into the right lane so he was right behind the green Toyota.

'I don't know.'

'I think,' said Malcolm, 'that it's the right thing to do. I'm going to follow this woman – after all, don't forget she got in touch with me on the recommendation of a fellow police officer. She clearly has something to tell us other than what a gentleman Harry Light is, and I want to hear what it is.'

Cecilia took the second exit down, stopped at a light.

'Do you think you'll go back to that?' Kate asked.

'Back to what?'

'Being a detective.'

Malcolm laughed. He laughed and laughed.

'Stop that!' Kate said. 'Why are you laughing?'

'Because.'

Cecilia turned left at the La Quinta Motel, then right at the Days Inn. They went down a block, past a Circle K, and turned again on to another street, this time a side street that seemed primarily residential.

'Because why?' Kate persisted.

'Because you asked me if I'd ever be a detective again.'

'And?'

'Well, look at me,' Malcolm said. 'I'm following this woman – basically doing an investigation. I even brought my gun, just in case. And I'm feeling a whole lot happier than I have for months. Plus it certainly beats watching birds and drinking too much Sam Adams beer.'

They passed house after house, all essentially the same stucco and red tiled roofs. The small yards were planted with stands of bright red cannas, magenta bougainvillea reached almost to the red tiles, shrines to the Virgin of Guadaloupe. The green Toyota Corolla kept going.

'I notice all this scary stuff doesn't seem to have hurt your appetite,' Malcolm commented.

'What's that supposed to mean?'

'Take it at face value.'

She wanted to say she wasn't scared when she was with him, but he might take it wrong. What taking it wrong might entail, she didn't really know. 'Where *is* your gun, anyway?' she asked.

'In my shoulder holster.'

Kate blinked. 'Wow,' she said. 'You know, I don't think I've ever been in a car with a man who had a gun on him.'

She was silent then as they followed the Toyota Corolla down another street, one more turn, then it slowed and turned into the driveway of a small house, a pretty house, the stucco painted a rose pink, blue trim on the door, with a gray Ford Explorer in the driveway. The Toyota pulled in and parked right behind the Ford Explorer, and Malcolm parked on the street a little past the driveway. They watched as Cecilia got out of the car and stood beside it, looking over at them.

A couple of kids skateboarded towards them down the sidewalk. They waved at Cecilia as they whizzed by. Cecilia beckoned at Malcolm's car.

'Tell you what,' Malcolm said. 'I'm going to go inside with Cecilia, and you stay here.'

'Why?'

'Just to be on the safe side. Is your cell on?'

'Yes. No. It needs to be charged.'

'Here, take mine,' Malcolm said. 'Press here—' he showed her – 'and you get nine one one.'

'Nine one one? Why?'

'Just a precaution.'

'Look, I don't want you to do anything you think is dangerous.'

'I don't think this is dangerous. I think it's just fine, but I still want you to lock the doors and wait. I'll come out and motion for you to come in once I've checked it out.'

Kate laughed. 'You mean once the area is secured?'

He opened the door of the truck and got out. 'How is it,' he asked before he closed the door, 'that you can go from stark terror to casual jokes in the space of a couple of seconds?'

It was one of those questions that didn't seem to require an answer. Kate watched as he went up the driveway. She saw Cecilia glance over at the car, then both of them walked up the sidewalk and Cecilia opened the door. They vanished inside.

Thirty-Four

Kate waited. She waited and watched as a mom with a stroller meandered down the other side of the street and a big red truck drove by – a low rider with fat tires and hip hop music blaring out. The two young boys on skateboards whizzed by again. She longed for her iPod, but it had run down too and needed to be charged. All she had was Malcolm's cellphone.

With pictures. Ian, Sally, Malcolm and herself at the table, all red-eyed and with foolish grins except for Sally who looked worried. She went back quickly through the cellphone pictures. Here was a dark picture, you couldn't tell what it was at all, then one of an angry-looking blonde woman in what appeared to be a store, and then some pictures of what seemed to be back yards in Dudley, more people, their faces ghostlike.

She went back more and found, of course, Cindy. This time full length in running shoes and shorts. She was smiling; she didn't look sad at all, but bright and shining. Maybe she was in a mania phase. Or maybe she had decided. Kate had heard somewhere that when people finally made the decision to kill themselves, they felt really happy.

But where was Malcolm? Should she start to worry? How long had he been inside? Why hadn't he said something like 'wait fifteen minutes then call the cops'? She wished she'd looked at her watch when he'd gone inside. She didn't really know how long he'd been gone, and time went by at an artificially slow pace when you were stuck in a car waiting.

Then a thought came to her, out of the blue. *All I have to do*, she thought, *is accept that no matter what happens in my life sooner or later I'm going to die.*

Then all at once the blue front door of the rose-colored house opened, and Malcolm came out. He was smiling. He beckoned to her. Kate got out of the car. She walked towards the front door, Malcolm smiling at her all the way.

'What's so funny, anyway?' she said.

'You'll see.'

He took her arm, an unnecessary gesture, and led her into the house. From somewhere inside she heard people talking and laughing. They walked through a slightly disheveled living room – saltillo tile, red curtains at the windows – down a short hall and into a kitchen: a fairly large kitchen dominated by an oilcloth-covered table. Five or six people were sitting around the table, Cecilia at the closest end.

She smiled when she saw Kate.

'Cecilia can do the introductions,' Malcolm said.

'Of course.' She stood up. 'Everyone, this is Kate, and Kate, over there is Chuey, and next to him is Ben, with his true love, Emily, and next to Emily is Belen, and next to Belen, I'm pleased to introduce my daughter, Anna Marie Romero.'

'*What?*' said Kate.

Anna Marie stood up. Kate recognized her then. Tall and pretty in jeans and a red peasant blouse.

'I don't understand,' Kate said.

'It's simple, actually,' said Anna Marie. 'Come outside where it's quieter, and I'll explain it to you.'

'My father?' said Anna Marie outside. She was so pretty, her dark hair like a cloud around her

240

head. 'For years and years he abused me, not like, um, sex, you understand, just yelling, and sometimes he'd hit me. He always had some reason for hitting me, like I was always bad, and for a long time I believed him.'

They were sitting on a small patio at the back of the house, on white plastic chairs at a wooden picnic table. Bright-pink bougainvillea spilled over the high bamboo fence, and bees buzzed in a cloud of purple verbena.

'I'm sorry,' said Kate. 'How awful. But you were still living at home when you, um, disappeared.' She was careful to make it a statement not an accusing kind of question.

'He hit my mom sometimes too. I wanted to look after her. But she said, *no, no, you leave, Anna Marie. I know how to handle him*. But I was afraid – I thought he would come to where I was living and kill me. And it's kind of hard to explain but, you see, staying home, at least I knew where he was.'

'Yes,' said Kate.

'And then I went to this poetry workshop, and there was Harry, teaching people how to write poetry. He was so warm, so interested in everything. We started seeing each other, not like dates, really, more like talks.' She paused. 'You were his girlfriend once, my mom said. I think he told me about you.'

'You *think*?'

'He didn't use a name. I was telling him about my father, and it came up – he said he was so ashamed and sorry about the way he acted when you were together.'

There was a silence. Kate looked away from Anna Marie at the pink bougainvillea spilling over the bamboo fence. She wanted to leave, to go back home, not listen to Harry apologize for his behavior through a surrogate.

'He said he didn't mean it as an excuse,' Anna Marie went on, 'but he was taking antidepressants, you know?'

'No,' said Kate, 'I didn't know.'

'He used to be a drinker then he went to AA. He got sober, but then he got depressed. I think he was maybe a little ashamed. But he'd been taking them for a while, and then his doctor switched him to a new kind. The pills worked really well, except he'd suddenly blow up, out of the blue, for no reason.'

Kate sighed. 'My question to you,' she said, 'is how long did you know him? He listened to all my problems too, in the beginning. He's good at that.'

'I'm telling you this,' said Anna Marie, her voice rising, 'because my mom said you thought Harry might have murdered me when I went missing. Well, you were wrong. He didn't. Here I am.'

'Does he know you're talking to me?'

'He saved my life, Kate. We worked out this whole plan together for me to get away from my father. He set it all up, got me a place in Phoenix with people he knew 'cause it was risky to stay with my relatives. He met me where I abandoned my car, and we drove here together, to Phoenix.'

There was a silence. Somewhere inside the house Kate heard people laughing.

242

'It was a big risk for him,' Anna Marie said. 'It hurt his reputation, having the people question him and all, but he did it anyway.'

'Do you still see him?

'Yes.' She laughed. 'He comes to Phoenix every now and then, and we have a deal. I have to make him *chili rellenos*. I'm not even a good cook, but he has this idea that all *Chicanas* are good cooks, and if he wants to be prejudiced, you know what? I forgive him.'

Afterwards Malcolm and Kate stopped in to pick up their stuff at Ian and Sally's, who of course weren't there, but they'd left a few things for Malcolm, including an iPod dock.

'If you don't want that,' Kate said, 'I'll take it.'

'Sure.'

They drove the long drive back from Phoenix. The Sierra Vista exit, the one they would take to Dudley, was coming up on the right. Malcolm put on his turn signal and switched lanes. The sun was getting lower in the sky, putting a glare on the windshield.

Malcolm took the exit and turned into the McDonald's parking lot. 'I need to stretch,' he said. 'Want anything – coffee, Coke, a snack?'

'Nothing.'

They got out together, walked around. Other than the cluster of fast food chains, there was only the desert that stretched away to purple mountains. The desert and, of course, the freeway, close by, cars and pickup trucks and big rigs lumbering along. Or appeared to be lumbering along; they were all going seventy-five, eighty-five miles an hour. If any living thing should step in front of them they would be killed instantly.

All around them was cement, sparse grass, six or seven or maybe even eight other fast food chains and a replica of a dinosaur in front of the McDonald's. A Triceratops? A Tyrannosaurus Rex?

'Here's the plan,' Malcolm said. 'You can stay at Dakota's tonight, or if you want to go home then I'll be more than willing to sleep on your couch with my gun.'

'That would be good,' Kate said.

'You're working tomorrow?'

'Yes.'

'I'm going to Tucson tomorrow to talk to Dr Paul Sanger.'

'Who's that?'

'An old friend of Wes and Carrie, according to Carrie's sister Rose, and also a friend of Polly Hampton, Wes's daughter. He came to Chico's release hearing. I didn't talk to him then. I should be back late afternoon. We can have dinner together, and I'll tell you what I find out.'

They got back in the truck. Everything was decided, as if they'd needed this particular landscape to decide on things.

Thirty-Five

Malcolm woke up on the lumpy couch in the living room of Kate's fully furnished rented house

244

to the sound of someone singing. French, it was French. Malcolm had a smattering of it from freshman semester in college.

'*Maman les p'tits bateaux. Qui vont sur l'eau*—' Kate. Kate was singing. '*Ont-ils des jambes?*'

He sat up, tried not to groan, swung his feet to the floor. His gun was on the coffee table. What—? Oh, yeah.

'*Mais oui*,' Kate sang on, '*mon gros bêta*—'

Malcolm went in the direction of the singing. Kate was in the kitchen, spooning coffee. '*S'ils n'en avaient pas. Ils ne march'raient pas.*' She looked happy.

'You're French,' he said. 'You never told me you were French.'

'My mother lived in France for a while when she was a girl,' said Kate. 'She liked to sing me that song about a little boat.'

'And where is she now, your mom?'

'She died. Three years ago. I miss her.'

But she looked happy. He realized he hadn't ever actually seen Kate looking happy.

Malcolm timed his trip to Tucson so he would get to the medical plaza off Oracle a little before lunchtime when, he hoped, the doctor would be free.

In the office, babies were crying. A red-haired middle-aged woman came to the sliding window and slid it open. 'Hi there! How can I help you?'

'I'm not a patient—' he began.

The woman's mouth twitched. 'Yes,' she said. 'I can see that.'

Malcolm smiled. 'My name's Malcolm

245

MacGregor. The doctor doesn't know me, but we have a friend in common, Rose Kelly. She suggested I look him up, and I'm only in town briefly. I was hoping, maybe during his lunch hour, I could have a word.'

'Hold on.'

Babies cried some more, mothers fussed. The woman came back in a minute. 'Half an hour – he'll meet you out in the courtyard by the fountain. How's that?'

'Just fine.'

Malcolm went and sat in the courtyard. Birds twittered. A lizard did push-ups on the rim of the fountain. From time to time Malcolm glanced at his watch. Half an hour went by, forty-five minutes, then just at the hour a man carrying a brown paper bag came out of Dr Paul Sanger's office. He wore a pink shirt and khakis and didn't look like the man Malcolm had seen in the court-room because he was wearing wire-rimmed glasses, instead of the big black ones. Malcolm imagined somewhere a Mrs Sanger, saying, '*Honey, you've got to get rid of those ugly glasses.*'

'Dr Paul Sanger?' Malcolm said.

'Yes. Malcolm MacGregor, I assume.' He smiled, shook Malcolm's hand and sat down beside him. 'Excuse me if I eat lunch. I only have half an hour.' He opened the bag. The pungent smell of tuna fish wafted over.

'It's terrible about Wes and Carrie. But you mention gun control in this state, and everyone gets up in arms, ha ha.' He paused. 'Sorry. Stupid, terrible joke. Or was it a joke? I'm not sure.' He took a few bites of his sandwich.

246

After a moment or so he said, 'Sweet Rose. So, how's she doing?'

'Very sad.'

He nodded. 'I can imagine. Carrie and Rose were pretty close. And how do you know Rose?'

Malcolm explained. He explained at great length: he described Chico and his grieving sister Lupita, he explained the circumstance of the murders and his thoughts on the matter as a police officer. It seemed the best way to gain support, sympathy, the man being a doctor and all.

'Huh.' Dr Sanger looked away, at some spot to the left of Malcolm's shoulder, as if there were something there of great interest. A large bird, maybe? Or a beautiful woman? Malcolm turned his head, looked too, but saw nothing in particular.

'Well,' said Dr Sanger after a while, 'it's plausible what you're saying about this Chico, about everything. I just don't know. Like Rose, I feel very sad. I hadn't seen Wes and Carrie for quite a while. They were planning to stop by to see me, after Dudley, then—' He stopped, shrugged.

'What about Polly? Were they going to see her?'

Dr Sanger gave him a look. 'No, but leave Polly out of this, all right?'

'Why is that?'

'Surely Rose told you they were estranged.'

'I know Polly didn't like Carrie. But how estranged exactly were they?'

'No, no, no.' Dr Sanger shook his head

vehemently. 'We're not going there. Please. Polly's a good person who's been hurt. She loved her mother dearly, and Carrie—' He shrugged.

'Drugs? Could they have had some involvement with drugs?'

He laughed. 'I don't know what Wes and Carrie were doing with their lives, but I'm pretty sure it had nothing to do with drugs.' He sighed. 'I just can't imagine them getting murdered. For God's sake, who would do it? It has to have been a mistake.'

'What were they like, as people? Was Wes combative, argumentative? Did he make enemies easily?'

'No, no. He was pretty mellow. Good athlete in high school. And Carrie—' He sighed again.

'What about her?'

'She was very beautiful in high school.'

'Like how? Seductive?'

'You could say that. I don't know if it was intentional, but she came across as seductive and withholding. You know. I have to admit back then I had a big crush on her. We all did. She had several long-term relationships, I understand, but I'd moved away by then and didn't keep track. She never married until Wes . . . And I think she really loved him. I know she did.'

'They lived so far away from here,' said Malcolm. 'So far you're the only person connected to them who's shown an interest in actively following the case.'

'What do you mean?'

'Just that I saw you in the courtroom at the

release hearing. Not that I would have recognized you if I saw you on the street, what with those new glasses.'

Dr Sanger laughed politely, the way people do when you make a joke they don't get but don't want to hurt your feelings. 'What new glasses,' he said, 'and what release hearing?'

'Chico's, of course.'

'I never went to any hearing for Chico. Why would you think I did?' asked Dr Sanger.

Malcolm was stunned. 'Because whoever it was gave your name to the security guard.'

'No shit?' said Dr Sanger, reverting to high school. 'That's weird.'

'Damn!' Malcolm said. 'The glasses. That was all you saw. Big black glasses. Who could it have been, I wonder?'

'No one I can think of. They were from back east, you know? It might have been, what do you call it, a lookie lou? Wow. You kind of caught me by surprise. I'll have to think on it.' He paused, reached in his pocket and handed Malcolm a card. 'Send me an email at the address on the card, and then I'll have yours.'

'Better yet, I'll give you my card,' Malcolm said. 'Just let me know if something comes to mind.'

'He slept on your couch with a *gun*?' said Windsong, his voice hushed as he stood with Kate in the produce section. He dumped a bunch of wilted chard into a bucket.

'Yes,' said Kate. 'I wasn't scared at all. He's in Tucson now, but he should be back by the time I get off work here at six. Then we're going to dinner, then he's going to burglar-proof the house. Aren't these—?'

'What?'

'The strawberries – they look like the ones I picked up.'

'No one,' said Windsong, '*no one* can tell one strawberry from another.'

'I meant the thingy that they're in.'

'They are the same,' said Windsong. 'We went through and picked out the good ones that weren't battered. We sold most of them, but – looks like what's left will have to go. Unless—' he grinned, holding one up, browning at the tip – 'you'd like one as a souvenir.'

God damn it, Malcolm thought as he drove away from the medical complex, I didn't notice, I didn't really look at the man who called himself Paul Sanger. I only saw his glasses, and I'm a cop, goddamn it. Who the hell was he, then?

He stopped at a fast food place, then changed his mind and went to a Mexican restaurant instead. He had time before he had to drive back to Dudley where he was supposed to meet with Kate at her house after she got off work. The restaurant had been recommended to him by Lupita – *if you're ever in Tucson,* she'd said, weeks ago.

God, Lupita, Chico. It was such a lame case against him, but proving motive was not a requirement in a trial, and there was still the cold hard fact of him holding the gun that did it. He didn't buy it, but a jury might. And maybe Chico

250

was better at handling a gun than anyone knew; maybe he'd had training, even – from, say, a drug cartel? And maybe he was a psychopath – hey, people were. Psychopaths could be good at seeming normal, sometimes even better than normal people.

And where the hell was Chico, anyway?

Malcolm sat in a black leather booth at the restaurant and ordered two green chili burritos, refried beans and fries, thinking, while he waited, about Wes and Carrie and their blameless lives. He knew better than that – no one's life was blameless – but still it seemed to him now that the murders must have been a case of mistaken identity, the wrong couple shot.

Which meant there would be no clues, no leads contained in the lives of the victims.

Then Kate – who was after Kate? He could see no connection between Kate and the Coopers. He'd had hopes about Hairy Lite, but not so much any more. Though, of course, you never knew. And that empty house bit – too bizarre. She had that ex in Vermont, maybe mad at her, but why? He'd cheated on *her.* Or so Kate said. Was Kate being straight with him?

Maybe there were things in her life she didn't want anyone to know about. The kind of things that get someone killed. Like what? What, what? His brain felt numb with thinking. Let it go. Let it go. It was his experience that answers often came when you stopped asking questions.

The order came. Excellent, down to the greasy as all hell fries. On impulse he called Kate's cell. He knew she kept it off when she was at work, but just in case. Just to tell her what he'd found out – nothing. Just to hear the sound of her voice. To make sure she was still alive.

He got her voicemail, didn't bother leaving a message.

He had the card for the real estate guy back in Jersey who was managing the house on Roscommon Drive, so maybe when he got back in town he would be helpful. The other real estate agent had said: what? He couldn't remember exactly, but soon. He should be back soon, maybe, even now. Yeah, sure, maybe he was back now. Maybe, maybe, maybe – what the hell. He pulled the card and punched in the real estate guy's number.

A woman answered. 'Hello?'

'Steve Anderson? Is he there?'

'This is his wife. Is this a client?'

'No. I had some question about a house he's showing, and—'

'I just asked if you were client,' she said. 'It sounds to me like you are. Look, he's been doing a lot of traveling, and he's exhausted. He fell asleep on the couch, and I answered his cell. Can't this wait? He'll be back in his office tomorrow.'

'Yes,' said Malcolm. 'It can wait. Thank you.'

He finished his lunch, left the restaurant, got in his truck and sat in the parking lot for a few minutes, staring out at the red and green Dos Equus sign in the window of the restaurant. The real estate guy had actually met this other guy who'd probably stolen the key and left it for Kate. Steve Anderson could be the key to figuring

252

out this empty house thing. He sat, wondering just how to handle Steve when he talked to him. He didn't want him to freak out or close down. It was hard on a phone; you didn't have as much subliminal information.

Then he started up the truck and got on Oracle, headed for the freeway, feeling a bit of semi-euphoria from eating good Mexican food and the fact he would be talking to a new lead tomorrow. A busy man with a life. But at the same time he kept thinking that something had to start making sense pretty soon, didn't it?

More and more he had the feeling that he was missing the big picture – and it had nothing to do with either Harry Light or Chico. Right now it looked like talking to this realtor was maybe his best bet, but you could never—

And who the hell was the guy in the Buddy Holly glasses?

Thinking so hard, he didn't even notice the guy who ran the red light, the guy in the battered pickup that was coming right at him. Then he did notice, enough to turn the wheel, but too late.

Kate drove to work that day, and around four she made a quick run to the post office – she hadn't checked her mail since she'd been back. Her box was jammed full, and they'd saved the rest in a box. She went back to work leaving the box on the passenger seat, and it was still there when she stopped off at the Circle K before she went home after work to gas up her car. She hadn't had the energy to go look through it; it was mostly catalogs, anyway.

After she gassed up her car at the Circle K she went inside to pick up some Sam Adams beer. It was the least she could do. When Malcolm got to her house, if he wasn't there already – she'd left it unlocked for him – it would be nice to be able to offer him a beer. And she had a pretty good quality frozen pizza in her freezer if it came to that. Or they might even go out to eat.

Back in her car she checked her cell. It looked like he'd called, but he hadn't left a message. She didn't see his truck parked anywhere when she drove to her house, just a gray Volvo parked on the street in front, maybe someone visiting her neighbor Estelle. Malcolm had probably stopped off somewhere to pick up some Sam Adams. She giggled. He would be there soon, she knew, because he'd planned to talk to Dr Sanger at lunchtime, which gave him plenty of time for the two-hour drive back.

She pulled into the carport, got out of the car, carrying the six pack of Sam Adams, went inside and put the beer in the refrigerator. She checked the freezer to make sure the frozen pizza was actually there. She'd left her cellphone in the car, and she was just heading out to get it and the box of mail when she noticed the door that led out to the porch was wide open.

Great. Malcolm was already here. He must have left his truck at his house and walked over.

She headed for the porch. 'Hey,' she said, on her way out there. 'How was Dr—?' She stopped.

A man in a baseball cap was sitting on one of

the porch chairs, feet up on the railing as if he owned the place, but it wasn't Malcolm.

For a moment she got very still inside. She saw the yard beyond the porch in a strangely vivid way, the patch of grass browning.

'Hi, Kate,' said Harry Light. 'Your door wasn't locked, so I just came in. Good to see you – it's been a while, hasn't it?'

Thirty-Six

'What are you doing here?' Kate asked.

'Don't be mad.' Harry Light stood up.

Kate backed away.

'Hey, hey, hey.' Harry held his hands out, palms up, as if to show he had no concealed weapons.

But, thought Kate, he could have that gun. It could be – where? Waistband of his pants? That's where they carried them in movies.

'Where are you going?' Harry said.

The porch wasn't visible from the street. Seeing him here right in front of her, he wasn't exactly formidable to look at – dressed in khaki shorts that showed off his knobby knees, wire-rimmed glasses – a poet, not what you'd call a man of steel. The baseball cap was because he was getting bald. Or balder. He always worried about that.

Maybe he was even completely bald already, the process sped up from the stress of it all. Good.

She hoped so. *How could I have run off with him*, she wondered. *How could I?*

'You had a gun,' said Kate, 'in the bedside chest of drawers.'

'Jesus Christ, that thing? It's still there, and it's not even loaded. It's for just in case someone breaks in. I can wave it around and scare them away.'

'Lift up your shirt and turn around.'

He did; there was nothing there.

'My friend Malcolm should be here any minute,' she said. And it was true, he should be.

'Malcolm,' Harry said politely.

'Malcolm MacGregor. He's a cop,' she added pointedly.

'Malcolm, Malcolm. Sure. I know about him. Anna Marie's mom told me. He seems like a good guy from what she told me. Like I said, don't be mad. You can't still be mad. I couldn't believe you left like that, without any explanation. What did I do? What was the finishing blow, anyway?'

'Hard to say,' Kate said. 'There were so many.'

'Besides, come to think of it, I'm the one who should be mad. We could have sat down together and talked about whatever it was that was bothering you.'

'Whatever it was? It was your silent rage. We were supposed to discuss your silent rage in a rational manner? Rage lurking under the surface, just waiting for a reason to come out. Restaurants were the worst, as I recall. I left you right after a restaurant episode. One of too many.'

'Restaurant episodes?' Harry wrinkled his brow

theatrically. 'I don't know no restaurant episodes.' He grinned.

'It's not funny,' Kate said. She glanced at her watch. Surely Malcolm should be back by now.

'Oh no,' said Harry, with false concern. 'Is your friend late? I hope he's not hooking up with—'

'Why don't you just shut up,' said Kate in a rage. 'I'd really like you to leave, Harry. I don't know why you came here. In fact, I'm leaving myself.'

She went down the porch steps and around to the side, heading for her car. She needed her cellphone, and that's where it was, in her car.

'Wait,' said Harry, following behind. 'Wait, please, Kate. You're right, okay? You should have left me, I've always understood that underneath, but I've never wanted to accept it, what a jerk I was.'

Kate stopped.

Harry took off his baseball cap, not totally bald yet, put it back on. 'If it makes any difference, it wasn't really me who was acting like that. It was the medication I was taking. It was an antidepressant.'

'You think that absolves you? Bullshit.'

'It screwed me up. I'm off it now, okay? I'm on this other one that's much better.' There was a pause. 'Jesus, Kate. Half the country's on anti-depressants. I've been depressed my entire life. After all, I *am* a poet.'

Suddenly, Kate had a picture of Harry when she'd first met him, at the poetry seminar, talking

257

about his poetry and what it meant to be a poet. He was so vibrant, alive, wearing a brilliant Hawaiian shirt (in *Vermont*!) printed with parrots and palm leaves. At the end he'd raised his fist to the crowd of mostly women and shouted, '*Duende!!*'

Vaguely now she remembered what had attracted her to him, some sense he held a truth, though about what she still didn't really know.

'You are so full of it,' Kate said.

'Your leaving,' Harry said, 'made me think a lot. About who I was, how I treated people. It led to my helping Anna Marie. It was a big deal for me, you know. My livelihood could have been at risk if the rumors abut her disappearance got too bad.'

'But you can't fire people for rumors.'

'I operate on grants, seminars, that kind of thing,' he mused. 'But nothing happened. I was still in demand. Who knows? Maybe it added a little bit of danger to my image. Anyway, you probably won't believe this, but I've never had sex with Anna Marie. And she's a beautiful girl. It was a completely innocent act, my helping her.'

There was a silence.

'Anna Marie likes you a lot, Kate. She thinks you're great. You can trust me. Anna Marie did, and look, *look*, I saved her. *I saved Anna Marie.*'

'Okay,' said Kate begrudgingly. 'You saved Anna Marie.'

'All I want to do now is make it up to you, the way I behaved. Let me take you out to dinner, Kate, okay? Please. And your friend too, if he ever shows up. Leave him a note. We can walk down there now. Cafe Roka – I checked around – it's the best restaurant in town.'

There was a gray Volvo parked in front of Kate's when Malcolm, head bandaged, parked his truck on the street just down from her house and walked up to her carport. After he was hit by the other pickup truck and had to go to the emergency room – head wounds bled a lot – to be treated and had dealt with the other guy's insurance etc. It got later and later. He'd called her, but no one answered. He left a message and drove on back. At the Sierra Vista turn-off he called her again, but still no answer. Strange.

Her car was in the carport, which didn't mean much since she usually walked most places. He peered in, saw a big box on the passenger seat and next to it her cellphone. He knocked on the door of the house, then opened it. Something that had been stuck in the door fluttered to the ground. He picked it up. *Malcolm*, it said, *I'm at Cafe Roka. Come on down. Kate.*

It seemed even stranger that she would just take off for the best restaurant in town – what was she doing, sitting there alone, ordering? Stranger still that she would leave her cellphone in the car. She never left her cellphone anywhere; it was always with her. He went inside.

'Kate?' No answer.

He had an urgent need to pee, so he did, then looked around. Sam Adams in the fridge – she didn't drink the stuff so it was obviously meant for him. Everything was pretty much in order,

259

except one of the chairs on the porch was pushed back further than usual – if he hadn't had law enforcement training he would never have noticed.

He left the house, checked her car door. It wasn't locked, so he opened it and got the cell-phone. There were his calls under 'missed calls'. The one from Tucson and the one from Sierra Vista. He hoped to hell she was where her note said she was, 'cause without her cell he didn't know how he could reach her; but why wouldn't she be?

He took off, drove downtown to the Cafe Roka.

It was a week night and close to twilight. A few couples lingered on the street; a couple of teenage boys sat on the top of one of the benches in Pedlars Alley, holding their skateboards. Malcolm parked a couple of blocks away and walked back to the restaurant. The windows were lit up with a soft orange glow and at the table by the window a smiling couple raised glasses of wine to each other. Then he realized who the woman was.

Kate, it was Kate, smiling so happily at the man across from her who was—

Hairy Lite.

Hairy Lite – wasn't that who he'd been protecting her from for days now? Hadn't she remained unconvinced, despite his, Malcolm's, assurances, that he'd probably had nothing to do with all the stuff that had been happening to her lately? Now she appeared to have changed her mind. This was good, yes, it was. She looked quite happy in there, quite at ease, not all

260

nervous and full of anxiety as she often was. Happy like she'd been this morning with him, but still happy now – so, obviously, she didn't need him to be happy. In fact, he might even be an unwelcome interruption to a pleasant interlude.

Doing his best to fight against the sense of betrayal that came over him and losing, Malcolm turned on his heel and went back down the street the way he'd come.

Harry cut off a small portion of the stuffed pepper appetizer he and Kate were sharing, chewed and swallowed. 'Pretty good,' he said, 'for a little town like this.' He took a sip of red wine. 'Now.'

'Now what?'

'All the stuff you've told me: the brakes going out on your car, that trip you took to New Jersey – God – New Jersey of all places.'

'*Sorry*,' said Kate, miffed. 'Not poetic enough for you?'

'No, I'm the one who should be sorry.' Harry reached over and put his hand on hers. 'I'm being a jerk. It's such a completely *bizarre* story. Then Ellen, dead. You may be surprised to know that I've met Ellen.'

'Really?'

'I knew people back east, not just you. I remember Ellen. Dark-haired. She did some documentary films?'

'Yes.'

'She was at some party I went to where there were probably a lot of your old friends. We may even have conversed. Ellen was pretty in a quirky

261

way. I'm sorry to hear that's she's dead,' he added piously.

Kate ate most of a red pepper: it was delicious, stuffed with a creamy white cheese.

The waitress came and cleared the empty plate that had held the peppers.

'Oh, my goodness,' Kate said suddenly. 'Where's Malcolm? He should be here by now.'

'The cop,' Harry said. 'Are you, um, what? Tight with him?'

'He's helped me a lot.'

Harry nodded. 'Smart move there, Kate. It sounds like you need a cop around.'

'I left him a note saying where I was,' she said distractedly. 'I should call him.' She fumbled in her purse. 'Shit. I think I left my cellphone in my car.'

'It'll be fine,' Harry said. 'After all, like you said, you left him a note. Does he carry a gun at all times?'

'*No.*'

'Oops. I'm being a jerk again. No, what I think is, we can narrow down who might have been doing those things to you. Some old boyfriend. Or even the unfaithful Rick. He's an artist, fiery temperament and all that.'

'There's no reason for him to be mad at me.'

'Kate, Kate. You can be really shitty to people, you know. Look what you did to me.'

'We already discussed that. I had every right.'

'You did, I'm not disputing it: you left me without a second look, without even a goodbye. You made the correct healthy choice under the circumstances.'

The waitress appeared, set down plates of salad. 'The dressing tonight is a raspberry vinaigrette,' she announced.

Harry gave her a big smile.

'Thank you so much,' said Kate.

'For all I know,' Harry went on, 'you were shitty to Rick and he fled to Hannah's arms for consolation. But that touch of masochism that led him to you in the first place has resurfaced. The romance cools with this new woman – he wants you back, so she decides to take matters in her own hands. She – what's her name?'

'Hannah.'

'Hannah? Hard-hearted Hannah—' Harry snapped his fingers – 'the vamp from—'

'Never mind, Harry, okay?'

'Anyway, Hannah sets this whole thing up out of rage and jealousy. Or, wait! There was that guy you told me about,' Harry went on, 'that you used to go out with before Rock, I mean, Rick. What was his name? It began with an 'S'. Stanley, Seymour – no, it was Stuart, I think. Stew. You told me about him – he got so mad when you broke it off he flattened all your tires. So maybe Stew is still, ha ha, stewing.'

'His name wasn't Stew,' said Kate coldly, beginning to realize that leaving Harry the way she had was not only healthy but incredibly healthy.

'Whatever.'

Malcolm went back to his pickup truck and paused, hand on the door handle. *What are you doing*, he asked himself, *acting like a stupid teenager*. He walked back the way he'd come, pushed open the door of the Cafe Roka. The hostess came forward.

'I'm meeting those people.' He tilted his head towards Harry and Kate. Right away he could see that Kate was glad to see him.

'Malcolm!' Her face lit up, then darkened. 'What happened to your head? Are you all right?'

He'd forgotten entirely about the bandage. 'Fine. I had a little run in with a truck.'

'You must be the famous cop,' Harry said. He held out his hand. 'Harry Light.'

Malcolm took his hand. 'Malcolm,' he said. He pulled out a chair and sat down.

'We were just discussing Kate's dilemma,' Harry said. 'Who's been harassing her? My guess is an old boyfriend. She doesn't treat them as well as she might. What's your take on the matter?'

Malcolm and Kate stood on the street outside Kate's carport, a vantage point from which they could see Harry Light's gray Volvo. They watched as it backed up—

'He's going to hit the railing,' Malcolm said.

He did.

The Volvo went forward, backed up again, and made a semi-turn turn into a driveway. Then it backed out of the driveway, and they watched the tail lights going down the street until he turned and was gone.

They went inside.

264

'Sam Adams?' Kate asked.

'Absolutely.'

They sat together at Kate's dining-room table. Malcolm took a big swig of Sam Adams.

'Just out of curiosity,' Malcolm said, 'what did you ever see in that guy?'

'Escape, I guess. I don't know.'

'Well, I certainly don't care if I never see him again. *Kate's dilemma*,' he said scathingly. 'Aren't we twee?'

'Twee,' Kate said. 'Sometimes you surprise me.'

'Why's that? I was an educated guy before I became a cop.'

'What did Doctor Sanger have to say?' Kate asked.

'Carrie was a big flirt in high school, and he wasn't the guy with the big black glasses who introduced himself to the security guard as Dr Paul Sanger.'

'Of course,' said Kate. 'Nothing is what it seems. I'm almost getting used to it. Oh, and by the way, Harry knew Ellen. He met her at some party years ago. Do you think that might be relevant to anything?'

'Who the hell knows?' Malcolm said.

Later that evening, after it got dark and Malcolm had had a few beers and Kate was still remembering the wine from Cafe Roka, Kate plugged her iPod shuffle into the iPod dock Ian and Sally had given them, and they danced outside in her yard, full of weeds and dusty grass. They danced under a new moon to 'Fun', singing about being young. They whirled around together; they twirled around separately. Kate got the giggles and laughed so hard that she lost her balance and had to sit down.

Thirty-Seven

Grackles yelled at Malcolm from the Arizona cypress trees that surrounded the courthouse, and a big black crow seconded their motions. Malcolm went inside through the bronze doors, dumped the contents of his pockets into the plastic bucket and held his hands high while the security guard ran a wand over his body.

'Hector Rodriguez working today?' he asked.

'Sure is.'

Malcolm went up the stairs to Judge Collins' courtroom. The door to the courtroom was open, but it looked empty. Hector was sitting on one of the chairs outside, staring down at his cell-phone. As Malcolm came closer he could just see the game Angry Birds.

'Morning,' Malcolm said.

The game vanished. 'Well, hello there,' said Hector, standing, looking alert. 'It's Mesa PD. How ya doin'?'

'Okay. Fine. And you?'

'Can't complain.'

'I had a couple of questions for you. Remember the guy at the Flores hearing? The one who said he was there for the victims?'

'I sure do. Or, at least, his glasses.' Hector grinned. 'Big black ugly glasses. Dr Paul Sanger.'

'Good memory,' Malcolm said.

'I try.' Hector bent his head modestly and brushed at imaginary lint on his shirt.

'Except he wasn't Dr Paul Sanger.'

'Yeah?'

'Yeah. I spoke with Dr Sanger. He wasn't here that day.'

'Then who was it?'

'That's what I'm trying to find out.'

'Wow. I bet. Rumor has it,' Hector said, 'you're working for the defense right now.'

'I am. If there's anything about the guy you can tell me other than the glasses I'd like to hear it.'

'Just medium,' Hector said. 'Medium everything. I mean, his hair was kind of brownish. He wasn't tall. He wasn't—' He stopped, looking over Malcolm's shoulder. 'Hey! Veronica!'

Malcolm turned. A pretty dark-haired young woman in a red dress and stiletto heels came over.

'Veronica here is Judge Collins' secretary,' Hector told Malcolm. 'She had a conversation with the guy.'

'What guy?' Veronica said.

'Dr Paul Sanger. At the Flores hearing. Guess what? That's not who he was.'

'Are you sure?' Veronica asked. 'But he was very nice, like a doctor. Polite. Gentlemanly.'

'Really?' Malcolm said.

'He said he liked my dress; it was the floral

267

print—' She glanced at Hector. 'He said his wife had one just like it.'

'A name?' said Malcolm. 'He didn't, by any chance, tell you his wife's name, did he?'

'Yes, he did. Esmeralda. He said his wife, Esmeralda. Excuse me, I have to run.'

'Esmeralda,' Hector said to Malcolm.

'Esmeralda,' Malcolm repeated.

'Yeah.' Hector laughed. 'Wanna bet? Interesting. Maybe it doesn't mean a thing, but still, it's interesting, huh? Anyway, I'm all for Chico – that's between you and me, you understand. I remember him from juvie.'

'From juvie?'

'Aw, he got in a little trouble with drugs, you know how it is, high-school kids.'

'Really,' said Malcolm. 'Just the once?'

Hector's face was utterly blank, wiped clean of any expression. 'Oh, maybe twice, maybe more, I can't remember.'

Malcolm left the courthouse and sat outside on one of the stone benches, the same bench he realized he'd sat on at the hearing for Chico, when he'd read the file. The grackles cackled, the air smelled rich with pine sap. Had Lupita mentioned that Chico had gotten in trouble for drugs as a juvenile? He couldn't remember anything specific. Surely he would have remembered. Well, juvenile records were sealed, and it probably didn't mean anything, anyway.

Were there other things that Lupita hadn't told him about Chico, things possibly relevant? He needed to talk to her. Maybe Chico had fled to

Mexico, to join a drug cartel as one of their major hit men. Maybe killing those tourists was just a way of proving himself.

Slow down.

He also needed to check in with Stuart Ross. He'd been spending way too much time helping out Kate. His cellphone chimed. 'Malcolm MacGregor here.'

'Hello, sir, this is Steve Anderson of Evan Bright Realty. I believe you've been wanting to talk to me?'

'Mr Anderson, yes, yes, I have.'

'Abbie filled me in on the details.' He chuckled. 'Man, oh man, what a mess. Only good thing is, no real harm done. Anyway, I'm getting the locks changed; we should have had done it back then when the key went missing. I kept telling myself it had just been misplaced, you know? I guess 'cause I'm a lazy bastard.'

'Abbie told Kate,' Malcolm prompted, 'that there was one guy you felt suspicious about?'

'Sure was. And that was pretty recent, too. I almost didn't show it to him 'cause the owner wanted to take it off the market, but I thought, oh, what the hell. He makes me a fantastic offer, the owner might reconsider. Anyway, once we got talking, he seemed kind of interested but not interested, if you know what I mean.'

'A name,' said Malcolm, 'did you get a name?'

'Matthews, his name was Bill Matthews.' He paused significantly. 'Or so he said.'

'Bill Matthews,' Malcolm repeated.

'Yeah.' Steve Anderson laughed. 'That should

269

be easy to trace, huh? How many Matthews out there, huh? But here's the thing, I also remember his car: it was a blue Toyota, and it had out-of-state plates.'

'What state?'

'You know, for the life of me, I don't remember, if I ever knew. It just kind of registered in my mind – out of state. Not New York, though; there's a million New York plates around here. Bill Matthews, that's what he said his name was, but I keep thinking of him as Gary Busey. Yeah. Gary Busey.'

'Gary Busey?' He said it like a question, but he already knew the answer.

'The actor, you know, played Buddy Holly in *The Buddy Holly Story*. 'Cause of the glasses – they were big and black.'

For a moment, Malcolm was struck speechless. He sat on the stone bench under the Arizona Cypress trees and watched the cars and pickup trucks making the turn to the courthouse, coming up the slope to the parking lot, coming from all over the county hoping for a little justice. So there was a connection for sure now between Carrie and Wes's killer and whoever was after Kate.

But why?

'Hey, buddy,' said Steve Anderson, 'you still there?'

'Yeah, yeah,' said Malcolm. 'You got a precise date for when you showed the house to this Bill Matthews?'

'Not really. But it was pretty recent – less than two weeks ago.'

'Well, Mr Anderson, thank you very much for your time. I appreciate it.'

Afterwards, he sat quietly for a moment. *Less than two weeks ago, perfect. That would make it just after the murders.*

What was it he'd been thinking about before the phone call? Chico. Chico's juvie record. Well, the hell with that. Things weren't making sense, but at least the things that weren't making sense were connecting.

There was one other thing too that had been bugging him – the snapshot Kate had shown him of the woman on the beach at Tall Pines Lake. The only personal item in the whole house. Was it just left behind by mistake by the owners? Or left behind by someone later, maybe someone in big black glasses? But this was all crazy, too crazy.

'Think. *Think*,' said Malcolm to Kate as they sat in her rented house at what passed for her dining-room table, eating nuked pasta that came from a bag and salad that came from a bag too. It was all remarkably good. Everything he ate now, Malcolm reflected, was remarkably good, his appetite whetted by stress. Oh, lovely stress, you felt so alive in it.

'You don't have to come up with anything right now,' he said, 'but let it sit there in your mind. Everything that transpired between you and Carrie. There might be one small detail – something you didn't pay attention to at the time.'

'Maybe I should be hypnotized?' Kate said brightly.

For a moment Malcolm looked as though he might seriously be considering it. 'Naw,' he said. 'Could be nothing. But the killer might think there's something. At this point we have to hope he's feeling safer though. Look, I have to go back there.'

'Where?'

'New Jersey.'

'Why, exactly?' Kate asked.

'Steve said out-of-state plates, so there's a good chance he stayed in one of the motels. I've got the date, plus the date you were there. Now there's a strong connection I need to do a more thorough investigation at the scene. I called Officer Dodds.'

'Office Dodds,' Kate asked. 'You mean, so he can help?'

'I can't take a weapon on the plane with me, but I don't feel good doing all this unarmed. He can get me a gun,' Malcolm said.

'Bill Matthews,' Kate said. 'Talk about a common name.' Suddenly, she put down her fork and began to cry, little shuddering sobs. 'I, I, I've never heard of a Bill Matthews,' she sobbed.

'Come on,' said Malcolm, more to cheer her up than anything else. 'Everybody's heard of a Bill Matthews.'

Thirty-Eight

It was late afternoon by the time Malcolm's plane landed at the Newark airport, and even later by the time he picked up the rental car and hit the freeway. One of these days he'd get one of those smartphones with the GPS app, but for now he had directions to a house written down. He drove directly there. A brick one-story in the heart of suburbia, kid's bicycle in the driveway, basketball hoop on the garage door.

Malcolm parked, started to get out of the rental car, when Officer Matt Dodds came out of the house, carrying a plastic bag from Target. Malcolm got back in, lowered the window.

'Afternoon!' Officer Dodds said.

'Afternoon!'

'Good flight?'

'It landed,' Malcolm said.

Officer Matt Dodds handed Malcolm the plastic bag; it was heavier than it looked. 'Much obliged,' Malcolm said.

'You take care now,' said Officer Dodds.

He'd gone online late the night before and looked up all the motels in a ten-mile radius of the house on Roscommon Drive. Basically, that included the area where he and Kate had stayed the last time and then a couple more a few miles down the freeway. If the guy had out-of-state plates, there was a chance he might have checked into one of them. Also a chance he'd be wearing the big black glasses. Also a chance, Malcolm thought, by now feeling weary of chance, he would have paid for the motel with a credit card and the card just might have his real name on it.

Unless, of course, his name actually was Bill Matthews.

It was all worth checking out – many a case had been solved due to plain old stupidity on the part of the perp. Even smart guys could be stupid once in a while.

He'd brought his badge from Mesa PD, figured it would give him some credibility. He planned to hit all the motels, and it would only take one, just one, person remembering something, which might lead to something else, which might lead to this whoever he was, this Bill Matthews guy. He had a theory, though it was usually best to avoid those, but he'd had this theory for a while and was still liking it – the actual shooter wasn't connected directly to Wes and Carrie, but was acting on behalf of someone else who was connected to them. A hired killer.

But how, *how*, did Kate fit in? Was he right in thinking she knew something she didn't know that she knew? Or the killer thought she did? He wished he could stop thinking for just a little while, stop obsessing – he'd heard of old retired cops who never stopped thinking about certain unsolved cases, lay on their death beds, surrounded with what was left of their estranged families, still mulling over certain details, still thinking, still figuring out.

Then a new thought occurred to him. Something he wanted to ask Rose, Carrie's sister. He called the cellphone number she'd given him, but no one answered, and a female robot informed him she had not yet set up her voicemail.

He checked into the same motel in the suburban area – Jack in the Box, Burger King, McDonald's, Kentucky Colonel, Wendy's and

Kroger's – where he had before. There was a different clerk at the check-in desk than the one who'd been there the last time. He flashed his Mesa PD badge, but the kid working there had no memory of a man wearing ugly black glasses, driving a Toyota with out-of-state plates who might or might not be called Bill, or William, Matthews, at the dates he supplied. No one at the desks of the other three motels in the same area remembered anything either, but they all took Malcolm's cell number in case of a sudden memory – anything: some little altercation, a casual remark that struck home, odd behavior.

And then, why not? He wasn't really tired, so he drove the five-mile stretch to the next batch of motels – two at a smaller plaza, just a Subway and a Pizza Hut, and found no one there with any memory of a man with ugly black glasses. Surprise. But in spite of everything he had a feeling he was getting closer, closing in. After all, he'd left his card at every motel in a ten-mile radius. He drove back.

His room was one door down from where he'd stayed before, a few doors down from Kate's old room. He stopped in and took a long shower. As if for old times' sake he ate at the same McDonald's where only a few days ago he and Kate had been, sat in the same booth on the same hard orange seat, had a quarter-pounder with cheese.

Tomorrow, get up early, start checking with the daytime staff in the motels. Also, he wanted to talk directly to Steve Anderson, the realtor, show

275

him the picture of the woman in the bathing suit at Tall Pine Lake. Why? Because it didn't quite fit in with the basic emptiness of the rest of the house. You had to pay attention to the details. What was that expression? The devil's in the details.

He looked up Evan Bright Realty on his laptop, found out it opened at nine. He planned to park out front in his rental car around eight thirty and try to catch this Steve Anderson on his way in. He spent a sleepless night thinking about all this and more.

Without him as a bodyguard on her couch, Kate was staying over at Dakota's. There she would be relatively safe, but how long could this go on? And what did relatively safe mean, anyway? At some point in his sleepless night, after Letterman, during the reruns of tired old sitcom shows, it came to him, as if he didn't already know it, that no matter what you did you could never make another person entirely safe.

Then dread, the black dog, came over him suddenly.

Nothing, nothing he had done had ever helped Cindy as she moved forward slowly and inexorably to her death. It seemed to him he had to save Kate or he would die too.

Kate mostly walked everywhere in Dudley, but after work she drove her car to Dakota's so it wouldn't be just sitting there in her driveway waiting for someone to plant a bomb in it or something. She parked it under a street light several doors away from Dakota's. The box of mail was still in the back seat where she'd left it two or three days ago, so she took it with her to sort through later, along with the box of takeout – Moorish chicken kabobs with quinoa tabbouleh – from the High Desert Market.

'So,' said Dakota as they sat on her patio eating the takeout. 'Where's your boyfriend now?'

'He went back to New Jersey. And he's not my boyfriend. I don't intend to have another boyfriend for a very long time.'

'Suit yourself.'

So Dakota would shut up, Kate went into the house and brought out the box of mail and began to sort through it, tossing catalogs and things addressed 'Resident'. 'There is nothing,' she said, 'nothing here. Oh, wait. This is from my friend Mandy in New York that I stayed with. A DVD she made of a bunch of videos – me and a lot of other people being stupid when we were young. Let's watch it later.'

'Is your ex in it?' asked Dakota. 'Rick?'

'Probably. And Ellen, who turned out not to be Ellen – the old friend?'

'One of the Ooblecks.'

'Yes. She'll probably be in it too. You know what? I don't think I'm ready for this. Maybe tomorrow night.'

'You know what else?' said Dakota. 'Let's do a dinner and movie night tomorrow, invite Biker Bill. We kind of owe him. I've got that Jim Jarmusch movie, *Dead Man*. Biker Bill loves Jim Jarmusch. We can watch your DVD after.'

Thirty-Nine

Melody got someone else to babysit the gallery and spent most of the morning in thrift stores – not only locally, but in Douglas too, the next town over – before she found what she was looking for. Then she hung around the county offices that afternoon until she saw the tamale lady drive up in her old battered Ford.

'*Señora!*' she called out to her. '*Tamales?*'

The tamale lady nodded her head vigorously '*Si, si.*'

'Green corn?'

'*Si.*'

She bought a dozen, stopped by the Co-op – Hi, Windsong! Hi, Posey! – and bought some of the Co-op's all-organic salsa and some sour cream. She carried her bags up the hill and into the house. She put them in the refrigerator way at the back where he wouldn't see them. She wanted them to be a surprise.

'What you got there?' he called out to her.

'Nothing,' she said.

'Melody?'

'What?

'I've been thinking . . .'

She went into the living room. He was on the couch with a book. He told her he planned to read everything ever written by Roberto Bolaño. She'd gone to the library and checked out everything they had. Right now he was on *The Savage Detectives*, which was going to take him a while.

'Thinking about what?' she asked.

'That gun.' He scratched his face – he was growing out a beard, and it was itchy. 'The one your ex left here. You said it wasn't loaded?'

'That's right. It's not.'

'It might be good if you got some ammo for it.'

She sighed. 'Everyone says not to, that if someone breaks in and tries to steal it, they could shoot me.'

'Melody, cheez.'

'All right, all right.'

Around six, which was when they were in the habit of eating, she steamed the green corn tamales and made a salad. He tried to come into the kitchen while she was doing this, but she wouldn't let him.

She didn't have a dining room – they ate at a table in one corner of the center room. She set it with the salsa, the salad and the sour cream.

'Ta-dah!' she said as she carried out the tamales.

He was happy, and they ate eight of them. She had three, and he had five.

Afterwards she brought out the shirt and the hat she'd found at the thrift store. The shirt was Hawaiian, printed with palm trees, the hat a straw fedora. Chico tried them on, and they both fit him perfectly.

Everyone looking for Chico, everyone, thought Melody with pride, but it was her door he came to late that night, blood all over his head but alive. Alive.

Forty

First thing the next morning Malcolm grabbed a coffee at McDonald's and cruised Roscommon Drive, car window down in the morning cool, obsessing a little. At 350, the yellow roses were still blooming. A woman walked her dog. The green grass was dewy and sweet smelling.

Then he drove to Evan Bright Realty and parked a few doors down. It was eight thirty. Two women showed up first, talking animatedly, one of them plumpish and carrying a box of Dunkin Donuts. About ten of nine a third woman in a bright-red suit came along and vanished through the glass door. Then nobody.

Malcolm yawned and glanced at his watch. He'd had about an hour's sleep last night. Ten after, quarter after. Damn. Might as well see what was happening. He got out of his car and went inside. Four desks, all of them occupied, three by the women he'd seen going in and a fourth by a man. Either he'd been there before Malcolm arrived or there was a back door.

They all looked at him as if he were their potential next best friend, and God knows working for a realty company in this day and age you needed all the friends you could get.

'Steve Anderson?' Malcolm said.

The man stood up, good-looking in a waspy forgettable sort of way, and came towards him, hand outstretched. Big grin. '*C'est moi,*' he said.

The woman closest to Malcolm rolled her eyes.

'Mr Anderson,' Malcolm said.

'Please, call me Steve.'

'Steve. I'm Malcolm MacGregor. We spoke on the phone.'

For a second, Steve Anderson looked surprised. 'No shit,' he said. 'You came all the way from Arizona?'

'That I did.'

'Then I'd say you deserve a medal. You're really hot on this. Tell you what, I'm not engaged at the moment, and I haven't had breakfast. There's a Denny's right down the street. We can go there and talk. I'll buy you a cup of coffee.'

At Denny's, they sat in a booth. Steve described in detail the man with the ugly black glasses – brown hair, big nose, chapped lips ('I noticed that 'cause he kept licking them, you know?') – and what had transpired between them as he devoured the lumberjack slam breakfast, which included eggs, pancakes, sausage, bacon, toast and home fries. Malcolm sipped coffee.

Nothing Steve told him added anything new, really, to what he had told Malcolm on the phone.

'Ah!' Steve pushed his plate away, wiped his mouth. 'Good Lord.' He picked up his coffee cup, then set it down without taking a sip. 'Good *Lord*,' he said again. 'I have to say, this whole thing is some story. What I can't figure out is why someone would want to play a trick like that on your friend.'

281

'I don't know. That's what I'm trying to find out.'

'So she sends you.' He laughed. 'Can't blame her if she never comes back here. So, she's safe and sound in – where is it in Arizona you're from again?'

'Dudley.'

'What was her name again?'

'Kate. Kate Waters.'

'Ahh. Kate. Ka-Ka-Ka-Katie. It's just nutso, you know what I mean, the whole thing, and—' Steve Anderson smiled – 'even more surprising is that she fell for it. What I don't get, to be honest, is you flying all the way from Arizona to check things out. It seems like a stupid trick, but—' He shrugged. 'It was just a joke, after all.' He paused and looked bemused. 'Wasn't it?'

'It's linked to a homicide investigation,' Malcolm said. 'A double homicide, actually.'

'No shit!' He leaned back in the booth. 'No fucking shit. Wow. I mean, like, how linked?'

'I'm not sure, exactly. That's why I'm here.' Malcolm slid the copy of the photograph of the woman at Tall Pine Lake out of its Manila envelope and pushed it over to Steve Anderson. 'You got any idea who this is?'

Steve Anderson looked at it, held it up to the light by the window. 'Nope. Not a clue.'

'On the back it says Tall Pine Lake.'

'Sure. Tall Pine Lake. That's a hundred miles or so from here. Lots of people from this area have a cottage there. Been there myself but I never—' he shrugged and pushed the photo back – 'saw her there. Not that you can tell what she looks like, anyway. What's the point of showing me this?'

'It was in the house, that's all.'

'Probably left there by the relatives.'

'It was in one of the bedrooms. On a bedside table. Do you recall seeing it there?'

'As a matter of fact, I do not. Huh. Funny. You'd think I'd notice something like that.' He shrugged. 'But maybe not. *Weird.*'

The waitress came over with a full pot. Malcolm shook his head; Steve gave her a big smile and covered his cup.

'What was the name of the owner of three fifty Roscommon, by the way?' Malcolm asked. 'I'm not sure I ever knew it.'

'Madigan. Emily Madigan.'

'Emily Madigan,' said Malcolm. 'Anyway, I'd like to have the number for the relatives – see if it rings a bell with them.'

'No prob.' Steve whipped out his cellphone. 'Got it here in my contacts.'

Malcolm punched it into his.

'How long do you plan to be around?' Steve asked.

'I booked a flight out, red-eye, day after tomorrow.'

Steve sighed. 'Well, anything I can do to help—' His face radiated goodwill, concern. 'Give me a call.' Then for a second he looked lost. 'Whew,' he said.

He seemed like a good guy.

Suddenly, Malcolm was worried for him, almost like a premonition. 'Don't do any investigating on your own, okay?'

Poor old Steve, thought Malcolm as he drove to the plaza with the two motels to check with the daytime staff. He'd probably ruined his day. Or maybe not. Some people were jazzed up by crime, disaster, tragic events.

At the two motels, he got nowhere again. 'Where's a good restaurant?' he asked the woman at the second motel. He'd kind of forgotten about breakfast, just the cup of coffee at McDonald's and then another at Denny's, and here it was a little late for lunch. He'd considered a sandwich at Subway, but thought, no, a real meal. At least he'd earned himself a decent meal, just for trying.

'You like steak?' the woman asked.

'Sure do.'

'Then try Rancher Bill's.'

Malcolm slid into a dark leather booth at the Rancher Bill's Steak House. Rancher Bill, indeed; there probably wasn't a ranch within a thousand miles of here. Annoying music played in the background, sounding like imitation Sons of the Pioneers. But a steak is a steak is a steak, if it's a good one.

A waiter showed up, wanting to know about anything from the bar.

'Sam Adams, if you got it,' Malcolm said.

'Very good, sir,' he said, as if he'd been watching movies lately about ritzy places with high-class waiters. 'Your waitress will be right along.' He left a laminated menu.

Malcolm perused it. Adorned with brands and branding irons, cowboys, lassos and cacti, it offered Cowboy Bill Prime Ribs, Billy's Rib-Eye, South of the Border Flank Steak, Rancher's Best Sirloin. The waitress showed up – she was tall, and dark and plump, in cowboy boots, white shirt with bolo tie and a chamois colored buckskin fringed vest. He ordered the rib-eye, medium rare, with fries.

'Dressing?'

Malcolm looked at her blankly for a second. 'No,' he said, 'I thought I'd come nude.'

The waitress giggled. Her face turned bright red. 'For the salad; it comes with a salad.'

'Then ranch,' said Malcolm. 'Of course.' What was happening to him? He was turning into a clown.

Waiting, he called the number Steve had given him for the relatives of Emily Madigan.

'Hello?' said a tiny feminine voice.

'Hello. I'm looking for a relative of Emily Madigan?'

'This is Jody. She was my aunt. Is this about the house?'

'Not exactly,' said Malcolm. He introduced himself, explained.

'Oh my goodness,' said Jody. 'Oh my goodness,' she said again. 'I was there when we cleaned out the house. It was sad, you know? You have this whole life built up with stuff you think is important, and then you die and, well, the stuff you leave behind, it's just junk.'

'A profound thought indeed,' said Malcolm.

'That why I'm putting my trust in Jesus Christ.'

There was a little silence. The waitress appeared and plunked down a salad.

285

'The photograph,' Jody said then. 'I don't think we would have left something like that behind. Tall Pine Lake? I've heard of it, but none of us ever went there. We used to live in Jersey, you know. Of course,' she added with a laugh, 'my aunt might have had a secret life. But, no, I don't know what it was doing there.'

'Well, thank you very much,' said Malcolm and clicked off.

The rib-eye appeared, the fries. The rib-eye, to his delight, was cooked just right, juicy and oozing pink, the fries properly greasy. He ate it all except the salad. He just didn't have room for the salad.

Then he called Rose, Carrie's sister. She answered this time.

'Tall Pine Lake?' he said, without much expectation.

'What about it?'

'Does it mean anything to you?'

'Sure. We used to go there as kids. My grand-parents owned a cottage.'

'*Really*? Just as kids then? Never as grown-ups?'

'Not really. My grandparents died when I was twenty. The cottage was sold.'

'What about Carrie?'

'You mean, did she ever go there as a grown-up? Yes, actually, she did go there. Several times, in fact. Kind of a nostalgia trip. She told me one time our grandparent's cottage was all fixed up, in the worst way. Not quaint any more.'

'Like when?'

'I don't really remember specific dates. It's one

286

of those memories that just floats up out of nowhere. Sorry.'

'Rose, I'm going to take a picture of a photograph and send it to you, okay? It'll be a couple of minutes.'

'Okay,' said Rose. 'Listen, I've got some crafts people here, we're about to start a class. I'll get back to you.'

Malcolm paid the bill and left the restaurant. The light was better outside, and he managed to get a pretty decent shot of the photo, which he sent to Rose as a picture message. Carrie had spent time at Tall Pines Lake. A link, a concrete link. He didn't want to expect too much, but it was hard not to.

He got in the rental and back on the freeway to the plaza he found himself thinking of as his and Kate's. Out of a sense of nostalgia and urgency both, he called Kate, got her voicemail but didn't leave a message. Then he felt foolish.

Aimless, Malcolm cruised back to the house on Roscommon Drive.

He'd been through the house already, but he wished now he could do it again. Even though he remembered checking everywhere, there might be a place he'd missed. In a way, he knew there probably wasn't, but in another way, cases were solved when things that had been overlooked came to light.

Malcolm called Evan Bright Realty to see if he could get the key to the house, but no one answered. A robot informed him they were closed for the day but his call was very important to them. He called Steve's cell, got his voicemail.

'Give me a call,' he told Steve's voicemail.

He went back to the motel. His sleepless night caught up with him then all at once, and he collapsed into sleep.

His cellphone chimed somewhere far away. He reached for it in his sleep, opened his eyes. Rose.

'Hi,' he said.

'Where did you say you got that picture?' she asked.

'I'm not sure I ever said. It was in the bedroom of a house at three fifty Roscommon Drive in—' Jeez, what town was this, anyway? – 'a town in New Jersey.'

'That's strange,' said Rose, 'very strange.'

'Why is that?'

'That's definitely Carrie in the picture. It was one of her favorites. But what was it doing in some town in New Jersey?'

'Who took it?' Malcolm said urgently. 'Rose, who took that picture?'

'Some old boyfriend.'

'*Who?*'

'I can't remember exactly. But it was one of those pictures she always had with her, you know? Shoot. Let me think about it, okay? I'll ask my mom too – sometimes her memory's really good, you just never know when.'

Malcolm fell back asleep, just as he was thinking he should call Kate, tell her the woman at Tall Pine Lake was Carrie. What would she make of that?

Forty-One

After work, Kate picked up her car at Dakota's and drove it over to her rented house. She and Dakota had discussed it and decided having Kate's car in Kate's driveway would keep someone from breaking into Kate's house – unless, of course, it was to murder Kate, ha ha, and then she wouldn't be there. Plus, then no one would know Kate was at Dakota's. Then they ordered takeout for dinner, since Dakota didn't think she could cook anything that Biker Bill would like.

'What!' said Kate. 'You can cook?'

'Shut up.'

They ordered a large all-meat pizza: sausage, bacon, pepperoni with extra cheese. Biker Bill came over at seven wearing stiff jeans and a clean T-shirt, just the faintest hint of marijuana as an aftershave. They ate half the pizza outside on Dakota's patio and the other half inside, in front of the television, watching *Dead Man*. Biker Bill stretched out on the couch, Dakota and Kate on chairs on either side.

Halfway through, just when William Blake was meeting up with Nobody, Kate's cell chimed. Malcolm. She'd been meaning to call him but hadn't gotten around to it. She took it outside to the patio. It was dark by now, eight o'clock, stars peppering the sky.

'How's it going?' Malcolm asked.

'I'm at Dakota's. We're watching a movie with Biker Bill – we had him to dinner since he's been protecting us.'

'Great! What's the movie?'

'*Dead Man.*'

'Ah.'

There was a tiny silence while neither of them mentioned what would happen to Biker Bill if whoever had killed Wes and Carrie aimed at him while he was protecting Kate and Dakota.

'Well,' Malcolm said, 'looks like I've identified the woman at Tall Pine Lake.'

'*Very good*,' said Kate. She laughed. 'Anyone we know?'

'Yes.'

'Yes? Really?'

'Know isn't exactly the word I'd use, but the woman is Carrie Cooper. Rose, her sister, identified her.'

'Rose,' said Kate. 'Yes, Rose. Of course.'

Another silence.

'You know what?' said Kate. 'This doesn't make any sense. No sense at all. Unreal. I'm tired of it all. Can we change to a different script? Maybe a romantic comedy?'

Then she was sorry she'd said that.

Johnny Depp floated off in a boat to the spiritual world, and Biker Bill snored softly on the couch. Dakota ejected the DVD and put in the one Mandy had sent Kate.

People Kate had known years ago appeared on the screen, faces coming close, noses first, then receding. An apartment, a couch, a table with people eating, a birthday party. There was Mandy, and then Kate herself in a big black sweater with shoulder pads.

'God,' said Kate.

Dakota giggled.

'There's Ellen,' said Kate. Sweet, dark-haired Ellen with her manic laugh. Kate felt a twinge of sorrow.

Rick appeared beside Kate, bearded temporarily. He waved. Then a new video popped up: everyone a bit older, a wedding party, yes, Kate remembered the party but not who got married. There was Kate herself in an ugly dress. Then another video, a later time. Kate not in it. Three youngish men sang a song together. A silly song, made up. Jake and Jessie and Buzzie. Buzzie . . . what was it about him, she started to wonder – yes, he'd joined the military. Dead, maybe, dead in Afghanistan? No in Iraq – then the video changed again, to some sort of gallery opening.

There was Mandy coming out from behind a cluster of people, a shy smile, then there was Rick to one side. No beard now. He and Kate used to go to the city together from time to time, then he started going alone 'cause she got so busy with the arts center. He held up his hand in front of the camera, turned away, bent his head. His arm was around—

'Wait,' Kate said. 'Pause that.'

Dakota did.

'Now go back, just a bit, and hit play.'

Kate watched. She saw Rick earlier this time; watching Mandy, she hadn't noticed him. He was with someone, holding hands. He was with someone holding hands, then he saw the camera, held up his hand, turned away, bent his head. His arm was around—

Hannah.

How could it be Hannah? This was years before Hannah had arrived in Rustic, Vermont. He'd never said he knew her. Wouldn't he have mentioned it? *Oh, by the way, an old friend of mine is coming to town.* Yet there he was with his arm around her, years before that. Around the time he started going to the city alone. He went a lot, really – making useful connections, he liked to say.

Seeing Hannah.

'Shit.' Kate stood up.

Biker Bill stirred.

'What's wrong?' asked Dakota.

'I've had enough. I need a break.' Kate went outside again and stared up at the stars. Rick had been cheating on her with Hannah for years. Literally years, and she hadn't had a clue.

Forty-Two

Malcolm woke with a start. How long had he been sleeping? Just a few hours; his watch said eight o'clock. But why was it so light outside? He got up slowly, still in his street clothes, went to the window. It was quite light outside,; it was that daylight saving time they had here. Arizona

292

didn't have it. Then he realized. Not eight p.m. It was eight a.m.

No one had gotten back to him since Rose's call last night – not Rose, about who had taken the picture of Carrie. Not Steve either. Well, it was early still. He turned on the television, making sure there was not some disaster taking place that would change his life forever.

It looked like not.

He took a long hot shower. Breakfast – he needed breakfast. He hadn't had dinner even. Then Evan Bright Realty. Get the key, go through the house once more – the last, final, *final* time, he promised himself. Then he thought he'd stop in and talk to law enforcement – they might be a whole lot more helpful if they thought this involved a double homicide.

Malcolm went to the same Denny's he'd gone to with Steve and ordered the same thing Steve had ordered yesterday – the lumberjack slam. Bacon, sausage, eggs, buttermilk pancakes, hash browns. Coffee. He thought about orange juice too but didn't want to overdo it. He was almost finished when his cell chimed.

Rose.

'I remember who took that picture,' Rose said.

'Who?'

'Except I can't really remember his name – just that it started with a B and was kind of funny. I never met him. Plus, if I did meet one of Carrie's boyfriends I didn't bother to pay much attention 'cause it would be someone else the next time. But this boyfriend lasted a while.'

'Yeah? A "B". For Bill, maybe?' Could there actually have been a Bill Matthews in Carrie's life?

'No, not Bill. And wow! You know what else? He was really, really mad at Carrie when she broke it off. She left him for Wes. I'd sort of forgotten the whole thing, but now I'm remembering. It was a while ago, you know?'

'You'd be surprised,' said Malcolm, 'how long someone can nurture a grudge.'

'Anyway, one thing I do remember Carrie mentioning is he was an amateur actor. You know, had big roles in amateur productions.'

'Aha. But no name. Damn.'

'Listen. There's some people I can call, maybe they know. If they do then I'll get back to you.'

'Okay, *great*.'

Then Malcolm sat quietly for a few moments. An actor. Okay, that would work. A guy shows up in the courtroom wearing a disguise, posing as Dr Paul Sanger. He'd have to either be someone who knew Wes and Carrie, to know about Dr Sanger, or a hit man hired by someone else who did. Like the old boyfriend whose name started with a B? The man posing as Paul Sanger and the man who did the shooting didn't have to be the same person.

He felt as though he had a whole bunch of fragments, but nothing seemed to hold together. Especially how this involved Kate. How the hell did she come into this? It made no sense at all.

He felt like calling her, so he did. Got her voicemail; she was probably at work, not lying on the ground, shot dead by a hit man.

Malcolm paid and left the restaurant, headed for Evan Bright Realty. He parked where he had before, got out of the rental. He paused at the big plate-glass window, looking at the houses for sale. 'Drastically reduced!!' it said on one. 'Motivated seller!!' on another.

Foreclosures everywhere. All the empty houses.

He walked into Evan Bright Realty. Four desks, two were empty. At one of the desks a woman was on the phone, and at the other, a woman smiled at him expectantly. The name on her desk was 'MARCI WHITAKER'. Oldies but goodies were playing softly somewhere. Stormy.

'You're Steve's client, right?' Marci asked.

He nodded. 'Is he around?'

'He's out with a client.'

'Shoot.' Malcolm snapped his fingers. 'I just wanted one more look at the Roscommon Drive place.'

'Now I remember,' Marci said. 'You're the investigator. Steve told us all about it. It's really—' She paused as a couple came in the door. 'Excuse me,' she said to Malcolm. She stood up.

'The key? To Roscommon?'

But Marci had lost interest in any conversation with him. 'Ask her—' She jerked her finger at the woman on the phone. 'Or it might be on his desk.' She brushed past Malcolm. 'The Pomeroys!' she said to the couple. 'So good to see you. We can head over there right now.'

The woman was still on the phone. Her sign said 'ABBIE FLINTSTONE'. Malcolm could see Steve's desk; he knew it was his due to the sign on it that said 'STEVE ANDERSON'. He walked back, past the Abbie Flintstone woman and a trophy case containing trophies won apparently by the employees – an athletic bunch. He could see a silver trophy of a woman swinging a tennis racket, but on Steve's desk he could see no key.

So he waited.

The woman got off the phone after a while. 'Lots of trophies,' he said to her.

She smiled. 'The former owner – he's passed – was a basketball star in college. He brought his trophies in, and then someone else did, and it kind of snowballed, you know?'

'I'm looking for the key to three fifty Roscommon,' Malcolm said.

'It's not on Steve's desk?'

'No.'

'Let me see – maybe—' She stood up. 'Be right back.'

Waiting, Malcolm checked out the trophies: a big one in the middle for the basketball star dead owner and the rest grouped around it, along with some medals. He was dimly aware that now Elvis was singing 'In the Chapel' on the oldies but goodies station. And then suddenly something happened, something changed, snapped, and at that point, when he looked back on this day, everything seemed to take place in slow motion.

'Found it!' Abbie dangled the key to Roscommon Drive in front of Malcolm. She looked at his face. 'What's wrong?'

'Where's Steve?' Malcolm asked.

296

She looked taken aback. 'I don't know. Don't you want the key?'

'I want to know where Steve is. Marci said he was with a client – do you know who that might be?'

'We always say that,' said Abbie, 'that they're with a client. To show we're always on the job, you know?'

'I *don't* know.' Malcolm had his cell out, calling Steve, but just got his voicemail again. 'Do you have any idea where he might be?'

'Probably with a client, like I said. I just can't tell you who at the moment.' Abbie looked huffy. 'What's this all about, anyway?'

'I'm telling you this as a member of law enforcement,' said Malcolm. 'I need to find him. I think he's in danger. Serious danger.'

'Oh my God.' Abbie put her hand on her heart, theatrically. 'Steve's wife, Mary Ann. She probably knows where he is.'

'And how can I reach her?'

'I – I actually don't know his home phone number. I'm not sure they even have a landline. I think they both just have cells, but I don't have her number.'

'Does she work? How can I find her?' Malcolm asked.

'Oh dear, oh dear,' said Abbie. 'She used to work. At the garden center in the local Target. But she got laid off a few weeks ago.'

'Aha,' said Malcolm. 'So there's maybe been a strain on their finances?'

'I'm sure there has been,' said Abbie. 'But they were lucky. Steve inherited some money from an aunt about the time Mary Ann was laid off. But what does that have to do with—?'

'Nothing,' said Malcolm. 'Probably nothing. Steve's car, what kind of vehicle does he drive?'

'A silver green Honda Accord. Listen, I can tell you where they live, if that helps.'

On his way to the address Abbie had given him, Malcolm called Kate, got her voicemail and a message saying 'this voicemail box is full'. Damn, damn. He texted her: *call me right away*. She would be at work, probably, joking around with Windsong, not paying attention to her cellphone. And what was he planning to tell her, anyway? He didn't know anything for sure. Not yet.

He pulled in front of Steve's house, a two-story Cape Cod with a big front yard. There were no cars in the driveway at all. He got out of the rental.

Next door a woman in tank top and shorts was watering a bank of zinnias.

'Hi there,' Malcolm called. 'I'm looking for Steve or Mary Ann Anderson?'

'Right there's Mary Ann,' said the woman, pointing.

Malcolm turned. A yellow Volkswagen Bug was turning into the driveway. At that moment his cell chimed. Steve.

'Hey, buddy,' Steve said. 'Heard you were looking for me.'

'I was.'

'Abbie said something about me being in danger.'

Malcolm watched as a dark-haired woman, a little chubby, got out of the Volkswagen. 'Sorry. I was being an asshole. I was trying to get hold of you, and I figured that would get her attention. I had a couple more questions for you – want to meet up for coffee, maybe at that Denny's?'

'Sure thing. Let's say in a couple, three hours? I'm with a client right now. I'll get back to you on that.'

'Okay,' said Malcolm. 'Fine.'

The woman went round to the back of the Volkswagen and opened the trunk. She took out a couple of grocery bags.

'Wanted to talk to your wife,' said Malcolm loudly into his cellphone although Steve was no longer there. 'She's right here in front of me. Okay, great!'

The woman turned and looked at Malcolm. 'What?'

'I'm a friend of Steve's. Malcolm, Malcolm MacGregor. You must be Mary Ann.'

She smiled. 'Yes.'

Malcolm walked over to the Volkswagen. 'I've been trying to reach Steve, that's why I'm here, and then he called me just now. Here, let me help you with those bags.'

He picked up the two biggest, one of which seemed to be mostly an economy size of Charmin toilet paper, and followed Mary Ann round the side of the house. Mary Ann balanced her bag and unlocked the door. He followed her into the kitchen, big and full of light. Geraniums bloomed in the window over the kitchen sink, amazingly lush.

'You can set them right there,' she said, pointing, 'on the counter.'

He put the bags down where she said and noticed that up close the amazingly lush geraniums appeared to be polyester.

'Nice place you have here,' Malcolm said.

'Now I know who you are,' said Mary Ann. 'The investigator. That poor woman sitting in that empty house all alone all night. What a stupid trick. Honestly, some people. But Steve's enjoyed meeting you. He doesn't know any policemen.' She smiled, dimples flashing. 'I guess it's kind of a vicarious thrill.'

'Well, your husband's quite a guy himself. I noticed his trophy over at the office. Wow, I was really impressed. He got any more of those?'

Mary Ann laughed. 'He's so proud of that, but, wait – yes, he does have more. You haven't seen the half of it. Come on, let me show you.'

He followed her into a big room, a den, fireplace on one side and on the other a glass case with a display of medals.

'Wow,' said Malcolm 'How'd he get all these?'

'The military. He trained as a sniper. He's proudest of that one,' said Mary Ann, pointing to the one in the middle. 'It's for expert shooting. It's the highest you can go in the military.'

'How long you guys been married?' Malcolm asked.

Mary Ann almost, not quite, blushed. 'Two years. My first husband died a few years ago.'

'Carrie. Carrie Cooper. Does that name mean anything to you?'

Mary Ann shrugged. 'No. Why? How?'

'Someone Steve might know?'

'I don't think so. He had a girlfriend once named Carrie, but not Carrie Cooper.' She paused. 'I only heard about her through a friend of his. He never talks about her – I guess 'cause she broke his heart. Or not.' She giggled. 'Maybe he broke hers. I know Steve seems like a good old guy that nothing really bothers, but underneath he's really sensitive. And now that I think about it, I'm not even sure her name was Carrie. I think it might have been Sally.'

'That Steve,' said Malcolm. 'You know, when I was talking to him we found out we knew some people in common. I'm wondering, who was the friend that told you about Carrie – or maybe Sally?'

'The friend? It was Randy, Randy Wells. But Steve called him Elephant.' She giggled. 'He was just a tiny bit overweight.'

'Randy Wells!' said Malcolm. 'Elephant! Hey. I think I know him too. You got a number for him?'

'I've got a number. It's his cell.' She recited it, and Malcolm put it in his contacts. 'He calls Steve all the time. He lives in the City. They were friends from years ago.'

'Well,' said Malcolm, 'I'd better run. I'm very impressed with those medals, by the way. I'll have to tell him. We're meeting for coffee a little later.'

Mary Ann laughed merrily. 'What? You're going to drive to Phoenix?'

'Phoenix?'

'That's where he is. He said he was going to meet you for coffee?'

'Yes.'

'Don't take it wrong; he's really a joker, you know. He's at some real estate thingy. He was kind of in a hurry; it was a last minute decision. He left last night. He's at the Something Garden Resort.'

'Desert Garden?' said Malcolm.

'That's it.'

'A real estate thingy. Like what? A conference?'

'Sure. I mean, probably. He goes to them all the time. Give him a call and ask him. Now, what was it you wanted to ask me?'

'What?' said Malcolm. His cell gave a little blip, text coming in. He ignored it.

'You told Steve on the phone, I heard, you said you wanted to talk to me.'

'Oh, that. Never mind.'

He called Steve, back out in the rental car. There was no answer. Then he called Frank Cruz of Mesa PD and reached him at his home number.

'Mac! Hey! Where you at?'

'New Jersey.'

'Of course.'

'What's up with you?' Malcolm asked. 'Are you busy?'

'I'm just torturing a few illegals, then I thought I'd have some breakfast.'

Breakfast. It was three hours earlier in Arizona. 'Look, could you check out something for me? See if there's a real estate conference at the Desert

302

Garden Resort and, if there is, see if there's a guy named Steve Anderson registered. Then get back to me as soon as you can.'

'Sure thing.'

He called Kate again; no answer there. He called information and got the number for the Dudley Natural Foods Co-op. It rang and rang, then a recording came on. It didn't open till nine thirty. More than an hour away.

Damn, damn, damn.

He called the number for Randy Wells, but of course no one answered there either. Just in case, he texted Kate:

Know anybody called Randy Wells aka Elephant?

He was booked on a flight late tonight, red-eye special. He needed to get back there sooner. Airport. Standby. Son of a bitch. He hit the steering wheel hard as he could.

Forty-Three

Steve knew plenty of people at the Desert Garden Resort. Even though he hadn't slept all that much last night, he was up and about at seven a.m. – which, after all, was ten a.m. his time – having breakfast at the long breakfast bar set up specially for the conference with overcooked scrambled eggs, dry bacon, burnt coffee, waffle batter and an assortment of tiny boxes of cereal. He filled his tray, took it to a tiny table, sat down.

'Hey, Steve, buddy, didn't know you'd be here. How's it hanging?'

Steve looked up. 'Ron Partridge, Madison, Wisconsin! Hey, hey, hey. How are you, man?' Ron Partridge was a bore.

'Good good. And you?'

'Fine.' Steve crunched a slab of bacon, for some reason thinking of the movie *Groundhog Day*. He edged away with his tray and spotted someone else he knew across the room: Samantha Crowley from Duluth, Minnesota. He waved in a desultory fashion and she waved back.

He was thinking:

One – see at least three people who know me.

Two – pick up name tag.

Three – good to go.

He'd promised himself when the whole thing with Carrie went down that he would make her pay. He'd loved her, he'd treated her well, and she had dumped him like he was nothing, nobody, and for who? A fucking insurance salesman. He'd waited for his revenge. He knew he had to wait until everyone had forgotten he and Carrie even knew each other. He thought about it all – how things had seemed to work out, then how things had screwed up. Kate. He couldn't believe it! Kate, of all people, walking down the street in Dudley. One-date Kate.

'*I'm sorry*,' she'd said. '*I've forgotten your name.*'

She'd recognized him all right, just didn't know why, out of context like he was, but she might remember, any time. He hadn't been able to take that chance, still couldn't.

He headed out to the parking lot, got into his rental car. Three and a half hours to Dudley. Three, if he really stepped on it.

'Kate, Kate. Hey, Kate, wake up.'

Kate opened her eyes. Dakota was standing there.

'What?' Kate said.

'It's almost nine.'

'Nine?' said Kate. She had a terrible headache.

'You said you were working today. And you're usually up by eight. I didn't want you to oversleep. I have to run some errands.'

Kate showered slowly, even though she was running late, still trying to take in the fact that Rick and Hannah had been seeing each other long before she'd thought. All that time with Rick before Hannah showed up was now meaningless. Out of the shower, she saw it was close to nine thirty. She picked up her cell to call the Co-op, but it was completely run down. She'd meant to charge it last night and had forgotten completely.

The hell with it. The hell with all of it. She got dressed quickly, walked to the Co-op. She was only slightly late, and as she walked in the door she realized she'd left her cell behind on the kitchen table.

Three hours later, a tall blonde with bright-red lipstick and big dark sunglasses sauntered down Main Street, peering into the shop windows. She wore black capri pants, a black baggy T-shirt and carried a big red straw tote. She sauntered down a side street, passed the Silver King Hotel, took another turn, and there it was, the Dudley Natural Foods Co-op. A sign in the window said 'SB1070' with a slash across it. Another sign: 'Humanitarian Aid Is Never a Crime'.

So, so, so, so, so, so politically correct. The sun shone on the big plate-glass window, reflecting back an image of herself. She touched her hair, adjusted the sunglasses, went inside. A hippy-looking guy, so, so, so 1960s, was at the cash register. It was two thirty p.m.

'Afternoon.' She was using her southern accent, the one she'd used when she played Blanche DuBois in, oh my God, high school.

'Afternoon,' he said. 'Let me know if you need help.'

She nodded, not wanting to chance too much conversation. She drifted through the store knowing there was nothing here she would buy, just looking. Looking for Kate.

And there she was near the back, talking to some young guy. Satisfied, the woman with the big straw tote bag, heavier than you might expect for something made of straw, turned away and headed for the door. The Co-op hours were posted on the outside: nine thirty to six thirty. Now she would have to wait a while. No rush. Wait and watch. She had all day and into the evening. Evening was maybe best.

Not like last time. This would be close quarters, quick, before any possible witnesses would even know what was happening.

'Have a nice day,' the hippy guy called after her.
'You too!'

* * *
306

The Co-op phone rang.

'God,' said Posey from the back. 'That phone's been ringing all day. Oh shit. Before I forget, someone called for you, Kate, right before you got here this morning. I'm sorry, we got busy and I just plain forgot.'

'Who?' asked Kate. 'Did they leave a name?'

'It was a guy, that's all I know.'

Malcolm, mostly likely. She'd left her cell at Dakota's. She got off work at seven. It could wait until then.

It was fantastic to be out on the street. The man with the scruffy beard, Hawaiian shirt and straw fedora sauntered casually down the Gulch, a tourist, anonymous. Well, kind of. The shirt and fedora said something; something cool, he thought. Nineteen fifties, maybe – hep cat hipster from the Islands. He loved the 1950s, loved them madly at that moment in time walking down the street in the year two thousand and something.

There were the zoot suiters too; those guys in the big suits with the enormous shoulder pads. Was that the fifties?

Chico reached the end of the Gulch and took a right, over towards the grassy park at the Mining Museum. It would be so sweet to sit on a bench and watch everything go by. He felt it coming – a change in his life. Not, of course, this obvious one, but one more subtle. No more crucified baby dolls. Something new, something different; he wasn't sure what, but he could feel it coming. But, wait, it would be even sweeter to sit on a bench with a newspaper. It would be kind of a

307

shield, plus it was a symbol of the old days when people sat on benches and read newspapers.

He stopped in at the Copper Queen lobby and picked up a copy of the *Arizona Daily Star*. Amazing how light it was; the poor old paper was dwindling fast. He carried it out into the sunlight again, down the steps to the grassy park where he took a bench. Cars and pickup trucks went by on the street; he heard the wail of a police-car siren far away on the highway that bypassed the town.

A couple passed him by, youngish, trailed by a small boy.

'Ethan, come *on*,' said the woman.

He looked at Ethan in sympathy, looked past Ethan at a tall blonde woman in the act of removing a pair of sunglasses. She held them up to the light, then took a tissue out of her red straw tote and began to polish them.

She looked familiar in a vague way. Something stirred in Chico's mind. Familiar in a vague, important kind of way. Why was that? She certainly wasn't a local. In spite of the bright-red lipstick and the blonde hair, one thing he thought for sure – she was ugly. She was one ugly lady. He'd seen her before, had thought the same thing, but where, where? She put the sunglasses back on and sauntered past him.

Then he remembered. *Shit.*

He waited until she was about a block away, nearing the post office, then he stood up and began to follow her.

Forty-Four

'You look tired,' Windsong said to Kate out on the sidewalk after they finished up. 'I can give you a ride – I brought my old truck today 'cause I'm helping a friend move out. He lives pretty close to Dakota's.'

Kate got in. She *was* tired today, hadn't fallen asleep till late, late, late, thinking about Hannah and Rick. Everything in the world just seemed fucked up. She had no idea what she was going to do with her life, and that seemed particularly pressing right now – making some sort of decision, though about what she didn't even know. She sighed.

'Cheer up,' said Windsong as they bumped along in the pitted streets of old Dudley, tax base a bit small for excessive road maintenance. 'Things could be worse, or they could be better – it's a draw, so why bother even thinking at all, that's my motto.'

'God,' said Kate, 'you're so sickeningly emotionally healthy.'

He pulled into Dakota's. 'I'm kind of worried about you,' he said.

'Why?'

'Dunno. You take care. Maybe I'll stop by a little later, make sure everything's all right.'

Kate was touched. 'Sure,' she said, 'if you like.' She got out and waved goodbye. She went inside.

'Dakota?' she called. 'Are you there?'

No answer.

But there was her cell lying on the kitchen table. She picked it up. Several calls, all from Malcolm. One text message. She was about to read the text when the phone rang. Malcolm.

'Hello?'

'At last,' said Malcolm. 'I've been trying to reach you all day.'

'I left my cell at Dakota's when I went to work. Sorry.'

'Where are you now?'

'At Dakota's. Just home from work. Where are you?'

'I just turned off the I-10 at the Sierra Vista exit. So I'm about forty-five minutes away. Listen, I found out some funny stuff about the realtor.'

'The realtor? Are you kidding? Abbie?'

'No, no, the guy. You never met him, as far as I know. Steve. Steve Anderson. Ring a bell?'

'No.'

'Shoot. I was hoping it might. He's a trained sniper.'

'*What?*'

'It has to be connected somehow. Trained snipers don't come by every day. Could be, he had it in for Carrie, and by extension Wes, 'cause of some failed romance, or it's a possibility he was hired to kill Carrie and Wes. Don't know by who. Maybe Polly Hampton.'

'My God.' Kate sat down on a kitchen chair. 'What does this have to do with me?'

'That's what I can't figure out. But look, Kate,

310

he has to be the one who lured you back to New Jersey.'

'But how did he know those things? About Ellen.'

'Could have read that interview that I read, the one online where you talk about the Ooblecks. Researched all of you and picked the one that was dead to lure you to the house.'

'It just doesn't make sense!'

'It has to – I'm working on it. Look, he's supposedly at a conference in Phoenix right now, but he could be in Dudley. I'll be back soon, but I want you to be careful. Stay away from the windows, lock the doors. I'll be back as fast as I can get there. I stashed my gun in my truck when I left it at the airport, so it's with me now, and I can be at Dakota's straightaway.'

'Your gun,' said Kate faintly.

'My gun.'

'At least,' said Kate, 'Biker Bill should be around. Let me see if I can tell if he's home without leaving the house.' She went to the window, peered out. His motorcycle wasn't parked in the driveway. But still, he could be back any minute.

'Is Dakota there?' Malcolm asked.

'No. I don't know where she is. I can call her.'

'Do that. Tell her to stay put, wherever she is. Okay? Just for a little while.'

'Did you text me?' said Kate.

'Yeah, right, I did.'

'I haven't looked at it yet. What about?'

'To see if you knew anybody called Randy Wells.'

'Sure. A long time ago in New York.' She laughed. 'We used to call him Elephant.'

'Jesus Christ. How well did you know him?'

'We were never really tight, but we both hung out with the same people. What about him?'

'Steve Anderson's wife told me Randy is Steve's friend. Friend and confidant, supposedly.'

Chico had been following the blonde for a couple of hours, and now dusk was setting in. It hadn't been all that strenuous, really. She'd gone over to the Dudley Coffee Company and sat in a corner, drinking coffee. Chico bought himself a plain coffee Americano and sat in another corner, at a table surrounded by tourists.

He'd told Melody he was going out for an hour or so. She would be worried he might have been identified, arrested. Nothing he could do about that. He didn't have a cellphone; they'd taken it from him at the jail. For a while he was caught up in the hum of people talking, the vibration of the whole outside world.

Then the blonde looked at her watch, stood up.

Chico stood up too, watched her go out the door. He waited a bit, then went out too. It must be getting on towards dinner time if you were an early diner. What time was it, exactly? He didn't have a watch. He'd always scorned watches, being an artist. *I have my own time*, he'd say.

Stupid punk kid.

The blonde went up the street and made a turn. Then another turn. Where was she going? The Co-op? It was about to close, if it wasn't closed already. But then she stopped, stood in a doorway just down the street. Waiting, it looked like. For what? For who?

Chico stopped too, stood behind a tree.

The door of the Co-op opened and Windsong came out with someone he didn't know but he'd seen around, new in town: Kate, that was her name. *Kate.* Kate was the one Melody told him about – she was in the photograph with the woman who was murdered. Carrie. Carrie Cooper. The news had made it sound like Carrie might have said something to Kate connected to the murders, but it hadn't panned out.

Oh, no, Chico thought. *Shit.* What if she *had* told Kate something and only the blonde knew it? The blonde who'd been buying him drinks at the St Elmo Bar.

Windsong and Kate walked to a truck parked just down the street and got in. He watched it as it lurched down the street and made a turn.

Then Posey came out – Chico knew Posey pretty well, actually. They'd always gotten along. He was glad he wasn't visible, just in case she might recognize him. Posey came out with Ryan, the manager. The blonde stepped out from the doorway and walked towards them.

They spoke.

Chico heard a name on the breeze. Dakota. He knew Dakota, another artist. She lived over on Yucca Street. Posey waved her hands. The blonde waved hers. Ryan pointed in the direction of Windsong's truck. The blonde turned away and strode down the street away from where Chico was hiding.

Ryan got in a car.

Chico remembered something, then something else. In fact, a lot of things were starting to come together.

Posey was alone now.

Chico stepped out from behind the tree.

Kate locked the doors and the windows, turned off the lights and in the dark in the living room she called Mandy in New York City, realizing as it rang that it was past ten o'clock there.

'Hello?'

'Mandy,' she said.

'Yes? Kate, what's going on?'

'Randy. Randy Wells. Remember him?'

'Sure. Elephant. Actually, he's lost a lot of weight. He looks pretty good now. So, what about him?'

'I haven't seen him for years and years, but he's connected somehow to this whole Ellen thing.'

'Randy? I don't think so. I mean, why? He was always a goof, but never – you know, *mean*.'

'Not directly connected, maybe, but someone he knows is. Someone called Steve. Steve Anderson.'

'Steve Anderson. But you know him, Kate. That's Buzzie. Buzzie Anderson.'

'No kidding. *Buzzie*.' Kate sat down abruptly on the couch. 'His real name was Steve?'

'Yes. I think he even kind of had a thing for you, back then.'

'We went on a date once. It wasn't much fun.'

'When did you see him last?'

314

'Oh, years ago, I think. Actually, for some reason—'

'What?'

'I don't know.'

'Elephant and Buzzie are both on the DVD I sent you.'

'I know, I know. Thanks, Mandy. Maybe I'll check it out again.'

She got off the phone. The DVD was still in the player. She turned on the TV, turned on the player and had a sudden thought.

Where was Dakota, anyway?

She texted her. *Where r u?* Got no immediate answer. She hit play, and the DVD started up. She hit fast forward till she got to the part with Elephant and Buzzie. Paused it.

And remembered where she'd seen Buzzie last.

Chico called Melody around seven thirty.

'Where are you? I've been really worried,' she said. 'How did you get a cellphone? It says Posey Prince.' A twinge of paranoia entered her voice. 'What are you doing with *her* phone?'

He explained. He explained as best he could.

'Oh my God,' Melody said. 'Please, please be careful. What should I do? Should I call the police?'

'So they can take me back to jail? Of course not. Listen, it will be okay. I'm following her to Dakota's right now. I'm going to play it by ear. Don't *worry*.'

'What do you mean, don't worry?' Her voice veered upward. 'Are you kidding? *Hello? Hello?*'

But there was nothing but silence.

315

Melody went to a drawer in the kitchen. She took out the gun that had belonged to a former boyfriend. It was loaded now. Chico had done that. He was so smart sometimes and so stupid other times. It would be a big mistake to be in love with him.

She knew that.

She put the gun in her purse and went out the door.

Chico could see the phoney blonde up ahead of him. She had a gun in that straw tote, Chico would bet on it. Things were getting clearer and clearer now. Maybe he should have had Melody call the police, but what would that do? Why would they believe him? No, he'd just end up back in jail. Something concrete had to happen. But not too concrete. No one should get hurt.

The streets went up and down, treacherous, full of ruts. The blonde strode on – legs of steel, legs like a guy, and as far as he could tell definitely headed for Dakota's. He knew a short cut. He darted down a side street, came out. Yep, she was still on her way, and now he was slightly ahead.

A weapon. He needed a weapon, just in case. A rock. Or maybe a tree branch, poke her eyes out. No. A rock was better. A big one.

Malcolm was just coming over the divide and into town when his cell chimed again.

Kate.

'Listen, I figured it out, and it has nothing to

do with anything Carrie might have said to me.' Her voice was breathless, excited. 'It's the blonde woman.'

'What blonde woman?'

'The one I saw the day of the shootings. When I got out of my car at the High Desert Market. I knew she looked familiar, but I couldn't place her. So I said to her, "I'm sorry, I've forgotten your name."'

'And?'

'She'd dropped her purse. She said that – her voice was kind of husky, but at the time— Anyway, looking back, it wasn't a woman. It was *Buzzie* in a blonde wig.'

'Who the hell is Buzzie?'

'Steve Anderson. And listen to this – Posey just called me. She's seen Chico; she let him use her cellphone. Chico asked her where I was going with Windsong, and Posey told him he was dropping me off at Dakota's.' She paused. 'You don't think Chico—'

'God damn it,' said Malcolm, almost shouting now. 'I don't know what to think about anything. Don't go near the doors or windows. Stay down. I'll be there as fast as I can.'

Forty-Five

Kate looked at the digital clock on Dakota's microwave. Seven forty-eight. She listened. Heard no noise. Then there was a noise, a snapping sound, a sliding sound. Malcolm said he was coming right away. What if someone – Buzzie? – was really out there and he saw Malcolm and shot him? No, Malcolm was a policeman. He would know how to do things.

Buzzie. God. He was always kind of a dork. She hadn't known him long, and they had had a date and it was incredibly boring. He'd been kind of rude and resentful afterwards, as if she'd somehow cheated or tricked him.

She heard another snapping noise, this time on the other side of the house.

Melody walked up the hill to Dakota's house, where Chico had told her he was going. Why? Why Dakota's? Dakota was way too old for him.

She could see Chico just in front of her, under the street light. He was behind a big Chinese elm. Melody made a circle, avoiding him, coming up closer to Dakota's. But what was that? There was a big blonde woman hunched over by the drainage ditch.

Dakota's place was dark; it looked like no one was there at all. Melody paused and waited. She had the gun in her hand, and it was loaded. Now she had to figure out what to do next.

Maybe just wait.

And then there was a hush. Kate felt it, inside Dakota's house, doors and windows closed and locked. A deep hush. Then, faintly, background sounds that would normally be automatically filtered came to the forefront – the distant sound

318

of car engines and truck engines, the hum of people's voices faraway.

And then Kate's phone chimed. She jumped. Dakota.

'Hi,' Kate said, 'where are you, anyway?'

'I got into an argument with this asshole sculptor.' Dakota laughed. 'I meant to call you before, but it slipped my mind. I'm just coming up the street.'

'No,' said Kate. '*Wait.*'

'What? My phone's going out. What did you say?'

Shit. Dakota was just down the street. Kate forgot herself and stepped out on to the porch, then down into the street to look for Dakota. And saw Malcolm's truck coming her way. Thank God, Malcolm was here. She would be safe. Saved.

Then a blonde woman stepped out from behind a mesquite bush, just a few feet away from her, both hands raised. She was holding a gun.

For a millisecond, everything in the whole world stopped.

Then all hell broke loose.

Gunfire came from two different directions, and a large rock sailed through the air and hit the woman just as she fell. Her blonde hair came off. The roar of a motorcycle came from down the street. Biker Bill rode up, swerved, just missing Steve aka Buzzie Anderson as he lay bleeding on the street.

He stopped. 'What the fucking hell!' he said.

Malcolm, Chico and Melody all appeared from somewhere. And from down the street came

– wow! – Windsong, stopping by to check on her. And Posey! Windsong and Posey. News traveled fast in a small town.

'Better call an ambulance,' Malcolm said, 'though I think he might be dead.'

They stood together, murderers, some of them.

Kate took a deep breath. She looked at Malcolm and Dakota, at Chico and Melody, at Windsong and Posey, at Biker Bill – all these people, just helping one another. What a wonderful world.

Forty-Six

Or not murderers, as it turned out. Steve 'Buzzie' Anderson did not die of the wounds received that evening in old Dudley on the street in front of the house belonging to Dakota Silverstein. He was transported to the Copper Queen Community Hospital and from there air-evaced to Tucson Medical Center, suffering from a concussion brought on by being hit with the large rock thrown by Gilberto 'Chico' Flores and two bullet wounds – one in the right shoulder from a shot fired by Malcolm McGregor, and the other in the left hand from a shot fired by one Melody Young.

As he was recuperating, a Cochise County grand jury found probable cause to charge him with two counts of first-degree homicide for the murders of Wes and Carrie Cooper, as well as several other less serious charges.

All charges against Gilberto 'Chico' Flores

were dropped, and on the strength of his sold-out show on the Gulch he got a one-man show at a pretty good gallery in Phoenix scheduled for some time in the spring.

As for the rest of them, they continued on, working at restaurants, at food co-ops, in studios, as private investigators for defense attorneys; mourning their former lives, their dead wives and their old selves as they began to create new ones.

'That song you were singing?' Malcolm said to Kate as they were having Senegalese peanut soup one day at El Serape restaurant. 'That your mom used to sing to you? About the little boat?'

'What about it?'

'How did it go, in English?'

'Something like this – Mother, the little boat that goes on water, does it have legs? Of course, my little silly, if it didn't have legs, it couldn't go.'

'Ah.' Malcolm swallowed a spoonful of delicious peanut soup. 'Sounds like a poem by Harry Light.'